THE
HERO

or

Shell Shock: A Love Story

Published in Canada by Red Deer Press, 195 Allstate Parkway, Markham, Ontario L3R 4T8
Published in the United States by Red Deer Press, 311 Washington Street, Brighton, Massachusetts 02135

10 9 8 7 6 5 4 3 2 1

Red Deer Press acknowledges with thanks the Canada Council for the Arts, and the Ontario Arts Council for their support of our publishing program. We acknowledge the financial support of the Government of Canada through the Canada Book Fund (CBF) for our publishing activities.

Library and Archives Canada Cataloguing in Publication
Almond, Paul, 1931-, author
The hero / Paul Almond.
(The Alford saga ; bk. 7)
Issued in print and electronic formats.
ISBN 978-0-88995-512-7 (pbk.).--ISBN 978-1-55244-342-2 (epub).--ISBN 978-1-55244-343-9 (pdf)
I. Title. II. Series: Almond, Paul, 1931- Alford saga ; bk. 7.

PS8601.L56H47 2014   C813'.6   C2014-904688-X
                C2014-904689-8

Publisher Cataloging-in-Publication Data (U.S.)
ISBN 9780889955257
Data available on file

Design by Daniel Choi
Cover image courtesy of iStockphoto

Printed in Canada by Friesens Corporation

THE
HERO

or

Shell Shock: A Love Story

Paul Almond

Red Deer Press

Rev. Eric and Rene Almond.

For my mother and father,

whose journey I never knew,

until I wrote this book.

PART ONE: 1926 AND ON

CHAPTER ONE

That man at the end of the platform — he's the key. But something about him denies access. Unlike the others waiting for the train, we'll have to approach him and his story cautiously. No plunging ahead with—"Hey, how are you?" No confrontation — oh no. So let us draw near slowly, wend down any long lanes of memory, ease along trails that might render clues, even use his own writings which we shall discover, and make our way gradually from observation to participation, fact working with fiction, until we can confidently move beside him...

First, let's watch from a distance. See how he stands, smoking his pipe, khaki haversack resting on his hip, apart from the group, staring out into the wide bay beyond. Note those newly washed trousers. And his clean cloth cap, flannel shirt collar freshly pressed, and the knitted wool sweater and heavy jacket. Well, it's June, and the weather here in on the Gaspe Peninsula is still chilly: across the railway tracks, tiny buds are only now reaching out from winter limbs to grasp the last rays of the modest sun. Beside him on the rough platform boards, a worn canvas bag (tied shut with a rope) leans against a frayed suitcase. So he's going on a long journey. But why?

The others in the station cast covert glances in his direction. It seems they know him. Why don't they go over, engage him in conversation? They all appear, even for farmers, rather well-off, and substantial.

The red-ochred wooden station with its overhanging roof sits on the curving wooded shores of an estuary. Around it, Port Daniel stretches half a mile east, stopping at a hill that rises into the badlands, and on through them to Gascons, Perce, and finally, the end of the line, Gaspe. Behind the village, a lagoon gathers the river from the highlands in the interior: haunt of moose, caribou and wolves. This whole wooded peninsula, rarely pierced by any local, is framed on the north by the great St. Lawrence River and on the east by the Gulf of St. Lawrence, bounded itself by Newfoundland.

Look, our man has turned, taken a few steps, and eased himself onto the loaded baggage cart. Look at those boots. Army boots. Resoled a few times, doubtless, but still serviceable. And did you catch that quick gleam from a small button on his lapel? A crown, topped by the curved words, *For Honourable Service*, above three maple leaves. A significant detail, no doubt. It shows he fought in the Great War, 1914-18, almost a decade ago. Indeed, that hunched figure on the cart emanates a world of experience — that few others hereabouts have undergone. So yes, they would all know him to be a veteran. Perhaps they can imagine what he's been through and that's why they leave him alone.

Passengers are chatting among themselves, some saying their goodbyes, others taking a short train ride up to New Carlisle or Bonaventure, and three or four heading to the big city, to Montreal.

Right now, our veteran is staring out over the blue waters of

Chaleur Bay. As usual, the ever present gulls are cresting waves stirred up by the beginnings of a storm; no fishing boats this late in the day. No great leap to surmise he is not looking at anything in particular, but rather backwards into the past.

A storm is coming. Let us think... The only major event told by the old-timers was of a British 74-gun man o'war, sheltered in this estuary from a similar spring blow in the early 1800s. Could our veteran be thinking of that? That moment when a single midshipman jumped ship: James Alford, his grandfather? Our veteran might not know the full story: that this huge ship with its three gigantic masts and twenty-one sails, the *Bellerophon* (famous for the battle of Trafalgar and later bringing Napoleon to Portsmouth) was only 180 feet long — a quarter the length of HMS *Dreadnought*, the WWI battleship our veteran would indeed know.

His grandfather had leapt off that ship into the same icy waters his grandson is now staring at, collected himself, made his way through these same woods ringing the same shore, past where this railroad station now sits and back up the Port Daniel River, to eventually settle in Shigawake.

Had we been on this station platform half an hour ago, we would have seen that midshipman's youngest son, Jim Alford, now stooped and grizzled in his 80s, shaking hands with his shorter, and it must be admitted, handsome, departing veteran son. We'd have noticed how quickly the old man turned away to hide the moisture starting into his eyes and how his tall figure hobbled stiffly back to the waiting express wagon drawn by Lively, a horse also approaching the limit of his earthly existence. Once aboard, Jim certainly slapped the reins, for Lively was not tied up, being accustomed to obedient waiting. Then Old Poppa, as Jim Alford was known to his family, would have set off westward along the main gravelled road over Port Daniel mountain, and thence to Shigawake, an hour's ride. Fathers and sons, at partings like these, don't stand around mumbling inanities if the train is late. Oh no, old Jim would never delay when his heart was breaking; he'd push on home to help their hired man and Earle, his son, finish up some last minute harrowing on their rolling farm.

But what's this? The station crowd has stirred and become animated. Have they heard something?

Our veteran gives a quick glance down the platform, seeing their excitement quicken. They have heard something he has not. A distant train whistle perhaps? Is he slightly deaf? Another clue. Might he not have served in the Artillery? A definite possibility, for those howitzers banging away every day for months on end would surely cause a hearing difficulty. He takes the last puff of his pipe, taps out the contents against the iron shelf of the baggage car, blows into the barrel and puts it in his pocket. Glancing up, he sees two crows chasing a hawk, just as they did on his first departure from Port Daniel Station, in the autumn of 1915, twelve years ago. He straightens, takes off his cap to smooth the neatly-parted black hair, a smile flavouring his lips. Is he remembering that first excitement as he left for university? But we can now assume that our prospective undergrad never got there — diverted by enlistment officers to join up and head over the Atlantic into the battlegrounds of France.

From his pocket he pulls a much creased blue envelope. Another clue to his destination? He stares at it briefly and then carefully stuffs it back into a jacket pocket. His black eyes, almost smoky, shut out further questions as might a furnace door conceal a well-stoked fire within.

A train whistle — this time closer. The former soldier eases down from the baggage cart and stares out across the waters. Yes, between the trees a plume of smoke funnels into the windy sky. He stoops, hefts his belongings closer and straightens, glancing at the others who are now beginning to mill about, exchanging farewells. But he remains, as before, apart and alone.

Before we join him on the train, shall we find out what brought him here, where he is going, and more particularly, why? For this we must turn to his own writings, and conjure up his recent past.

CHAPTER TWO

O ur enigmatic gentleman on the platform has filled a worn black looseleaf with scraps of writings. His own words (hereinafter rendered in italics) written earlier in the autumn of 1926 on his battered Underwood portable at Bishop's University, some hundred miles south of Montreal, tell us about his view of "Life".

A beautiful flower garden overlooking the Bay de Chaleur — lilacs, tulips and roses, the most wonderful colouring and sweet perfume, a haunt of hummingbirds and wild canaries.

But the wee laddie did not care to weed in this Beauty Spot — although his mother was trying to teach him to love her flower garden — Mother's Paradise. Oh, no it was almost as bad as going to school, but sometimes when pulling out a weed by the roots, he found a fat angle worm. Then the young laddie's eyes would glisten and immediately the worm would go into his pocket to keep company with his jackknife and fishing tackle. Then when mother wasn't looking, he would sneak back over the hill to the wonderful trout streams and small lakes, the wee laddie's paradise! Mother worried when he went off on these solitary hunting and fishing trips, alone except for his faithful collie dog, Charlie. But the excitement of those silent pools where the big trout lay on the bottom, refusing the tempting angle worm...

Happy memories of childhood — the only perfect happiness because free from worry, care and sin.

That was life.

In their steel helmets, with gas masks, pack sack, rifle and bayonet, a line of khaki-clad troops were struggling over shell holes and dead bodies, through barbed wire, trying to dodge the bursting shells on their way to the Front. The Great War for Civilisation: England at death grips with Germany.

Coming back from the trenches and passing our line of troops lay the men on stretchers: ghastly, awful faces and mangled limbs. Machine-gun and rifle fire opened up as a Hun plane flew over on a bombing raid. It was raining a downpour, and the mud was simply dreadful.

The young officer looked at the drawn, tired faces of his men and thought of the garden at home on the Bay de Chaleur. Next morning they were going "over the top" on a raid, which meant that many would never return to their flower gardens in Canada but would sleep instead among the Flanders poppies in faraway France, "pushing daisies" as soldiers say.

In that soul-destroying half hour before dawn, waiting for the attack, while our artillery was pounding the German trenches and cutting lanes in the barbed wire entanglements, he heard, "God I am fed up," as someone said, "this awful shelling and mud..."

The young officer thought of his old rugby coach and spoke a few words to the men in his section. "I believe, boys, that God Almighty hates a coward, so I would rather die than be a quitter! Our objec-

tive is the German third line..."

The whistle blew, the artillery fire lifted, and over the top went the raiding Canadians through that Hell of No Man's Land. The objective was never reached because German machine gunners mowed them down. The wire had not been properly cut — there was no retreat, simply because there was nobody left to retreat. They had all died in front of the German wire like heroes, faces to the foe.

The young officer was lying wounded in a shell hole waiting for death, when a comrade crawled over and said, "I can help you back to our lines. Anyhow, we will either get back or die together, for I will never leave you."

Divine unselfishness! Magnificent heroism!

This too was life.

A marvellous sunset, pure red, lit up that Western sky in British Columbia. The sun was going down like a tired old man who has done his work well and left behind a wonderful glow in the memory of his friends for kind deeds and unselfish acts. This afterglow thrilled you with silent wonder — so beautiful that it almost hurt: words would have been profane. Marvellous colouring, purple, rose, and little clouds like islands of pure, bright, shining gold in a deep blue sea, the islands of departed heroes.

The man was smoking his pipe outside a tent belonging to the Geodetic Land Survey of Canada — a government party of land surveyors. His friend was lying on the grass at his side. Perfect companionship, where words were unnecessary because mood speaks to mood, sense to sense, feeling to feeling.

Just below the camping ground lay one of those mountain lakes which are unequalled in Canada for sheer beauty: snow-capped peaks towering up into the blue. A slender stream ran down from the hills, winding its way along and falling — a cataract of sparkling, bubbling spray — into the silent lake, surrounded by the mysterious forest with its tall Douglas fir, murmuring pine, white birches, maples and poplar, with rustling, shimmering leaves.

God's own peace! Mother Nature in one of her charming, restful moods trying to banish scenes of war from the lined faces of the returned men, whispering to them of love, peace and happiness. A delicious sleep on pine needles, so absolutely sound and restful. What a contrast to the noise of the raging guns and artillery fire on the Western Front only two years before.

In the first streaks of dawn in the eastern sky, a bird broke that blissful stillness, followed by the wonderful chorus when they sing their morning hymn at dawn — what musician could attempt to rival them with his mechanical instrument?

The joy of existence; the feeling that it is just good to be alive.

And this also was life.

Revealing about his life up to now, certainly, but no hint as to this present voyage. Nor to the origins of the blue envelope.

Perhaps we should speed up this process by going back seven years to Shigawake, our man's home, to a scene that well have taken place, though nowhere recorded.

* * *

In 1919, right after the war, our veteran was raking up fallen leaves in the garden of his family farm, known as the Old Homestead, when a horse and buggy came down the road from Paspebiac at a fast trot. Slowing, it turned in. He paused to watch it go up the driveway: a woman driving, smartly dressed for sure, but no one he knew, so he went back to raking. Some of these leaves he would deposit on certain plants as mulch against the winter frost.

"Eric!" His mother's voice rang out.

He turned. The little white-haired lady on the front steps waved.

He dropped his rake and headed towards the house as around the veranda came the visitor.

He reached the foot of the stairs and stopped. There, on the top step stood a vaguely familiar figure. He frowned as he took in her stylish boots, the fur collar above a long straight coat open to reveal a dress with descending patterns, her brown hair neat under a fitted hat, obviously from the finest milliner in a big city. Clever makeup heightened her cheekbones and accented her lips.

Both figures stood staring at each other. Tears welled up in the lady's eyes. "Eric. Thank God. So you survived..."

Eric looked at her in wonderment. "Raine? Are you my Raine?"

As she nodded, he leapt up the stairs and put his arms around her and hugged tightly, his mother watching.

After a time, Eric loosened his embrace and held her at arms length, still staring. "Raine, how you've changed!"

"And so have you, dear Eric." She took a handkerchief from her small, elegant clutch purse and wiped her own tears from her cheeks. Her formerly skinny frame had fleshed out into a fully formed figure.

"Well, I'll just go in and get yez both a cup o' tea." Eric's mother opened the front door.

"Wait! Thanks very much, Mrs. Alford, but first, I'd like to take Eric back to the Hollow. I'll have the tea when we return, if that's all right?"

Moments later, Eric fetched the well-worn staff leaning against the back wall and walked with Raine up the slanting path that cut across the hill behind. Not speaking, hearts full, they could feel the silence between them laden with promise. Halfway up, Raine said, "You've been through so much, Eric. I heard from others what it was like over there. Terrible."

"And I guess you have been through a lot, too," he replied.

They stopped at the brow to look back down on the Old Homestead. To the east, St. Paul's white wooden spire caught the sun; to the west, other farms of Alford lineage, and just below, the Temperance Hall soon to be moved below the road to host a United Church congregation.

Eric gestured: "Women's Christian Temperance Union. WCTU. Stands for: Women Combined to Torment Us." He laughs. But seeing Raine's smile fade, he went on, "I'm dying to know..."

After a time, Raine began, "Well... the day after you left — that night really, because I was afraid that 'family' o' mine would follow me in daylight, and bring me back — I set off. I was so tired, because I hadn't eaten, bein' upset at your leaving. And anyhow, there never was anything in our shacks to eat."

"I hoped and prayed," said Eric, "after what those relatives had put you through, that you'd soon get away." The past, its incest, hunger and deprivations, remained unspoken between them.

Raine nodded. "I guess I musta walked all the way to Paspebiac by dawn, and I felt like dropping, but I kep' on. I had to lay me down to rest from time to time, but I made it to New Carlisle by nightfall. It looked like rain so I wanted some barn where I could find me a haymow. When the farmer seen me, and I guess I looked pretty bad, he and his wife, they took me in and fed me a darn good meal. They had me sleep in the house, and after a big breakfast I went on, and you know Eric, I got to Bonaventure the next day!

"I figured by now I was pretty safe. So, I started to look for work and you know? The second store I went into, the man's wife had taken sick, and I started helping out, sweeping and cleaning. But I couldn't get you outta my mind."

"I had an idea, Raine dear," Eric mumbled, "that once you got away, you'd be fine. And did you stay in Bonaventure long?"

"Well..." Raine set off with him across the flat field atop the hill, "I'll try to make this short, because I want to finish before you and me, we go down to see that family of mine."

Eric's sudden look betrayed his anxiety. He had made sure to avoid those folk in the shacks and their side of the brook since his return. They might well have blamed him for Raine's departure. But now, he'd stand by Raine, no matter what.

"You see, one French fella who kept coming in, he had a club foot so he couldn't go fight no war. But he was good-looking, and kind, and his head was sure full of ideas. I kep' waiting for a letter from you, but none came, and finally, well ..." She paused, and glanced at her companion.

Thoughtfully, Eric walked on with his staff, thumb hooked in the notch.

"Well, he was going off to Quebec City in the summer to make his fortune, and he asked me to come. I'd been seeing him all winter, off and on, and we'd been pretty good friends all spring, too. When I seen no letter was likely to come, I took off with him." She paused. "We were married in Quebec."

She glanced sideways to see Eric stop and look at her, and then break into a big smile. "Oh Raine, I'm so happy for you. Is he good to you?"

"Good to me? I'd say! Gave me two beautiful children, and I help him with his work, too. You know, in the five years since you left, we took advantage of the war and got ourselves a little business."

"Oh yes? What kind?"

"Well, you know them haversacks you fellas had in the trenches? Sorta carry them round your neck and they sit on your hip? Well, they take a pile of sewing, and we figured out a way to get farmers' wives to work at home on that there canvas, and we made a pretty good go of it. My Edmond, he's real smart."

"But I bet it was you who talked to the wives..."

"Yep, and I collected the bags and I gave out the pay; good fun...

We made us lots of money, as you can imagine."

Eric shook his head in amazement. "Two children, too! How wonderful, Raine. Where are they now?"

"Left with my storekeeper in Bonaventure where we got off the train. He and his wife were so happy to see me, they offered to look after them while I came down here. I was hoping I'd find you and we could go together to see my folks. When I kin see their reaction, maybe I'll come back tomorrow with the children. He lent me his horse and buggy to come down. People are so nice to me."

"As they should be, dear Raine."

"And you, Eric, what about you?"

Eric shook his head, and did not reply at once. Finally, he mumbled, "Can't talk about it, Raine." They walked on in silence. "I guess I've been affected... Well, I don't do much around the barn, or help out enough on the farm." He brightened. "But you know... I met someone, too. During the war, on leave in England." He glanced at his companion. "I even can't stop thinking about her."

"I know what you mean..."

But then as they reached the brow of the hill, Raine stopped short. Below them lay the Hollow with its pig pasture, its cleared meadow where cows grazed, and back beyond, a tawny forest of dying leaves, some still orange, mostly drab browns interspersed with the rich green of spruce, and lighter green of cedars by the brook that wended down to the millpond. To its right stood the greying timbers of the hard-working sawmill of Eric's brother-in-law Joe Hayes, married to his sister Molly. He winced at the whine of the saw like a distant Jack Johnson, starting high and dropping, flashing him back for a moment to those shells raining down on the Artillery.

Raine took a few steps toward the edge and stared at the three shacks on the opposite bank. Half clothed children ran around outside under washing flapping on a line.

Eric studied Raine, a solitary but stylish figure as she stared, transfixed, at the site of her humble beginnings. Neither moved for a long time.

Suddenly Raine turned. "I can't! I just can't go down, Eric. You've got no idea —"

"I think I do, Raine." He turned to follow as she hurried away. "How could I forget bringing you back an apple or a sandwich? And then finding out how they treated you. How often I prayed to the Good Lord, when I was training and later in the firing lines, that you would escape safely."

"Just like I prayed for you, Eric." She glanced over her shoulder. "But I ain't comin' back here no more. Never again."

They walked on in silence for a time, and then Raine said, "And what's her name, this lady you met in England."

"Rene, short for Irene. (but pronounced Reenee) Funny. A bit like your name."

Raine smiled. "Do you write each other?"

"No."

"But Eric, you must have been back home a while now? When did you get here?"

"In March this year."

"And you didn't write?"

Eric shook his head.

Raine stopped. She looked at her companion, handsome, but showing the ravages of war in his eyes and on his face. A scar where a piece of shrapnel had entered his cheek still glowed red. "What do you mean you haven't written? Don't you care? You said you couldn't get her outta your head."

"Yes, but..."

"But what, Eric?"

"Well, you see, Raine, she's ... well, she's kind of rich. Out of my station. I made a decision when I said goodbye, that it would be over." Raine let out an exclamation, and he went on, "Well, I didn't want to saddle her with no long-distance romance. The best thing was to cut it short."

"And how do you know what she's thinking?" Sparks flew from Raine's eyes. "What about her? Don't you imagine she's got feelings? Couldn't you tell she liked you, too?"

Eric shrugged. "Well yes, I suppose she did... she might. But I told you, Raine —"

"You told me what! That she's rich and you're poor? That's crazy, Eric. Just think of the distance between me in that there ramshackle shack, messed about by my uncle, starving, no clothes to wear, and you in this here big farmhouse out on the front road — all the food you ever needed, all the clothes you ever wanted — what about that? Did it matter to you? No sir! Anyway, you told me it didn't."

"Raine, of course it didn't."

"Well, you think she's any worse of a person? The fact you live here across that great ocean on a farm won't make any difference to her, no matter how rich she is."

Eric was silent, thinking. "But I told you, she didn't write me —"

"It's not her job! You're the man. What are you thinking? You get home and write her this very day, or I'll never speak to you again!"

And then for the first time on their walk, Raine gave a peal of laughter, making Eric smile and, finally, relax — the old Raine coming to the fore...

"We can't have that, Raine! I'll write her today."

CHAPTER THREE

Eric received a letter back, we may be sure. So can we surmise that the blue envelope he fingered on the platform came from Rene?

In this extract from another essay written in 1926 on that battered portable typewriter: *"...In the summer of 1921 on the Prairie in Alberta, we were surveying pals, and put in a season with the Geodetic Land Survey of Western Canada there."* But no real follow up. So let us imagine Eric sitting with two companions, a surveyor and a paddler, around a campfire, talking...

"Now what in the name of heaven made you take up surveying?" The speaker, Arnold, a hefty, apple-cheeked farm lad with a spunky disposition, had enormous muscles, which made him their chief paddler. "A fella like you, Pop, with all that there experience, why take a job like this?"

Eric, the enigmatic veteran, who for all his youth seemed older than his years, sat cross-legged, smoking his pipe, not replying to Arnold's provocative question. We can imagine that he would have preferred a bit of peace to this extended wrangling, customary whenever the other two got together.

"Listen you — " snapped Dutil, the Surveyor, "Eric, he t'ink this de best job in de whole world!" His black eyes glittered with annoyance as he rubbed his long nose with a forefinger, while his other hand massaged an ear stabbed earlier on the trail by a dead twig.

"Yeah, Dutil?" teased Arnold. "You think she's the best job because you got nothin' else. But Pops here, he's crossed the ocean, seen France and them European cities. What he musta learnt in that there war, eh? So why not pick a better money maker?" Not hard to see that he was throwing this out as a means of tormenting his superior.

"You don't think I been travelling, me?" Dutil retorted. "I been all over dis country. You get surveying ticket, you work all over. I say, she be a fine job."

Eric raised his head and glanced at the Surveyor. One presumes he saw two sides to the argument; both companions loved their heated debates as they sat around a small campfire apart from the rest of the survey crew, who had retired to their tents.

"De best way for making money, too," went on the Surveyor. "Why you leave your farm to come paddle wit' us? Money! That's what."

"Okay, money." Arnold picked up a long stick and poked the fire. "But I like the woods. I like bein' by a lake. I like nature. Him too."

Eric nodded his agreement.

Dutil turned to Arnold. "You wrong! He tell me when we start: he need money. And best way for get that, surveying. The food, the sleeping, she all paid."

He looked over at Eric. "Is he right?"

Eric glanced up, and then back into the flames, without speaking.

"I bet he's got a girl." Arnold grinned. "That's always the reason..."

"Yep!" Dutil snapped. "In England. He tell me. He need money for see her."

"Is that so, Eric?"

Eric gave a noncommittal shrug, which was neither a yes or a no. Silence settled for a moment and then cheeky Arnold spoke up again. "If it's money yer after, much better to get an education. Learn a business. Surveyors, they don't get ahead."

"Oh yes oh yes oh yes, next thing, you be Administrator."

Arnold burst out, "Administrator!" He snorted. "You think Pops would like that?"

Eric shook his head, apparently agreeing.

"Listen, I got this here cousin," continued Arnold, "he went to McGill, learned engineering, made a pot of money. But you don't have to learn no engineering, Eric, you can study history, anything, even become a professor yourself, learn mathematics, go get a job in one of them there labs inventing stuff. Lots of money, once you get yourself a university degree. My cousin did."

Eric glanced over, and seemed to be absorbing that.

"No matter what you fellas say," Arnold finished, "an education, that's the way to money!" And then the three of them lapsed into silence, Eric smoking, Arnold stirring the fire, and Dutil rubbing his itchy long nose.

Back to Eric's typewritten excerpt:

I reflected about trees and life: There are tall murmuring pines, big blue spruce and friendly white birches, the wonderful maples, the little cherry trees, the straight ash, rustling poplars, small crooked alders — all different! Much the same in life — we are born with dif-

ferent characteristics and talents. It is impossible to make a friendly white birch into a murmuring pine or a crooked little alder into a maple. All you can do is to see that the best conditions of growth are possible so that they will be the finest trees after their kind.

Men are not born equal and it is hopeless to try and make great geniuses out of everybody; but we can try to help them all be good in their own small individualistic way.

We spent two perfect months in that country. Then I threw over surveying and went to Bishops University.

McGreer Hall,
Bishop's University,
Lennoxville, Que.
November 1922

Dear Rene,

Thank you so much for your fine letter. I got it a long while ago but I keep it close. I've been out in the bush for a couple of months with a surveying party, and now, you'll never guess -- I'm enrolled as an Arts student in Bishops University. It is a wonderful old place, been around for years — Gothic Revival stuff, and some of Quebec's most historic buildings, including St. Mark's chapel. My older brother Jack, whom you know, went here, and his son Gerald is here now. I'm excited at the prospect of three years just learning. At the end of it, I'll be sure to get me a fine job that will allow travelling...

Even though I haven't been writing letters like I should, I have you in mind. I would even say you're with me night and day — but I don't want you to be caught by this. I imagine by now, you have a fine young man who is looking after you and you're probably having a great time.

If you get a chance, write me again and tell me how your dancing is going. I don't know who this Pavlova person is, but I gather from the way you wrote about actually dancing on stage with her, it was a big event. No one can tell me anything about her on the Gaspe Coast, for sure, nor on our survey trip. Ha-ha. Now that I'm at university, I can ask around and find out more. I wonder what the Mater said to your being on stage! I know her attitude.

Any word from your nice sister Hilda, who you last wrote was hitch-hiking alone in Africa from Rhodesia down to Johannesburg? Don't take it wrong that I'm not asking about that sister of yours, Leo. I'll say no more on that subject.

Well, back to my studies. Now that I'm here, if you do write, I'll be able to reply a lot sooner.

Your friend, Eric.

Meanwhile, let us look at more of Eric's collegiate life. Fragments from his later essays will enlighten us before we encounter the cataclysm, that, alas, interrupted this idyllic existence:

There is an old saying that "the Lord looks after fools and drunks." He was looking after me all right when the Principal gave me a room in my residential university with an open fireplace. Here, I would sit dreaming in front of the blazing wood with thoughts of friends, life, love, beauty and death. Sometimes a few college friends would gather around smoking their pipes in the glow from burning embers, or the soft, mysterious light from a few candles on the mantelpiece. The atmosphere was not conducive to hard study, more for restful day-dreaming; but wonderfully adapted to the making of friendships with swapping of stories and ideas about life.

Although he seems headed for an uneventful college career, and certainly underplays the leadership which, as an older student, he would display, this article in *The Mitre,* the University magazine, gives us hints of real dangers about to pounce...

The students of this University have known for some time that it has been the desire of the Principal to see organized a contingent of the Canadian Officers Training Corps. The visit of General MacBrien last November, when he addressed the students on the nature and purpose of the Corps, helped to fan the interest, which many of the students felt, into a real enthusiasm.

Since then, events have moved fairly rapidly...

Opening our veteran's war record, we see a form headed Active Militia of Canada, dated January 1923. Lieut. Eric Alford qualified for the rank of Captain *"by virtue of his overseas service"* and indeed was actually recommended for the rank of Major. Thus he became head of the University Corps, as a picture of the uniformed Corps in late 1923 confirms.

So he was running the Officer Training Corps, and even made quarterback on the rugby team, as this excerpt from the Mitre confirms: *"First year on the team. Filled the difficult position of quarter very successfully."* Oh yes, he enjoyed the games, and the Corps, and it sounds as if he was having the time of his life.

* * *

A small squad of about thirty uniformed men march along the Sherbrooke road towards Bishop's. A light rain has begun to fall and, in their teens or early twenties, these trainee officers are fidgety; they dislike parading in the rain, which is now getting worse. After their successful manoeuvres in a makeshift parade ground to the north-west, they swing along as best they can in the increasing downpour.

At the head of the contingent marches a short, well-built veteran — yes, our own Eric — followed closely by his second-in-command, Delbart, a tall, gawky undergraduate in his last year of Engineering, his small forehead enveloped by an army hat that gives his black eyebrows and jutting jaw a prominence they don't deserve. At the back, a drummer beats time; to help them swing along, they sing old songs from the Great War

Eric slows his step, falls in beside Delbart and, at the end of the verse, tells him another version of Tipperary. His Adjutant burst out laughing, and then calls out the new lyrics to the squad.

Grinning, they sing: "It's the wrong way to tickle Mary, it's the wrong way to go."

Eric scents the air, then looks up as thunder heralds heavier rain. He begins to look nervously left and right into the dripping woods and slows down, agitated. Instead of ordering double time to get back to college, he peers ahead into the rain. Behind him, the first marchers notice, but the men keep singing until the words end. In the dusk, their Major breaks step, and they see him start to crouch, swaying side to side.

Delbart, the Adjutant, quickens his step to come beside. "Something wrong, Sir?"

"The smell, the uniform, it's wet."

"Yes sir," Delbart replies, "I can smell it. Oh, you're remembering it from the Front? Always rain over there, I heard that."

"Same uniform, same smell." But Eric seems not focussed on the words, looking around nervously, fiercely alert and on guard. "And the guns."

Delbart frowns. Did he mean the thunder? Though the singing has stopped, the drum keeps up until Eric orders it to stop. Now, only the rain and marching boots can be heard.

The men grumble and look at each other, perplexed. They want to get home with this rain gusting into them. These army tactics are not what they expected when they volunteered so happily.

As they approach an open farm gate to their left, Major Eric looks up at Moulton Hill rising across ploughed farmland. He loosens his revolver.

Delbart speeds up again to join his leader. "Shall I call a halt, Sir?"

Eric stops, stares up the hill and then, with a loud command, calls out: "Bugler, sound the charge! There's the Ridge!"

This is met by puzzled looks. The Adjutant looks over his shoulder at the others who have broken step and straggle to a halt.

"Bugler, I said, sound the charge!" Eric's voice sounds high, cracked, urgent, and distraught. "We've got to take it! Orders!"

"Sir," Delbart says, "a bugler, we didn't bring one —"

Eric pays no attention, still staring up the hill. "Going to be tough, but we'll take it." He calls loudly again, "Bugler!"

Bewildered, Delbart looks around. The others become alarmed. The drummer has stopped.

"Is he yellow?" cries Eric. "Has he deserted? Court martial in the morning! No time now — we must take the Ridge." An answering roll of thunder confirms the order.

Eric takes a breath, breaks through the gate, and calls loudly, "Cha-a-a-rge!"

His Adjutant scurries after. Others linger, wondering.

Up ahead, Eric whirls. He sees the men holding back. He bawls out through cupped hands, "God Almighty hates a coward. It'll be ours! The Brits tried, then the Scots, and now us. We'll take Passchendaele! Charge!"

A great peal of thunder echoes his cry. Some start through the gate, others hold back, baffled.

Eric sees the confusion. He fires twice over their heads.

That does it. The men crouch and run after him.

He leads the way, then he stops and whirls. "Spread out!" he cries. "Those guns, they'll mow us down. Keep low, run zigzag!" He does so himself as he charges ahead of them all.

As commanded, thirty chilled and shivering trainees attack Moulton Hill over ploughed pastureland turned to squelching mud by autumn rains. They chase one another, stumbling and grumbling.

"I see what he's doing — making us feel what real battle's like. Perfect!" And "Yeah, enough of that parade-ground drilling. This is the real thing!"

Others object loudly. "He's gone crazy." "No, no, he's pretending."

"Those shots, you think that's pretending?"

But they keep on, sliding and slithering up the hill, growing steeper. Eric turns, gratified by his men following. He brandishes his revolver again. "We're making it! Keep it up! We'll take the Ridge yet!"

Zigzagging back and forth as commanded, the squad runs, tripping over the furrows, some falling, others jostling together, all panting hard.

Eric reaches the top and starts firing wildly in all directions. Some duck, others drop in to the mud.

Delbart runs up. "Sir, sir, I don't think we should be shooting. We'll disturb the neighbours."

"The Germans — you think they'll quit without a fight? You're wrong, Delbart, dead wrong!"

"Germans, Sir? No Germans here — closest is thousands of miles away, over the Atlantic. We're on Moulton Hill. Don't you see? Look, there's a farm house."

"Oh, so that's where they're hiding! Lying in wait?"

Before Eric can charge towards the farmhouse, Delbart grabs his arm. "Sir, Sir, hold on! Look, we were there yesterday, remember? Getting fresh eggs. He's our friend. Sir, they're all friends." Eric relents, confused. "It was a grand exercise, but now, Sir, look at the men, they're all muddied, they're worn out. It's over."

"Muddied? Of course they are." He stands for a moment, perplexed but alert.

"Sir, the hill has been taken."

"But where is the enemy? They wouldn't just disappear."

"No Sir, there is no enemy. It was a grand exercise. The men have learned a lot. We taught them what real battle is like. But now, let's form up and get back to college quick as possible."

"Back to where?"

"To college, Sir. We've got to get out of these uniforms. We have exams in a week. We've got to study."

"Study? College?" Eric appears dumbfounded. His revolver goes back into its holster.

Delbart relaxes somewhat. "Well done, men!" he calls out. "Wonderful manoeuvres. Back down. We'll form up on the road. Home on the double! We'll dismiss in the quad." He turns to Eric. "Well done, Sir. I even... I even believed it myself."

Eric nods silently. He starts back down the slope with the others, slipping and sliding. But the spark is gone.

He reaches out. Delbart comes to steady his leader and help him hobble down the hill.

Back to the Mitre: *"We regret having to report the resignation, due to ill health, of Major E. Alford, under whose enthusiastic leadership the Contingent came into being."*

Our tough footballer, our fine leader, has chosen to resign. Does this write *finis* to his University career?

CHAPTER FOUR

Immediately after, Christmas Break allowed Eric to go home, picked up at Port Daniel station by Old Poppa in the buggy and brought safely into the comforting arms of his family in Shigawake. Warned in advance by Canon Alford, Earle and his two sisters, Winifred and Lillian, restrained any criticism of his actions, as did their mother. She would have given him extra care and succour, too, for this is what Eric wrote about her in that 1926 autumn frenzy of writing:

She brought twelve babies into the world; washed, fed and clothed them — taught them their prayers, watched their habits and tried to interest them in the beautiful things of life, especially flower gardens. Tried to make them charitable and loving by bringing them with her when she gave gifts of food and clothing to poor people.

She worked hard to get us all an education, sending us to school and college, writing us letters every week, always with a piece of inspirational poetry inside, chiefly out of a newspaper. Then she sent us out to fight the battles of life, glad when her daughters became nurses and her sons soldiers. But when the War was on, she would walk the floor many nights in silent prayer and worry — no sleep for her.

Her hobbies were three, religion, flower-gardening and visiting the sick. She always had family prayers, morning and evening. Then would read us Bible stories until we dropped off to sleep. She made the most beautiful flower garden in the counties of Bonaventure and Gaspe, helping her neighbours start gardens by giving them plants, shrubs and herbs from her own. One of my earliest recollections was driving my mother to see a poverty-stricken family on Christmas Day.

I have known her to bring a girl into our home to have her baby when her own family had turned her out. I have known her take in two old people when their own selfish relatives had put them out in the cold, and keep them in comfort until they died. I have known her sit up all night with a poor tramp in the middle of winter when our next neighbour had refused him lodging. When anybody was sick in the neighbourhood, she was the first at their bedside.

She had watched her grandchildren and great grandchildren come into the world; now she is a feeble old lady facing west and waiting patiently for her call.

Safe in his own environment again, over the short weeks of his Christmas vacation, with no events to trigger any further flashes, Eric managed to recover. Back he went to Bishop's — his one means, he believed, of measuring up, of becoming what was needed when, or if, he were ever to see Rene again. Nothing had stopped him during those years of the most hellish war ever fought by mankind, whether bullets, incoming counter-battery shelling, shrapnel wounds in the hand and face, or even the dreaded shell shock.

From all accounts, Eric was accepted back at college as if nothing had happened. He even acquitted himself well, until many months later during the autumn term, he played football again. The team won a good few games, but the last one they played, the most important, they lost, and Eric, as quarterback blamed himself.

Shortly after there came a knock on the door of his room in Mc-Greer Hall at Bishop's University. Waiting outside was someone Eric described in an earlier essay:

He is a man of about fifty years of age, with dark brown, flashing eyes. Almost five foot eight inches in height, with the erect carriage and noble bearing which rightly belongs only to old army Officers.

A bulldog sort of a face, broad forehead, thick nose, heavy jaw and square chin, lines deeply carved in the cheeks and upper lip by suffering and fighting, but with humorous wrinkles around the eyes. This tremendous strength is offset by the dreamer's look and softened by sympathetic lines along the forehead. He appears big in every way, a magnetic, dominating personality and immense power of will, and a wicked temper firmly under control. Yes, some awful soul conflicts must have sculptured that face and grooved those lines of character.

He has experienced and observed life: Captain of his rugby and hockey teams at college, four years as a lonely missionary on the bleak Labrador coast, Chaplain Officer with the Canadian Forces in two wars, Rector of one of the largest churches in Montreal. He has travelled extensively, mixed with all kinds and classes of men, observed other races and customs, experienced life in all its aspects: on the lonely Labrador, on the battle-stricken South African veldt, in those muddy trenches in Flanders, in city slums, hospitals, asylums and jails. He has observed life's silent heroisms, its blackening sins, its tremendous struggles and soul conflicts, its divine unselfishness, its ultimate peace.

He has held babies in his arms, swearing them into that great adventure for Good, joined many hands in that perfect partnership of married love, closed tired eyes in death and given the last rites to soldiers, mothers, fathers and young girls. Yet he has looked on life with all its glories and failures, its sins and sufferings, and found it worthwhile.

Waiting for a response by the door stood Col. The Rev. John Alford. Was he surprised this late morning to find his younger brother still in bed? Or did he anticipate all this when he knocked hard on his oaken door?

Eric, head under the covers, did not reply. The door opened anyway and in came his visitor. Eric peered out from under the covers, sat up at once, and swung out of bed. "Jack! I didn't expect to see you here. What are you doing in Lennoxville?"

The Canon took a moment before responding. "Oh, I had some church business in Sherbrooke, and then I thought I'd come over here and visit!" Not hard to see Jack was making this up.

Eric started to dress hurriedly while Jack looked around. Some disarray! Not usual for his younger brother.

Eric grabbed his underwear and loose wool trousers and hauled them on. Then he got down on his hands and knees to look under the bed for his socks and boots. "I've got an exam to go to, Jack."

"Eric, the exam is almost over. It's nearly noon."

"Nearly noon? Oh dear, I must have slept in."

Jack did not reply but crossed to the chair and picked up Eric's shirt where it had been thrown, haphazardly, and brought it over. Eric hurriedly put it on.

"I asked where you were," Jack murmured. "They said you haven't been seen for a couple of days."

"Oh, I'm fine, Jack. Perfectly fine. I just haven't wanted to eat. Lost my appetite." He gave a weak laugh.

"Nothing wrong with that, Eric." Jack went back to the chair, put his elbows on his knees and leaned forward, staring at the carpet before him.

Eric hurriedly did up his shirt, and then crossed to the cupboard to choose a tie. "Sorry the room is in a bit of a mess."

"So I see." Jack raised his eyes briefly and went back to studying the floor. "But don't worry, I'm used to such things."

"I'm not usually like this, of course. It's just that recently ..."

"So I hear."

Eric turned. "Hear? What do you hear?"

Jack shrugged. "Do you want to tell me about it, Eric?"

Eric took out a tie and started to put it on. "There's nothing to tell Jack, nothing. I'm perfectly all right. Honestly."

Jack looked up. "Honestly?"

Eric avoided his look and came across to sit down and put on his boots, which he had found in the cupboard. Jack rose and came to stand above him. "Eric, I know something is wrong. I'm your brother. You can tell me. It won't go any further. Don't worry." Eric didn't look up, but stopped putting on his shoes, and placed his two feet on the floor and his head in his hands.

Jack spoke gently, "Eric, there are times when it all gets too much. I know. I've seen some of our finest veterans, our greatest heroes, I minister to them, this is nothing new to me." He sat beside Eric on the bed and put his arm round his shoulders. "Come on, Eric, what is it?" He gave his shoulders a little shake.

Eric continued staring at the floor. "Well, we lost a few games."

Jack said nothing, listening.

"I know you'll think that's nothing, but you see, Jack, I'm the quarterback. I'm responsible. It haunts me"

"Eric, games are won or lost, it's the nature of rugby. You did your best, I'm sure of that."

"Oh yes. I did my best. Sort of."

"Go on," Jack prodded gently.

"Well, that last game, I kept getting these thoughts... As the players hit me, well, that's rugby, but.... I couldn't really concentrate."

"I've seen that, Eric — a lot, in fact. I was head of the Chaplaincy Service, so our veterans... they come to me."

"It happens a lot?"

Jack nodded. "So you can keep on. What kind of thoughts?"

"Well, you see, it's like I was back there. In Belgium. On the Firing Line. But all the time, I keep seeing them Heinie coming at us. And we can't fire the gun. For some reason it jams. Or else the team isn't working properly; they can't get shells into the breech. We stand there, helpless. And the Hun, they come at us with their bayonets." He shook his head. "I thought when I resigned the Officers Training Corps, all that would be over. I thought I'd be free. And I was. Most of the year. But things started to pile up... Losing games..." He sighed. "Trying to study, but my focus, all gone..." Eric shook his head. "And they call me Pops, they all look up to me. But often, I just want to be left alone..."

Jack nodded, as if he knew this. "But those images you get, they never really happened, Eric."

Eric looked at him for the first time, and then stood. "Damn right, they never happened. We had the best gun! Nothing stopped us. Three years I was there. We never let the side down. Those damn Hun never broke through. We worked like clockwork. We were the best Howitzer team in the Brigade." He paused. His shoulders sagged slightly. "That's the trouble, Jack. It never happened. But that's what I keep seeing. These dreams, these pictures, they keep coming at me from all sides. So, maybe, in that last game when I was being hit hard, this damn picture would come at me, Huns with their rifles! And bayonets. I didn't play as well as I should."

"Nobody blames you for that, Eric."

"No, nobody blames me. In fact..." He walked around the room and then sat in his one deep armchair. He leaned back, stared at the ceiling, and then shut his eyes. "Last week, last Saturday, we had our picture took. We were in Sherbrooke for a celebration. End of the season. All the fellows got to drinking, we were cutting up fine. And then ..." He scrunched his eyes shut.

Jack leaned back on the bed, adjusted his pillow and looked at his younger brother. After a time, he said, "Go ahead, Eric."

Eric took a breath, and continued. "Well, we were celebrating and a young fella came up. I was sitting talking with a pipeful and my glass of whiskey. And he leaned down, tapped me. 'I'm coming to Bishop's — My older brother was killed in the war. I want to join your Officers Training Corps.' I turned to look up — and Jack... Jack, I saw Ralph Rideout, the spitting image. At the Front, y'see, I'd picked up his bloody head from the mud to give it a burial, just his head, and I'd carried it to a pool yellow with mustard gas, I can't forget that, never, I just can't. I said a prayer and threw it in... Well, I thought this was Ralph — back from the dead. I let out a great holler and the room went dead quiet. And then I heard them coming up the stairs to our hotel room, heavy feet. The Hun! Jack, I was damn sure the Hun was coming for us all. I had to save my team. I hauled out a revolver and aimed. I ordered the team under the table. Hide behind chairs!" Eric yelled now. "I'll blast that damn Hun when he walks through the door!"

At this, Jack, shocked, said nothing, trying to keep his composure.

"Well sir, I told our coach, Alfred, 'Get behind, I'm gonna blast him!'"

"And then ... then Alfred, he grabbed my hand, he knocked the revolver away, grabbed it, called, Come in! And put the gun behind his back.

"In came the night manager. He told us to keep the noise down. That's all. And he was right. But Jack, I coulda killed someone..."

"So no harm was done, then?" Jack sighed, relieved.

"No, no harm done. But, I can't stop these flashes, no matter how hard I try. I don't know... It might well happen again, y'see. There's just nothing I can do to stop them. I don't know... what to do. I'm... a bit lost," Eric finally confessed. He leaned back in the chair, breathing heavily.

Jack sat up on the bed. "Well, Eric, the best thing for us right now is to head off back to Montreal, and I'll get you on the train home. Last time this year, you had four weeks at the Old Homestead. And you felt much better."

Eric nodded. "But the exams, Jack. I gotta write the exams."

"You're not ready for that, Eric."

"Damn right I'm not. Every time I go to study, I find I can't concentrate, the flashes. The war. The explosions. I... I just can't focus. And worse, sometimes I'm so alert, for no reason, just wide, wide awake, as if anything might..." He lapsed into silence.

Jack nodded to himself and got up. "Eric, let's get your things together and we'll head off on the three o'clock train. You know how much better you'll feel at the Old Homestead."

"But the exams?"

"Don't you worry about them. Your Principal, McGreer, he was one of my chaplains in the war. I'll have a word. I'll try to make it all right..."

Eric nodded and, with a new lease on life, got up and went around tidying his room. He grabbed a suitcase from the shelf above the cupboard, put it on the bed and began to pack.

Jack watched his brother. "Eric, if this holiday doesn't work, there is a new military hospital out at Ste. Anne de Bellevue, not far from Montreal, just an hour's train ride. They look after veterans. If the Old Homestead doesn't do it, after Christmas, I'll make sure you can get in for some tests."

CHAPTER FIVE

*I*n hospitals in every province of the Dominion of Canada, soldiers disabled in the Great War for Civilization are living in endless suffering and death in life, which is worse than death itself, Eric wrote on his portable typewriter. *I had the opportunity of spending eighteen months in a locked ward of one of these so I claim first hand knowledge of my subject. I will liken this hospital to a gigantic man and divide this imaginary person into several parts.*

The bones and skeleton are the returned soldiers - the wrecks of the Great War. To clothe this skeleton is easy, only a few suits of grey and blue with locked doors and barred windows.

The heart beating so strong and true are the overseas nursing sisters — ministering angels to souls in torment.

The brains are the doctors and medical science fighting death and disease.

And the soul — I suppose the place must have a soul — they wrap a Union Jack around what is left of the Canadian Soldier and ship his coffin home to relatives, or they pull men up from deep down in Hell, put them on their feet again, and send them back into the game of life to work and play for a few more years. This soul is most unutterably sad but sternly beautiful, for I saw the most divine unselfishness and silent heroism that I have ever witnessed during my stay at this Military Institution.

Yes! We are the wrecks of the Great War! We show scars in our heads where the shells made a dent but did not kill. Our lungs are eaten away from the effects of gas. An exploding shell as we went "Over the Top" sent us up in the air, but did no physical damage. A German infantryman went to bayonet us and we were crazed with fear. Our legs were shot away. God help us! Our eyes are out. "Poor chap, a terrible inward struggle passing all understanding put him where he is," so the doctors say. Now nurses and orderlies lead us all around by the hand. They take us out for walks in our uniforms like a flock of frightened sheep. I am so frightened I walk on my knees.

Once we built bridges, painted pictures, made poetry, preached sermons, healed the sick, worked on farms, made wonderful flower gardens, but that was all before the war. Now we sit in corners and knit stockings, make little baskets, do bead work, while lady visitors come in and say, "My how perfectly splendid that stocking is. I must get you to knit me a sweater." Do you wonder I curse them openly?

It was Sunday and the boys were all gathered by strong orderlies, and paraded in their greys and blues to the little Chapel, the suffering torments plain on their faces and broken bodies. All had gathered to worship the Almighty Father, God of Love, Peace and Good Will.

The chaplain was a hero himself: he had been through two wars and gone with many a man to the scaffold. Indeed, a coward would not have been fit to speak to these broken heroes.

One soldier was cursing in a monotonous tone; others were fight-

ing in a corner, separated by orderlies. Then the chaplain's message rang out clear and strong like a bugle call: "I believe that no soul will be finally lost! Almighty God has a great pair of loving arms right around you... understanding all, forgiving all, suffering with you and helping you bear your cross." One of the broken soldiers from the rear of the chapel shouted, "Cut out that cursing and fighting! This damn parson is saying something worthwhile."

On Armistice Day the Union Jack was flung to the breeze from the hospital flag-pole — the flag they had given their lives for, with its three crosses and its matchless colours: red for self sacrifice, blue for love, and white for purity. The broken soldiers stood erect with the light of love in their eyes and saluted the colours.

"It's Tommy this, and Tommy that, and Tommy how's your soul?"

But it's this thin red line of heroes when the drums begin to roll!

These overseas nurses with their blue uniforms and white veils hanging down — God bless them! They love these broken wrecks of the war. They put their arms around them, wander with them hand-in-hand in Hell and try to pull them up to their Heaven. When Christ died upon the cross He took our sins upon Himself. Well, that is just what those sisters do with the returned soldiers. They make the special sin or suffering their very own.

It seems to me if you want to help a person, it is impossible to do so from a distance. You must touch! And those girls put their arms right around the soldier patient — blind their eyes to the repulsiveness, shut their ears to the cursing, and love and lift.

I have seen a nurse looking after a cancer patient so repulsive that an orderly might vomit when he entered his room. I have seen another feed a man who was gone mentally, morally and physically, just like a mother would feed a newborn babe.

But they often lose their fight and close the tired eyes of the broken soldier — who can then open his eyes to the Call of his Great

42

General. "Well done thy good and faithful servant, enter into the Joy of thy Lord."

And then sometimes they win their fight! If you could see the light in a doctor's eye when he has won a man back and set him free again, you would appreciate some of the joys of a doctor's life of service.

What of the soul of this soldiers' institution?

Who is that man feeling his way up from the village with a cane, led by a little dog? Oh him? He lost his eyes overseas in a gas attack. But he took a course in massage at a school for the blind, and now he massages soldiers.

One of the chaps wants to write a letter home to his wife to thank her for the photograph of his two little kiddies. He was a Flying Corps Officer overseas, but creeping paralysis has set in and he is losing a fight with death. The more you do for him the less he will do for himself, so help him if you dare! But this letter must be written, although his hands are too shaky to hold a pen and his mind too feeble to formulate a thought. "All right, my comrade," answers an artilleryman, "we will write this wonderful letter together."

"Dear Mary," the paralysis chap says. The artilleryman writes it down and inquires, "All's well, what's next?" The sick laddie answers: "I - do - not - think - I - can - write - today. Help - me - to - lie down - and straighten - out - my - legs - please... "

"All right, tomorrow then, old soldier," answers his cheery helper.

It took his comrade, who was also suffering intensely, four days to help him write that letter.

A soldier, a mental patient, was suddenly given leave to see his wife and kiddies. He heard another soldier remark that he would like some wild flowers. This soldier could only stay one day at home, then had to return to Hell. But all that day his wife and kiddies went out into the fields gathering wild flowers for the sick soldier.

"Everybody, please try to be good," the sister said, "just for half

an hour. A soldier's mother has come a long way to see her son."
The son did not know his mother — he did not even know his own
name, but how wonderfully quiet that ward was. Even the cursing
patients smiled at the gentle old lady.

One day a young parson, a mere boy just out of college, walked
into the ward escorted by a nursing sister. God never meant him
to walk into that ward and ask darn fool questions to those suffer-
ing heroes, but our boys returned good for evil, answering his silly
questions in a gentlemanly manner.

One man, dying from the effects of gas and suffering intensely
every morning, said, "I do not wish to give those little nurses or the
orderlies any extra trouble, so I smother my groans in my pillow."

Another hero opened his heart to one of his comrades at night.
"Yes, I am in pretty bad shape. I guess I am dying all right and
would just give the world to see an old girl friend. But who would
want a young girl to be tied to a broken old soldier? Not me! I would
shoot myself like a dog first. So I let her go and I pray for her every
night."

Yes, the soul of this hospital is most unutterably sad, but sternly
beautiful.

And you, my soldiers, who have your health and strength, so
keenly alive to the beautiful things of earth — would you turn
sometimes with a silent prayer to the Merciful Father, God of Love,
and ask Him to be with these souls in torment and comfort them?
They stood in front line trenches against the German army for you
and for me. They did not give their lives — that would have been
easy. They gave themselves to endless suffering, and death in life,
which is worse than death itself.

CHAPTER SIX

The Lions,
Brentwood, Essex.
July 1925

Eric dear,

I haven't had a letter for such a long time that I am worried. I know you go off on those dangerous trips into the wild forests of Canada. But you told me that you were entering university. And I've had a couple of letters from you since then from Bishops. I'm wondering what is the matter?

Perhaps you met a young lady there, a student, but that should not preclude our friendship. At least I hope not.

I never told you how romantic and exciting I found your descriptions of those canoe trips and expeditions into the winter woods on snowshoes or with dogs pulling sleds. It is so very foreign to us here. My friends love hearing about that wild and uncharted wilderness that you seem to understand so well. It is most exotic, so very different to us surrounded by our buildings and motor cars. Even now we're seeing fewer and fewer horses on the streets.

I confess I read some of your letters, not to Leo who doesn't appreciate such things, but to others at the Ginner Mawer School where I have been studying, as you know. You see, I do classes there even though I have graduated, just to keep my hand in. They all love hearing about your distant adventures — causes quite a stir when I bring in another letter.

Hilda has returned from South Africa but doesn't enjoy living with the Mater. The problem is, Leo loses no chance in taunting her, even hinting she's not pretty enough to get a man. Now, she's determined to leave again. She's even thinking of New Zealand, opening a dancing school in Auckland. It is not as adventurous as Canada, of course, but it's a long way from the Mater. I have been encouraging her.

As you seem to understand, Mater is not pleased with what I'm doing. I appear in recitals, and I love dancing on stage. I have even taken to helping Ruby Ginner with some of her classes, working with beginners. I don't know which I like more, appearing on stage, or teaching others. Fortunately, now I'm doing both. It's not beyond possibility that I will join Hilda or perhaps go on to Australia and start a school there. A bit of a challenge for me, but as you know I never mind a challenge.

Do write to me, or if one of your relatives gets this and something has happened to you, I really must know. So I'll send it to Shigawake, rather than Bishop's. I just can't bear the thought of you attacked by a bear or falling through some frozen lake — you have no idea how my imagination works to so upset me.

So write to me, my big adventurer.
Rene.

The Military Hospital,
Ste. Anne de Bellevue, Que.
November 1925

Dear Rene,

My silence has not been due to any accident, thank heaven. But it is due to something far worse, and I had no idea how to explain. Perhaps if we were ever lucky enough to meet one day, I could give you the full story. But for the moment, let me say that I am in a military hospital, where your letter reached me. I have suffered from nerves and shell shock again. You remember in England I had it, too. But I was sure I had recovered. I still intend to finish at Bishops, of course, and get my degree. But right now, nothing is sure.

I'll write you as soon as I get out of here. They say I'm getting better.

Warm wishes from your "Adventurer."
Eric.

So was that hospital the end of all hope Eric had for Rene? Not so fast. He wrote about his stay in hospital, as he did all the other essays: *"...during the time I was attending lectures and carrying on with all my work as a university student in Third Year Arts."* Autumn term of 1926... after the hospital. So he did make it back to Bishops! Though he didn't play rugby, choosing instead to write, presumably feverishly, many essays.

Somehow he must have recovered, gotten home to Shigawake, and then rejoined his University in September. Trust our veteran. Oh, and in a note he mentions a dog, which seems important, likely recommended by his military doctors.

My British bulldog Foch sleeps by the open fire in my room — a brindle and white, with a perfectly hideous, ugly face, tongue out, teeth showing, snorting, sneezing, puffing and panting. But a very lovable dog and a wonderful friend. Every once in a while, he brings me his ball to play with him or a rope to pull tug-of-war.

One of the students said, "Poor old Pop, after all the girls he must have met, now he has only a homely old bulldog for a sleeping partner." But I tell you frankly, you would never get a truer friend than this old bulldog pup of mine.

43 Macleay Street,
Sydney, NSW, Australia
February 1927

Eric dear,

I am writing this to your Shigawake home, because I'm not sure from your last letter whether you will be going there from hospital, or straight to college. But I'm writing now because I have a new address. This will come as a surprise, but I know you like surprises – I certainly do. You see, I did make the decision to go to Sydney, Australia, as I hinted earlier. I am here now. Being the first graduate of the Ginner Mawer School to arrive, I am very busy, as you might imagine. I have begun teaching. I am also trying to arrange to get dance on the school curriculum in

Sydney, and even now am instructing schoolteachers in the rudiments of classical Greek dancing. I also give a few talks, which are being well received and reported in the newspapers, believe it or not, and am even thinking about opening a school of my own. Dancing is very much in the news these days, with the tour here this year of Anna Pavlova.

Sydney is rather exciting, Eric. Australians are not at all as stuffy as we British. They are like Canadians, and have a good sense of humour, always laughing. And their accent! You would find this city a lot of fun if you were able to come.

I know you will be writing about your time in hospital, but it might take time for that to reach me here, forwarded from Brentwood. I just have your letter which assures me that you are soon getting out of that Military hospital. I am thrilled, of course, and from what little you have told me, your stay there will have been quite beneficial.

Yes, of course, I remember those times when you behaved a little differently. You should not worry about telling me. I know you to be very brave, and after what you have endured, it is wonderful you can function so well , rugby, running the Officers Training Corps — a born leader, don't I know it! As you say, your malady is only intermittent. So try not to worry.

It will take a good deal of time for our letters to cross now, with me being out here. I shall just have to wait patiently, but be sure to write as soon as you can find the time.

Meanwhile, I do have great faith in the future here. So far, I've been so lucky in my welcome from these warm and wonderful people.

Your faithful friend, Rene.

Finally, one crucial excerpt from Eric's typewritten dossier, this one written perhaps after he'd received Rene's letter:

A college friend asked me one night in front of my open fire, "Why are you so solemn and sad, Pop old boy?"

I said, I have struck my tents, and burnt all my bridges. No retreat: advance or die fighting. I am on the march. There is a spot I love, but I have left it forever...

A beautiful garden overlooking the Bay de Chaleur with one hundred and forty lilacs: white, purple and blue, a rose walk, white, red and pink, five avenues of trees with wonderful hedges,

spirea, hydrangea, larkspur, poppies and all other gorgeous flow-
ers. A little summer house under the apple trees called "Lovers Re-
treat" covered with Virginia creeper. When I think of the wonderful
colouring of the flowers facing the matchless blue waters of the Bay
de Chaleur — the afterglow of the sunset back over the hill with
that blue mountain ridge filled with lakes and trout streams, all
old haunts of mine. Then the moonlight on the sparkling waters of
the Bay de Chaleur at night — one trail of blazing glory to Fairy-
land.

Yes! Give me a flower garden by the sea and I am happy. But
now I am leaving the east and facing west.

In June after the exams, I go direct to that Pacific Coast on a big
adventure. I am saying goodbye to the Bay de Chaleur, burning my
bridges behind me. I am on the march.

The saddest word to me in the English language is Farewell. It is
the thought of saying goodbye that is making me sad tonight. Not
the thought of the glorious adventures with friendship, victory, de-
feat and suffering, which will surely come.

And now, having learned all this about Eric, we can rejoin him
on the station platform in Port Daniel, awaiting the arrival of the
Atlantic, Quebec, and Western Railway train from Gaspe.

PART TWO: 1927

CHAPTER SEVEN

Eric strode through white clouds hissing from the locomotive and watched the carriages slow down. Carrying his suitcase and haversack, he headed for the stool placed by the conductor for embarking passengers. Half a dozen gathered around, nodding to Eric as he joined them, stepping back to allow him first entry, as was only right for a veteran.

Making sure to choose his seat on the bay side of the carriage, now only partly filled, Eric lifted his duffel bag and suitcase overhead and put his haversack on the seat. A whistle blast announced departure. The train gave a jolt and lurched out of the station, moving slowly. Some of the passengers were still settling in, arranging their bags, talking among themselves. Eric clenched his eyes shut, opened them, shook his head slightly, and settled back to look out the window. He'd taken this trip already, to and from university and to check himself in at the military hospital. But now, an altogether different beginning...

His thoughts ranged over the details of his leaving: had he forgotten anything? Had he left everything in order? How would

Marshal Foch fare with the family? His bulldog had taken a liking to his older brother Earle, and more importantly, Earle to him. Momma would also see that Foch would be cared for. Such a shame to leave him, but nothing for it, the train trip would have been too hard. So in fact, all seemed in order.

Ahead in Montreal, difficulties loomed. His nephew Gerald, Jack's son, had been at Bishop's during the first of those unfortunate episodes. What memories of that remained? Were the episodes generally known? Was Eric considered, as he feared, a crazy loon? Had rumours of his attacks spread through the college? Or had everything been smoothed over, his brother Jack discreet, and those temporary set-backs ignored, as Eric hoped? Well, he would soon see. He'd written to Gerry to suggest lunch.

And the next challenge — his brother's church: Trinity Memorial in Notre Dame de Grâce. Canon John had worked all through the early part of the decade to raise the general public's awareness about returning veterans, many disabled, some physically and some, like Eric, with hidden ailments. When the money for the actual church building finally came together after heroic and tireless fund-raising, what would Jack's Trinity "Memorial" Church contain? What souvenirs of death and much mayhem? The few times Eric had passed through Montreal before, he had avoided going there; he wanted no reminders of the Firing Line. But he loved remembering those outings on leave with his brother in London, driven by such lovely chauffeurs, Rene and her caustic sister Leo. Sweet reminiscences. If it hadn't been for Jack's high rank, Eric would never have met Rene, the lovely volunteer driver, not in a million years. How far apart were their lives: she from a wealthy Brentwood family from Essex, and he from a lowly farm on the Gaspe. Only by the Gray's volunteering their large brown Daimler had he and his cherished lady friend met.

So yes, the war had brought — apart from comradeships and

acts of heroism — other benefits. But here he was, thinking of benefits, of Rene, when it was so very unlikely they would ever meet again. Banish such thoughts!

But don't let go of those times his brother had visited him at the Front, as Head of the Chaplaincy Service of the Canadian Forces. Eric remembered that on one occasion their visit had been interrupted by a counter barrage from the enemy, so they'd both had to race to a dugout for safety. Moments like that did nothing to trigger any disconcerting episodes: rather, what bothered Eric were the memorabilia he might encounter in the church. Well, he thought, I'll just wait and see.

Before he knew it, the train blew its warning for Kruse's Crossing. They passed the lane, and then, still not at top speed, the train chugged over the Iron Bridge across the Hollow. What images this crossing spawned: the Millpond, the distant greying timbers of the mill, and their old Tamworth sow in her pasture, circled by spruce rails (for it was deemed temporary). When Eric was three or four, the hired man would take him back in the wheelbarrow with two pails of slops: old potato and turnip peelings, rotten carrots, bits of beetroot, all in water from boiling their vegetables.

Back to the hollow to feed the red pig
Home again, home again, jiggety-jig.

The hired man, Howard, would sing this ditty to little Eric who clutched fiercely at the sides of the wheelbarrow with small hands.

And what about jolting back to the hay-fields and out again, past the Hollow, in the empty hayrack? Lying on the load to watch wild clouds streaking across the sky before an East wind heralding onslaughts of rain. Get that load into the barn fast! But other days, when the sun beat down and he hefted coils of hay onto the load — he'd even learned how to build loads himself, no easy task, going down that slanted hill-track behind the house, plenty of bumps and boulders to shift the hay as the horses galloped down at high speed, pulling back hard before they swerved into the thrashing floor and came to a halt. Off he would get and clamber up into the mow, where Earle would fork off the load hay to him and Howard for spreading around.

And then, oh glory! Down to the wharf stretching its battered timber-tongue into the mouth of the blue bay. They'd tear onto the lower lip where fishing boats moored, strip naked and leap screaming into the icy waters to get the hayseed and flecks of straw and sweat splashed away. And out fast, for sure, because you'd freeze in more than a minute, those darn waters were so cold!

And how he used to love milking the one cow in the barn in mid-winter, when the others, being with calf, had dried their milk — that one provided all the family needed for its winter milk, cream, and butter. In the darkened stable with its door shut against the twenty-below weather outside, the hot bellies of the cattle steaming, squirting into the slushy, foaming bucket as he worked first at the front teats and then the back, finally with thumb and forefinger squeezing out the last drops of milk, before rising to bring the stool to the front of the stable, setting down the bucket at one side, shooing away the two cats prowling for their long-desired drink of milk, until he poured some in a can and let them go at it greedily. Horses next. Through into the thrashing floor, open the bin for the oats, get out a dish and come tip the feed into small trays beside the mangers. Byes how those horses loved their oats!

Placing the milk bucket carefully aside, he'd grab the square-mouth shovel and clean down the "drene" (centre walkway) opening the door to the manure pit to shovel the warm-smelling manure out for spring spreading. Fine fertilizer, no doubt. That and seaweed from the beach, what more did a farmer need? And before breakfast, he would sit on the rail seat at back of the stable to relieve himself. So much better than that icy outhouse behind, the two-holer used mainly by the women. Then back into the house with a bucket of milk through snow flurries, hauling off his winter togs in the porch and carrying the milk proudly into Old Momma's kitchen. Yes, he loved that job, assigned before entering his teens. Earle had enough on his plate: feeding the cattle, pigs, chickens, so many chores.

But after the hearty breakfast: bacon from the porker killed in the fall, eggs they'd just gathered, soft fluffy bread baked by Old Momma, well, he could curl up and read. It was only later, when he came back from the war and tried curling up once again, that Old Momma had to snap sharply at Earle, who often complained.

"Now you fellas listen! It's a poor farm that can't afford one gentleman."

How often had he heard Old Momma say that! And finally, it had become lore. Earle stopped his complaining, Old Poppa stopped looking sideways at him; his sisters too accepted it — they always had — but mind you, when the sun was hot, into the flower garden he went. Why, he'd even built a small wooden gazebo with two crude benches where he could sit quietly, read perhaps, hearing buggies trot by, even an occasional motor car with American tourists.

These soothing images kept flowing through his gradually relaxing mind, and soon in the rocking railway carriage, Eric fell asleep.

Where Chaleur Bay narrowed to a point at Matapedia, the Gaspe train halted to wait for the bigger Ocean Limited, thundering in from Halifax on its way to Montreal. After some to-ing and fro-ing the Gaspe carriages were attached and then took off again. Eric made himself comfortable for the night.

Montreal. All the next day. His first challenge.

The train had been late arriving, but even so Eric had time to visit a couple of bookshops. Finally he met Gerald at the St. George's

Club up on the Boulevard. In the elegant lobby, his nephew gave him a long, hard look, and then led him through into a dining room with white tablecloths, suave waiters, some with limps, Eric noticed, and even the head waiter with one arm. Fairly brimming, too, with lawyers and businessmen, even a judge whom Gerald pointed out.

Gerald, noticing his look, said, "Yes, my father made sure this club hired as many veterans as they could." To which Eric nodded, pleased.

Soon, Gerald brought up the recent historic flight over the Atlantic. Was he just avoiding talk of college? "What do you think of that fellow Charles Lindbergh last month? Must have been crazy to try that." Transatlantic flights were all the rage, Eric knew: newspaper headlines around this time seemed only concerned with brave aviators.

"Well, he made it to Paris, Gerry." Eric settled himself and looked around. "Pretty fine club."

"Thanks. Lucky to get in. Poppa's influence, I'm sure: everyone here knows the Canon."

"But you're doing pretty well yourself. A rising young lawyer, they tell me."

Gerald shrugged. "Trying my best. But yes, yes, Lindbergh sure made it. Never seen such a reaction — the whole world went crazy. Men like him shouldn't be allowed to fly. You'd think they'd have stopped him taking off from New York in that little *Spirit of St. Louis*. Certain death, I would have said, like many of the others before him."

"He reached Le Bourget Field the next day. May 21st, by golly."

"First time ever." Gerald shook his head.

"Well, sometimes it's the crazy fellas get things done." Eric paused as the waiter limped up to take their order: a plate of roast beef of Merry Olde England and Yorkshire pudding with all the trimmings! He couldn't wait.

They went on chatting, Gerry telling Eric that the Canon was away at a midweek conference. "You should see his church, Eric. It's a thing to behold!"

Well, so far so good. He knew that Gerry would have brought up his illness had it been a *cause célèbre*. "I'm going to take this afternoon and really visit."

In no time their soup had appeared. "So you're headed West?"

Eric nodded, and changed the conversation: "And what's that young scallywag Lloyd up to these days? You know, I nearly got your brother killed in the woods a few years back."

Gerry put down his knife and fork and wiped his mouth with his napkin. "You can be damn sure my brother told me, and all the world, about that, Eric. You fellows got caught in some surprise rainstorm in the middle of February. Oddest thing I ever heard. Nearly ended your earthly existence."

"Yep. Made short work of our snowshoes. We had some twine, so we lashed spruce and cedar twigs to the frames, tried to carry on that way. We'd go about a mile then the twigs'd give way, dropping us to our arm-pits in that slushy, sticky, melting snow water. Was it ever freezing, too!"

Gerry shook his head.

"Wet through, we took axes, tried hewing boards out of a soft tree for skis. But they were worse, because one end would catch in front, throwing us on our heads. Up to your waist in water and mighty cold water at that. Drenched. No way of lighting a fire or sheltering in that downpour, so we had to keep going. Nearly froze to death back in the interior."

"I don't think Lloyd will ever forget that. But he went off with you again?"

"Oh yes, your brother Lloyd's one tough young fella."

"I think his Uncle is even tougher," Gerry added admiringly.

Eric sloughed off the compliment and asked, "Is he still doing that prospecting?"

"Getting interested in the stock market now, like everyone else. Making a barrel of money, all of them."

Eric nodded and continued eating. "These fellows here sure look prosperous. And this roast beef is the best I've had for a long time, Gerry. Thank you very much."

"Nice, isn't it? Thought you'd enjoy yourself."

Eric and his nephew continued chatting, running back over their families, avoiding any hints of Eric's stay in military hospital. Eric had seen Gerry appraise him keenly in the lobby. "You look just fine, Uncle Eric," he had said, sounding a little surprised.

After dessert, Gerald headed back to his law office, and Eric caught a streetcar westward towards Trinity Memorial in Notre Dame de Grâce. He regretted he'd been in hospital for its dedication in May 1926.

He paused before the large, grey, neo-gothic building and took a deep breath. But then from the large oaken doors emerged two men, in their lapels the button signifying "veteran". But Eric had no need of that recognition. One used crutches to get about on his good leg and his companion had a rather badly scarred face. Making sure his companion didn't fall, the man with the wounded face nodded at Eric, who for some reason found himself snapped into a salute, as the soldiers in that London restaurant had done when a Victoria Cross recipient entered.

They passed on and Eric climbed the broad steps, entered the oaken doors, up more stairs, and paused before the open Rector's office to his right.

The secretary, a short, stocky woman with greying hair, came forward. "Another veteran!" she remarked, "Welcome to Trinity Memorial." When she went back to her desk, Eric moved warily forward to check the nave. At the far end of the aisle, stained-glass windows glowed with a crucified Christ, below which tasteful white granite ornamented the chancel's setting for its large altar.

He walked slowly down the aisle, passing a somewhat older man sitting slumped at the edge of a pew, a veteran again, thought Eric, pleased: at least my brother's church is doing what it was built for... He noted the array of Great War flags high in each corner, turned left toward the side chapel, and then on impulse mounted a curved wooden stair behind the huge Messmer pulpit. The sounding board spread over his head like a giant engraved leaf as he tried to imagine what it would be like, preaching to that sea of filled seats, Sunday after Sunday. God had called his brother to be His servant even before he'd attended Bishop's University some thirty-five years ago. He wondered what that call would be like.

Back down he went, and around into the Lady Chapel. So far so good: no triggers from the war disturbed him. He stood quietly before the smaller altar under three small stained glass windows brought from a former church combined now with Trinity, as noted in the plaque:

Francis Armstrong Pratt, the former rector of Church of the Good Shepherd, became Associate Rector here at Trinity, when the two came together.

After a time, he went and sat in a pew. In this sanctuary, he might contact his Lord and Master. He allowed his thoughts to float free. They turned, as one might expect, to the future.

"What," he wondered, "should I do... My great adventure lies ahead. But beyond? I've left the Gaspe Coast. And now what?"

Preparing for his trip had preoccupied him to the exclusion of all else. Now that he had actually set off with only the future ahead to think of, what next?

Well, ask and ye shall receive... "Dear Lord, give me a message. Some purpose. Not right away, don't worry. But later — whatever

I'm doing, I promise to listen. After all, you brought me through those battles, those college courses, and that... hospital. I surely am yours. Talk to me and I'll obey."

Eric stayed a good long time in the side chapel of this church, built so that the Fallen would be remembered. He had been told a local women's group had planted 840 trees westward along Sherbrooke Street, called now by some the Road of Remembrance. Each tree bore a plaque in memory of a soldier killed in the Great War. He would remember that. He sighed and then, closing his eyes again, formed a prayer for the boys he'd left in Military Hospital, eking out, forever it seemed, their living death. He hoped he'd never have to go back.

CHAPTER EIGHT

1 0:15 PM Thursday night: June 24, 1927. Windsor station. The great CPR train, the Imperial, left Montreal with nary a jolt on its journey across the Dominion of Canada. The passengers had been allowed aboard half an hour early and Eric was already in the wide washroom, cleaning up; two passengers also occupied the other basins, one shaving, the other brushing his hair and trying, rather unsuccessfully, Eric noticed, to conceal a nasty scar on one side of his head. Even this long after the war, veterans seemed everywhere in evidence, making Eric feel not so alone. Two of them exchanged comments about their journey's beginning, but the third seemed disinclined to talk.

In no time Eric climbed into his lower berth. The night before on the Ocean Limited he had sat up all night, not wanting to pay extra for sleeping accommodation, so his rest had been uneasy and interrupted. Tonight, with the gentle rocking of the train, he soon fell blissfully asleep.

9:45 AM Friday morning. North Bay. Few got on, and the train chuffed off through endless woods. Charlie, the uniformed porter, made up Eric's berth while he was at breakfast, and when he came back, he sat watching heavy, dark forests flow by. So few towns and so little to see, so Eric turned to his haversack. He had brought along *The Life and Letters of Paul, the Apostle*, by Lyman Abbott, which he'd found on one of the many shelves in the Old Homestead — his sisters read a lot, as did Earle, who doted on Zane Grey. Then yesterday poking about the downtown bookstore, he'd looked for a book on Greek dancing, but nothing came up save for *The Eye of Greece*, a small guide published the previous year by The Acropolis Travel Bureau. Better than nothing. Were he ever to see Rene again, he wanted to be up on such things. He'd also found *Kangaroo*, by DH Lawrence, published recently, about the author's visit to Australia.

12:15 PM Sudbury. More woods. As the train roared on, the comfortable sound of its whistle penetrated the thick glass, reminding him every so often of the Regular back home, blowing for Kruse's Crossing.

With not much to look at in this northern Ontario, he let his thoughts wander. Luckily he'd been frugal with his army pay. He had asked sister Jean to deposit it for him in the Bank of Montreal, as brother Jack had advised. Add his officer's pay of $120 a month to his war service gratuity of $550, and also, beginning with his hospitalization, a small disability pension, and he'd accumulated a moderate nest egg. He'd also kept most of his modest salary from surveying. At home, he had tried to contribute to the farm, but his mother would hear none of it. He wondered if he would ever see her again. Lately, she had become so frail.

Having saved so assiduously for "a rainy day," that rainy day had come. He had bought a coach-class ticket, double the sixty dollars of colonist class, where passengers had to provide their own bedding and sit on hard seats; a first-class ticket would have been too extravagant. Coach bestowed the benefits of restful nights in a berth before he struck that exciting but unknown West Coast.

8.35 AM Saturday. Port Arthur. Eric was finishing breakfast when they neared the head of the Great Lakes; he had studied them in school. And soon, the woods gave way to farmland, slightly more interesting. But then, Eric began to ponder the wisdom of his journey.

Why was he going? Wanderlust? Or had something deeper driven him to venture west, so far from all he held dear? He pushed these disturbing thoughts away — perhaps he didn't want to acknowledge the romantic vision of Rene driving him ever onwards. Get on with some reading, he decided. Saint Paul, having travelled all over the Mediterranean himself, might have advice for this lonely figure on a train, heading he knew not where...

8:15 PM that evening: Central Station, Winnipeg. The Imperial pulled in before dark; Eric got out onto the platform to stretch his legs. He saw lots of passengers boarding here, so the berths in his carriage would be filled. And when he returned, he found, sitting opposite, a well-dressed young man: two prominent ears beneath neatly brushed short brown hair.

This upper-berth passenger introduced himself as Adam Hadley, eager to talk and full of energy. He began asking Eric questions, where he was going, and so forth. Although his eyes went straight to Eric's veteran pin, he did not venture there. Eric admitted that he had just graduated from Bishop's University.

"You're so lucky! No hope of a higher education in our family. And being the oldest, I had to support us. I only made it to Grade 10." Adam grinned, and went on proudly, "Got my first job in 1921 delivering groceries for $5 a week. From that, I moved up to delivering engravings for seven bucks, and then landed a job as an office boy in the Grain Exchange at ten a week!"

Eric gave the expected look of approval, and Adam went on, "Yep, I was convinced I was on the road to success. You know about the Grain Exchange?" Eric shook his head. "Ten storeys — it'll be the biggest office building in the British Empire! The status place to work in post-war Winnipeg, I'll tell ya. I delivered morning papers to the big houses of wealthy Grain Exchangers. Those fellas had come west to Winnipeg with nothing and made their fortunes. If they could do it, so could I." Adam paused, and went on, "Only thing we thought about was money. See, I grew up in poverty. Our family knew nothing else, like a lotta folk in Winnipeg during the war.

"My first big job was running messages back and forth between our office and the telegraphers on the trading floor of the Grain Exchange." Adam loved going on at the mouth, Eric saw, but he enjoyed listening to the eager young man. "Soon I was helping with the books and learning how to run an adding machine, and how to make out insurance policies. The office opened at nine and closed whenever the day's work was done, usually towards midnight. I sure got tired, but by Christmas I had won a hundred buck bonus!" He nodded, thinking. "Ran all the way home with an envelope of five dollar bills."

Eric smiled. Adam was enjoying telling of his own history, so representative of many Winnipegers.

"When navigation ended on the Great Lakes in December, the vessel-brokerage business came to a dead stop. I picked up some extra money as a part-time bookkeeper and by the time I was nineteen, I was making $150 a month, and my Christmas bonus reached $500."

That certainly impressed Eric. "Quite a story!"

"Oh yes. Bank accountants made less. You know, those banks refused to let employees marry until they were earning $1,000 a year! That took maybe ten years..." Adam looked concerned. "Am I talking too much?"

"Not at all, Adam. Fascinating, this life of yours out on the prairie."

"Well, sir, I bought a half-interest in a couple of race-horses, but I've been falling for one swindle after another. I even sent good money after bad to promoters of oil wells in Louisiana, gold mines in Colorado, and silver mines in Ontario. In between times, I took flyers in the grain market and lost. But you know, last year I had a nearly-new Ford sedan and smoked two-for-a-quarter cigars." Adam paused, remembering. "Now I'm on my way to Calgary because of something that could make even more money. Well, why not? Everyone's getting rich. Might as well keep at it."

Later that night in his lower berth, Eric reflected how out in the big world, all the talk seemed to be about money, people making it, and how bright the whole future looked. He wondered why he'd never been touched by that. You certainly needed money to survive. But not a subject to dwell on, so he drifted off.

After an early breakfast, Eric waited in an adjacent seat until Adam finally slid down from his upper berth and went off to eat. The black porter, Charlie, made up their berths: he took the sheets from below and above, threw them in a big laundry bag, folded the blankets neatly and placed them on the upper bunk, along with the brown wooden partitions he had slid from their slots. Then he pushed hard and folded the curved upper bunk into place in the rounded ceiling of the car. He grinned good-naturedly at Eric and they exchanged a few words, as they had been doing every so often. Eric liked the old fellow — well, not so old, but in his fifties at least — grey frizzled hair beginning to adorn the good-natured but slightly weathered brown face.

Eric opened his new Greek Travel Guide, hoping to unearth at least something on classical Greek dancing, but no luck. Adam, on his return, saw that Eric was engrossed and lazily watched the featureless fields roll by.

On the train went: 9:40 AM Sunday, Regina, Saskatchewan; 11.05 Moose Jaw, and soon —

4.10 PM Swift Current The train was sailing past great broad acres reaching toward infinity, it seemed, light green with spring shoots. Imagine farming out here, thought Eric — none of the rolling land at home that their horses had to deal with, hauling the mower or reaper tilted sideways, slipping, always slipping, so hard to keep going in a straight line.

Eric gestured out the window. "That prairie, it sure stretches far and wide. You know, I used to wonder what gave those cowboys such a free, fearless, sweeping look. It's this boundless land with its mighty distances. I worked near here, you know." He proceeded to light his pipe.

"And how did you like that?" Adam prompted.

"All right. But one special morning, well, she started off fine: meadow larks on every pole sending up bursts of song. Adam, that melody caught my soul and tore it right up into the clouds. But when the music stopped, back came your thoughts with a thump."

"Oh yes, I've heard them larks — not often, mind. Spent most of my time, as I told you in the city."

"Well sir, towards noon the wind started." Adam nodded; he'd seen it. "We hurried to our tents — just impossible to hold a precise level instrument in that gale."

"Sure can blow on the Prairies."

"By and by the gale increased to a darn prairie cyclone. That sand pelted us like a harsh cloud of furious, drifting snow. The lights in Swift Current blew off their posts." Eric drew on his pipe. "No man could stand upright. Our tents were laid flat and we buried our heads in the sand like ostriches, praying for mercy."

"I've heard of them cyclones."

Eric sat back. "Well sir, she finally stopped and, all of a sudden, there was this great peace. Some farmer's wheat crop, young sprouts all about three inches high, had blown over onto the railway tracks, poor fella. Glad I'm not back there now — give me the forest any time."

At the dinner service that night, Adam told him, "You know, I'm getting off in Calgary. Four in the morning. I hope that black fella, he remembers to wake me. You just never know with them Negroes."

"Charlie? I find him reliable. I've seen a few of these black fellows over in Europe, too, all fine. A shame the way they're treated — some awful stuff going on south of the border."

"They can stay down there, as far as I'm concerned."

Eric shrugged this off. He remembered that sort of intolerance during the war, specially where other nations' troops mingled in the odd estaminet. Never could understand it, even though no coloured fellas on the Gaspe Coast. He hoped on these travels he'd get to meet up with some and get to know them.

At last they piled into bed and said their goodbyes.

7:55 AM. Monday morning. Banff. Before arriving, Eric woke up and went into the dining car. Eating his breakfast, he saw out the window great snow-covered peaks and still lakes that heralded another good day of sight-seeing. He drank it all in, happy to be a real traveller, and at last they crossed into British Columbia. Eric soon fell asleep, but with a rest broken by dreams and worries — so much lay ahead: his arrival in Vancouver, and then... just so long as his shell shock stayed quiet, he prayed, more adventures.

CHAPTER NINE

In a state of repressed excitement, Eric got down his bags much too early. But right on time, at 7:45 AM, they pulled into Vancouver's Union Station. He breathed deeply and stepped onto the platform, helped by Charlie to whom he handed a handsome tip. Head for the information kiosk, he told himself, and ask for any veterans' organizations. Must be one here, he thought, and there was. He was directed to it, and carrying both bags, he found the makeshift sign: Canadian Legion Branch 60. Breathing hard, for he'd been carrying a good weight, he went up the wooden steps and opened the door.

Inside, a gruff old legionnaire got up to greet him, introducing himself as Alf Powys — Eric figured he'd been a Sergeant Major. He indicated a chair, so they sat and Eric took out his tobacco pouch and offered Alf a pipeful. "I thought it best to come straight here, from the train station."

Alf pulled out his cigarettes and both veterans lit up, chatting about their part in the Great War. Alf had been in the infantry, but after a severe wound had spent his time training recruits. Then he launched into his favourite subject: the Legion. "This here branch just got formed last November. We got left this house by one of our members, but we're looking to build a more suitable place. I'll tell you, Eric, we've had some history with the Legion."

"I bet," Eric replied. "We had quite a time too, in Sherbrooke, Quebec, where I was at college. Different bunches of veterans getting together, some French, some English, but no one could agree on what to call our organization or where to locate — I've heard it's been the same all over."

"Yes indeedy. Finally, a couple of years ago, out west here, we started crying a shame we couldn't all get together. So in Winnipeg, in November of '25 — went there myself — a bunch of us formed the Canadian Legion of the British Empire Services League, known as the BESL. Got it incorporated just last year in '26."

News to Eric, though he'd heard of some such formation taking place.

"Yep, before that, we was called the Dominion Veterans Alliance. So now, we're all together under the Canadian Legion." Alf, cigarette in his mouth, took his coffee cup over to a table with brochures and maps and asked, "I guess the first thing you'll want is somewhere to stay?"

"I'd be much obliged." Eric was pleased when the old fellow told him: "Best for you, being a former officer as I can see, would be this place up here." He jabbed his finger at a map. "Mrs. Collins, her husband was killed in the war, such a fine Colonel, left her with two children and a big house, but nothing else, 'cept of course that tiny widows' pension they gives. So she turned it into a boarding house, special rate for veterans. She prefers officers, she told me," he gave a wink, "but she'll take anyone. Not too expensive, friendly atmosphere, I think you'll like that."

"I surely will. Good to be around other military men; they understand what we all went through."

Eric stayed for a bit more chat, then set off in the taxi that old Fred rang up for him, there being no public transport to Mrs. Collins's fine old mansion on a leafy side street.

Once welcomed, he distributed his belongings in drawers, thinking all the while how remarkably good the Lord Above had been. This was all he needed.

After a bit of a rest, he followed Alf's advice and walked down towards Gastown, the old part of the city: full of bars, lots to see, but more especially, to a hotel known as the Europa, where Alf had mentioned that a former Brigadier, Sam Holtby, often took his whiskey. He had visited the Legion just a couple of days before looking for workers.

Eric reached the tall and most peculiar wedge-shaped building, a flatiron style, as he was to learn inside, and paused. Framing its wide doorway, two plain columns were adorned with an ornamentation of leaves —, didn't that look Greek? Rene always hovered, as one might imagine, at the edge of his consciousness.

Once inside the long and clubby bar, Eric ordered his drop of scotch and asked the bartender to point out Sam Holtby. Right away he took his tumbler over to where Sam leaned against the bar talking. Eric introduced himself and the other man moved off.

Luckily, Sam Holtby had also been a Gunner, and so they had quite a time discussing their Regimental service in the Great War. Sam had even known Andrew McNaughton, the Artillery genius, now a General, that Eric revered, and he vaguely remembered Dick Overstreet, Eric's former lieutenant. And indeed, after a couple of pipefuls and another whiskey, Sam Holtby turned to his new project.

"After that terrible fire at our athletic ground, a friend of mine on the city council asked me if I could do something about it. So

I got together a bunch of men to fix it up. But Eric, my foreman's not so good; had to get rid of him yesterday."

"Sorry to hear that, Sam.... Anything I could do to help?"

"Exactly what I was thinking. You commanded a gun under fire, and got wounded setting up a forward observation post at Amiens so you'll sure know how to handle a bunch of ne'er-do-wells. Not to say they don't work hard — they're mostly from the Prairies, and also from the backwoods up Island."

"But, Sam, I know nothing about construction."

"No matter, it's not the building part I need. It's someone to stop them going at each other, keep them in line, make them happy. They're well paid: I got the contract from the city, and I'm not looking to make myself a millionaire out of other people's money. And as we both know — if you need someone to rely on, don't look any further than an officer from the Canadian Field Artillery!" Eric grinned at the thought. "But I reckon you're looking for something more permanent?"

"No, not necessarily. This will do me just fine, Sam. I'm staying up with Col. Collins's widow. I just need to make sure I pay her rent every Friday, while I look around this wonderful city of yours."

"Well then, that settles it."

C/o Mrs E.L. Collins,
14 Nottingham St.
Vancouver, BC.
July 1927

Dear Rene,

Remember your letter with that new surprise address? I'm going to give you a surprise, now. I'm here in Vancouver, having crossed our great Dominion on a wonderful train called the Imperial, from Montreal to Vancouver. I already have a job, some friendly accommodation, and now I wanted to send you my new address, because for sure letters will reach me here quicker than in the Province of Quebec.

I even bought a guidebook on Greece, in the hopes that it would have something about that kind of dancing you're doing. No luck. But I also got *Kangaroo*, by DH Lawrence. They told me in the bookstore he's a pretty good writer, from the coalfields in England. I'm going to start reading it right away, to find out more about your Australia.

I've been noticing how many of the new buildings here are built in what the guidebook calls Neo-classical Style, which seems to be just Greek architecture. The provincial courthouse here, well, it's a regular Greek-looking building, recently built too. I guess that all fits with your dancing, for sure.

Well, I'll close now, and hope this letter finds you in good health. I've burned my bridges, and I've begun a new adventure. Who knows where the future will lead?

That future took a sudden turn two or three weeks later when Sam said to Eric one night, "In a couple of days, my son Kenny gets here from Honolulu."

"Does he now? What's he been up to? Holiday?"

Sam nodded. "After his degree from UBC, he got a kind of wanderlust. Took off for a while, with my blessing, mind. So I'm going down to meet him at the boat. The ss *Makura*. Pretty splendid ship, I'm told. Its arrival is sure to cause some first-rate excitement. Might you like to come?"

Eric had been seeing Sam at the hotel bar after work, a friendly way to exchange views of the job that Sam rarely visited, perhaps once a week, occupied with other projects. So Eric went with him to the Vancouver's port and watched the ship's arrival.

Having twice crossed the Atlantic on common troopships, Eric had never encountered the banners and noisy celebration greeting this great ocean liner. Crowds had turned up on the dock, some to meet relatives or friends, but many for the excitement. Long, sleek, huge, a tall mast forward of the bridge and one great funnel leaning back, the *Makura* looked to Eric a thing of majesty and beauty. What must it be like to travel on a ship like that?

So imagine his surprise, when having a drink later with Sam and his son, Ken, he found that the boat had originated in Sydney, Australia. He stifled his excitement and listened politely as Ken told his father what he'd been up to, and started on the history of a curious sport called surfing. "And after Duke Kahanamoku started it all — he lives now in California — there was George Freeth, an Irish fellow, but from Hawaii. Those sixteen foot boards they all use? He cut them almost in half; that's what I'm using. It's so much fun, Dad. You paddle out lying on the board, and then you turn around — this is at Waikiki Beach — and then, when you see a wave coming, you paddle with your arms to keep up and then once you get the hang of it, you stand up on the board and let the waves carry you in. I actually did it a couple of times before I had to come home. Can't wait to try it again."

But all the while, Eric was dying to ask him what it was like on the boat. When he got the chance, the youth filled him with stories of the shipboard accommodations and romances.

The next evening, something drove Eric to pass by the shipping office and enquire as to the price of a ticket to Sydney.

The pretty young saleswoman told him about the next ship to leave. "It is the ss *Aorangi*," she gushed, "the largest ocean liner afloat! It leaves in three weeks, July 27th."

Eric frowned. "Say the name again?"

"Aorangi. It was named after a mountain on New Zealand's South Island. Aorangi is from the Maori language: 'cloud in the sky.'" Eric smiled. Nice name, he thought. "And what a voyage it will be! It's as big again by half as the *Makura*." She seemed filled with pleasure at this handsome young veteran wanting to go across the Pacific to Sydney. "Do you know anyone there?"

Eric didn't really want to reply, but for some reason blurted out, "Yes. A young lady, in fact."

The girl blushed. "How exciting! Have you told her you're coming?"

"Not exactly," Eric stammered. "Oh no. Not at all."

"How thrilling! She'll be so excited."

"Well, I doubt that. I haven't seen her for eight years."

The girl's face fell. "Eight years! How do you know she isn't already married and got a family?"

"Well, we have been writing."

"Love letters?" The girl blushed. "I'm sorry, I don't mean to pry, but it's so romantic. You going off to see a girl that you haven't met for eight years. I think that's wonderful!"

"I didn't say I was going."

"Oh, but you must! You must! Here. Take this form. Bring it home. Fill it out and bring it back with a cheque. I love people doing things on the spur of the moment. It's so exciting. Our passengers usually book months before. And they're mostly old, and boring. Though," she added quickly, "some young folk are going, too. With their families. There's excellent accommodation still left open."

Eric took the form, wondering what on earth had ever possessed him to come in here in the first place.

She added quickly. "Oh," she clapped her hands together. "Oh, I do hope you go."

And on July 27, when the ss *Aorangi* blew its deafening whistle and pulled away from the quay, Eric Alford was aboard.

CHAPTER TEN

Eric had bought himself a berth in a cabin for six, which was almost the cheapest, but still took a good bit more than he had saved from the month under Sam. However, this was to be a long voyage — four weeks to be exact. By most standards, he was travelling light: only his bag, suitcase, and his haversack, whereas most passengers had steamer trunks stowed in the baggage hold.

Two weeks before the trip, Eric had returned to the ticket office with his cheque and his forms filled out. But first he had checked with Sam Holtby. Hesitantly, after a Scotch and a pipeful, he had broached the subject.

"Now why the hell do you want to leave, since you're doing so well?" asked Sam. "I thought you and me, we'd have a fair little partnership. I already got another job for you to do after we finish this athletic field."

Eric was prepared for this, having spent a sleepless night wondering how to justify his rather ridiculous impulse to his employer. "Sam, you'll have to forgive me, because it's kind of hard to explain. You see, in London during the war, I met this English girl."

Kenny, Sam's son broke in. "And you're going after her! Good for you, Eric."

"Well, it's not as easy as that. You see, I don't even know if she'll want me. As a matter of fact, we haven't seen each other for eight years."

Sam looked in astonishment. But Kenny's eyes glowed. "Well, when you wrote to her, she must have told you to come. Otherwise why book yourself a passage?"

"Damn fool thing to do," Sam said, "if you ask me."

How to answer these legitimate concerns? Eric started slowly. "Well, I just have no idea. Something told me — I'd been thinking about her all this time, while I was in university, and knocking around doing some surveying, and she... she kind of got pretty well locked into my mind."

"Oh boy!" shouted Kenny, to the dismay of the other drinkers in the bar. "A real love story. But you didn't answer my question. Did she not say to come?"

Eric shook his head. Sheepishly, he replied, "She doesn't know." He took a slug of whiskey.

Sam Holtby shook his head. "Darnedest thing I ever heard."

"Dad, I think it's real romantic. Like a Jane Austen novel." He turned to Eric. "We read them at UBC. See, Eric, one day I might even be a writer." Seeing his father's head swivel fast in his direction, he went on quickly, "Well, I mean, after I get this job we're angling for at the Stock Exchange. I can make a lot of money there, and maybe when I'm older I can spend my time writing."

Sam shook his head wearily. "My son ..."

"Well, Sam," Eric went on, "I know it's crazy. I've been telling myself it's crazy ever since yesterday, when I visited the ticket office. But the *Aorangi* —"

"Dad, that's the biggest one in their fleet, the biggest that goes to Australia. I wish I could have been on that. But I had to get back here in time to arrange this job."

"So you see, Sam," Eric went on, "I haven't bought the ticket, and I won't if you need me that badly. But the fellas there, I seem to have them sorted out. They're doing a fine job, and this construction foreman can handle them; so you might not even need to replace me. That's what I'm hoping," Eric added, weakly.

"Dad, you've got to let him go. This is the best story I've heard for long time. You never meet someone like Eric here, gambling his whole life on some vision of a girl he once met. I bet," he turned back to Eric, "I bet you'll knock her flat. I bet she's never had anyone do that for her, in her entire life. She'll be so excited..."

Sam lifted his eyebrows. "And on the other hand, she might not be." He glanced at Eric with an almost sorrowful look. "Eric, if you come back here with your tail between your legs, you'll have a job, don't worry."

* * *

The first while on board, Eric spent his time familiarizing himself with the great liner, bigger by half than the *Makura* as the girl had said, and one that took a good deal of exploration. The classes were segregated, of course, but some of the activities could be shared.

While most of the first-class passengers sat out in deck chairs, Eric contented himself with daily exercise around the great ship or leaning on the rail and watching the city of Victoria pass by on his right as they headed off into the great Pacific Ocean — twenty four hundred miles to Honolulu on the first leg of their voyage.

The first evening in the great tourist-class dining room, Eric couldn't help but notice a tall, well-shaped beauty with brown hair piled in a fetching coiffure, wide eyes roaming the room but always returning to fasten on him. She sat at a table of older folk whom he took to be her parents and their friends. No one her own age. He figured her to be at least twenty, taken on this voyage by her folks.

The next day she approached him as he leaned against the rail. He turned to look, somewhat surprised. What perfect features — even a pert nose, but in those oceans of her eyes he found himself floundering. Quite a stunning young lady.

"Hello, may I introduce myself? We need a fourth for our shuffleboard and I thought you might like to join us. I'm Sharon Black." She held out her hand.

Eric introduced himself and allowed as how he'd be pleased to join them.

After the introductions, an older man, who seemed taken aback by Sharon's choice — was he jealous? — explained the game to Eric, though the forty-foot-long "court" with compartments and a triangle at each end seemed self-evident. "We use these sticks, called cues, to push pucks, those weighted disks, down and hope one lands on a square with a high number. Quite easy really."

"Don't listen to Arthur," Sharon said, "I've played every day and I always lose."

"Maybe our veteran here will bring you luck, Sharon my girl," said the older man. His plump wife looked at him disapprovingly. "After we play all the pucks at this end, we go down to the other and start over again."

Eric found he soon got the hang of it, and became one of their regulars, even joining them when they switched to deck quoits, played with hoops of rope, a bit like horseshoes. A good queue of names always waited for games.

After the first game, Sharon and Eric retired to the bar for a drink before lunch. Eric wondered at this Torontonian, obviously from a good family. Why had she booked in tourist class? The others at her dining table were neither friends nor relatives, she admitted. "Mummy and Daddy were appalled at my choice. They said I should travel with 'my own kind.' They are so stuck-up. But I knew that I'd find more interesting people if I travelled this way. Up in first, they're all old. If you're looking for a shipboard romance, don't go first!"

Eric was taken aback, but grinned. "Well, good luck. I expect you will find lots of pickings down here on this deck among us all. There must be a pile of us."

She looked at him, with a slight frown. "Oh, I've been looking all right. But no one else has got what it takes. You're a veteran. You've lived. I can see all that in your eyes, Eric." She gave him a little wink and smile, patting his hand. "Going through a war. Does a lot for a man!"

Eric didn't want to amplify that statement. It sure did a lot — and not all of it good. But he pushed that memory aside. No dwelling on shell shock on this trip.

Faced with her forthright come-on, he told himself to confess right away: I'm taken. But he realized: What a ridiculous statement! Taken? What on earth did he mean? Only 'taken' in the sense he was on this damn fool errand after someone he'd met years ago. He chastised himself. "Quite a ship, isn't it?" he said quickly, to change the subject.

Sharon nodded. "But I know nothing about it. Daddy booked it for me."

So Eric decided to learn something of this great liner they were on, heading into the unknown. That evening he spotted the Purser at the rail, taking a cigarette, and went over to look out at the setting sun. Fortunately, they had not yet struck a storm and the sea had been welcoming.

"Well sir," the Purser said in answer to Eric's question, "it is a new ship indeed. Maiden voyage only two years ago, January

1925. We left Southampton, went to Los Angeles and Vancouver; I was aboard. Great trip. Then we moved to this route. And you know, every time we stop in Vancouver and Sydney, we spend a day and a half disinfecting her. Got to be careful, travelling these tropical waters; you never know what kind of germs get aboard."

"And she's the biggest steamship afloat?"

"Steamship? No, she's one of these new breed of large liners powered by diesel," the Purser told him. "Average speed around seventeen knots. And you wouldn't believe the amount of fuel we burn every day."

"Several tons?" Eric ventured.

"Over fifty a day!" said the Purser proudly. "She's going in for overhaul at the end of the year, but they're keeping us officers on salary while she does. I'm looking forward to a bit of a holiday. Been working full time these past two years."

With that information tucked carefully into his head, Eric went to his cabin, certain that on the morrow, he could entertain Sharon. His years of going to bed soon after dark on the farm and in the bush meant he retired early, well before the others here who loved the evenings' pursuits: dancing, drinking, and playing card games. Alone in his bunk, he wondered what on earth would come of this sudden turn of affairs?

CHAPTER ELEVEN

The RMS *Aorangi* breasted the great Pacific swells with ease: a gentle roll was all the passengers felt, except infrequently when they struck rough weather. Eric soon developed a healthy routine that involved, after digesting his breakfast, striding around the deck for a brisk "morning constitutional" as a tour of the decks was known. And before long, the long-legged young Sharon joined him.

"I just hope I'm not too brisk for you?"

"Oh no, I love hiking. I'm very athletic!" She smiled. Such lovely teeth, he noticed. Wealthy upbringing, lots of good food and, he suspected, strict parents: brush your teeth! Not like at home; their one dentist had only recently arrived.

"Tennis, swimming, sports, I love them. I ride a horse of my own in Toronto. I'm very active."

And so over the next while, Eric got to know Sharon pretty well, and her plans. She was not afraid to chatter about herself, certainly. "Freddie and I, we're getting married in the autumn, one of those big weddings, but it might be fun. I'm looking forward to Honolulu, though. We're going to treat it as a kind of a secret pre-honeymoon." They kept passing older rug-wrapped couples stretched on wooden arm chairs, staring out at the heaving horizon, hardly talking, some reading. "For the real honeymoon, we're going around Europe, and then poor Freddie, he'll have to settle down in his father's firm."

"Which is?" Eric asked.

"Oh, you probably haven't heard of it. It's in the brokerage business, and they're making nothing but money these days." She laughed gaily. "I like being taken care of in style." She waved and smiled at an older man who made as if to join them, but gave it up as they sped by. "It'll be jolly, with lots of parties, of course. But then, I will belong to Freddie completely."

"Don't you belong to him now?"

Sharon looked sideways at him without speaking. After a time, she said, "A little dalliance never hurt anyone, before having to give it all up and become a wife forever..." She looked sideways at Eric again.

After striding around the deck for an hour or so, they retired to the bar for coffee and Lamingtons, little Aussie sponge cakes dipped in chocolate and covered in cocoanut. Eric enjoyed her companionship, although he wondered at the hints she kept dropping. And the more he got to know Sharon Black, the more he liked her. Where would all this lead? It did seem as if she were throwing herself at him. Oh dear, hard to resist.

"And what is Freddie doing in Honolulu?" They were sitting at one side, having sampled the pastry table. One did nothing but eat on this voyage.

"Well, it's Freddie's last big holiday before settling down," Sharon told him. "He's taken up some silly pursuit called surfing. I have no idea what they do, but in his one letter, he seems caught up in it."

"I wonder if he uses a long board, or the short one?" Eric gave a sly chuckle. Her reaction came as he expected — she whirled: "What do you know about surfing?"

Eric shrugged, pleased. "Oh, nothing much."

"Well, if he enjoys it, so much the better. I have some new bathing suits, and I'm going to sit out on the sand and watch. He really likes to see my body. At night, he tells me, there's a great bunch of friends who turned up from Toronto for their holidays, and it should be fun. But then, of course, I'll be his alone." She looked at him again.

"Lucky him," Eric found himself saying, and then almost as quickly regretted it, for he knew she would take it as a kind of invitation. Which in a sense, it was. No doubt about it, she was a striking young lady. Later, when the ship held its formal dance on the weekend, he found himself with her again, doing his best to join in the latest shuffle.

"You know, Eric you're a very remarkable man," she began after a while. "Freddie is much younger. You, being a veteran, I mean, you're not old, but there is something... Well, a strength, as if you'd seen it all."

Eric had to admit, "I have seen a lot, probably."

"Not many men are as handsome as you, Eric. You don't mind my saying that?" Eric shook his head. Who would mind those words from lips as perfect as hers? "At the same time, you're so true to yourself. You have the manners of a prince, and the honesty of a farm boy. Intriguing combination."

Eric was no longer taken aback by her candour, but concentrated on doing the steps required on the dance floor.

Sharon noticed his difficulties and they soon retired to a side table. But then, being as pretty as she was, Sharon got one invitation to dance after another, some young and good-looking but married, others older but still obviously attracted. Eric watched them on the dance floor; he left a lot to be desired so far as danc-ing went.

After sticking it out for a while, Eric was about to give up. So Sharon turned down the next offer to dance to have a nightcap with him. After taking a good slug herself, she ventured, open-ly, "You know, Eric, I have a two-berth cabin. And the second is empty."

"Really? I thought the ship was nearly full."

She paused. "Well, it was." She glanced at him. "I think Daddy didn't want me bothered by anyone else, so he bought the other bunk." She sipped her drink and mentioned casually, "You might find it more comfortable there."

Eric shifted in his seat. She went on quickly, "I have a window, well, a porthole, and we can see out. It's so lovely in the morning with the sun coming in. We're on the south side of the ship, Dad-dy saw to that. Wouldn't you be more comfortable than with all those other people in your cramped inside cabin?" She went on quickly, "And you're welcome to it."

Rather a challenging turn of events! What could Eric say, but, "Well, Sharon, that's thoughtful of you; thank you very much. I will certainly consider it."

Her face fell. "That wasn't quite the reaction I was expecting." A slight frown furrowed her delicately arched eyebrows.

Eric knew she usually got everything she wanted. But this time, more of a challenge? "I'm sorry. I guess I'm not too pol-ished."

"Don't try that farm stuff on me, Eric. You must have seen a lot of life in those trenches, and also, I imagine, in those dread-ful places men went to in France. And even in England. I'm sure you're not as innocent as you appear."

Eric shook his head. "But maybe I really am..."

As they took their leave, she leaned across and kissed him on the cheek. Lots to think about later in his cramped inside stateroom.

Eric decided to take the free dancing lessons offered to help passengers enjoy their voyage. Betty, his teacher, was plain but had a tall, spry figure, lots of dark hair, dark eyes, and a small mouth. She certainly knew her stuff and Eric, being well-coordinated, was able to pick up a few steps. The second day he even looked forward to the afternoon lesson. She had an appealing flare, though at first seemed a little cold, or perhaps merely withdrawn.

On the last of his three private lessons — they were dancing pretty well together now — things took a decidedly sharp turn. They had gotten to know each other and he liked Betty: she had a vulnerable side, one that seemed in need of reassurance. She had been married, but her husband had left her in a hurtful manner. She used to be a dancer on stage but now at her age was forced to make a living by teaching.

As it turned out, she was also interested in more than just that. "You know, Eric, after dinner when they all play their silly card games, you might like to come see my cabin in the crew's quarters. We have to be careful, of course, because we're not allowed to fraternize with passengers. But my cabin-mate is understanding, and we have an arrangement..." She paused and looked at him, to gauge his reaction. Eric pretended to be concentrating on his dance steps. "I have a good bottle of single malt Scotch," she added, "and we could have a sip together."

There was no doubting her intention. Eric wondered how he should handle this. It was almost too much — two women on one voyage, both apparently seeking his companionship — and for the night. Not Shigawake, certainly.

She seemed so deflated by his hesitation that Eric felt he must accede. What would be lost by going to her cabin for a drink, anyway? But then he stopped himself. Once he got there, might it not be even harder to get away?

"But if you don't want to..." she murmured, "that's all right too."

Such a yearning in her voice. What was it made him pause? Eric asked himself. He certainly liked Betty and even felt affectionate after the lessons, but really, his heart wasn't in it. He began, "You see Betty, I'm taken already."

No sooner were the words out of his mouth than he realized he had spoken the truth. But what a ridiculous thought! He immediately chastised himself for it. Again, whatever did he have to base this crazy lie on? Some fool vision that had grown far too big in his brain?

"I completely understand, Eric." She looked at him with trusting eyes. "If only my husband had been like that. Faithful." She scrunched her eyes shut, though she continued dancing. "The bastard," she muttered under her breath. And then she brightened. She looked down at Eric, for he was a good three or four inches shorter. "You've been doing very well, Eric. I'm really proud of you as a pupil."

And so it turned out that when he danced with Sharon on the Saturday, Eric was able to hold his own on the dance floor. And now, Hawaii was drawing close.

Sunday night, Eric spent a particularly boring evening at a talk on aspects of Fiji, which the ship would be visiting after Honolulu — native girls, hot sun and beaches. As they were leaving Sharon came over to him. "Sounds almost as interesting as Hawaii..."

Eric nodded noncommittally.

"I watched you during the talk. I could see you were bored."

Eric nodded again; he was tired. Then, needing something to cheer him up, he suggested a nightcap. After they found a seat and ordered drinks, Eric noticed that Sharon seemed nervous. In fact, she finished a second nightcap while he was still nursing his first, and ordered herself a third. Then she turned to him and said, "Eric, I've been meaning to ask: I want some advice. And it can only come from a man. Will you help?"

"Of course, Sharon, anything you want." No hesitation there.

"Come with me." She knocked back her drink. Eric finished his and followed as she led the way down to her companionway, which fortunately was empty. She turned in at her cabin door and Eric followed.

"Now, I want you to sit there and shut your eyes."

Eric did as he was told. The cabin, compared to his own, was quite roomy. He sat down on the small chest on the left-hand side of the door, and Sharon knelt at the drawers under her berth. She turned to looked at him. "Eric, I told you to shut your eyes. I have a surprise."

Eric nodded and clenched them shut. He leaned back, crossed his legs and tilted his head to the ceiling. Soon he heard rustling and the movement of clothing. After a moment he heard: "Open your eyes."

Eric opened them, and then sat bolt upright.

There stood Sharon in a stunning white nightdress. Cut straight across, just above her full breasts, it had straight strips of embroidery looped over her shoulders to hold up the slinky material falling straight to the floor. Above the nightdress, Sharon had let her hair down, and it tumbled over her bare white shoulders. Eric was captivated — that skin just asked to be caressed.

"Eric, I want you to help me decide which one I should wear when I meet Freddie."

Eric moistened his lips. "Sharon, I don't think you could do any better than that. Not often I've seen a young lady as beautiful as you in a nightdress."

"Not often?"

Eric smiled. "All right, not ever, if you really want to know."

That certainly made Sharon happy. She smiled, turned round so he might see all sides and then spread her arms. "There, have you seen enough?"

Eric nodded. "Yes, quite enough."

"Now, shut your eyes again."

He did so and heard more sounds of clothing, the nightdress going up over her head, he presumed, for now he could visualize that, and then, another one being pulled down. In spite of himself, he could feel blood rushing to his face.

"Ready?"

"Yes," Eric muttered hoarsely. What would he see next?

"Open your eyes."

Eric did so, and took in the lovely Sharon, this time in a cream-coloured nightdress with a v-neck, heavily embroidered across her full bosoms. The material in this one seemed thinner. As she stepped forward towards Eric (on purpose?), the bright cabin light behind her illuminated the complete outline of her body, her long legs, her hips, and her slim waist.

"Which one do you like, Eric?" she asked, almost innocently, but with a little smile that told everything.

Eric tried to think about the dress, not what was in it.

"This embroidery, it's from Paris, you know. Hand done. Daddy helped me choose it. I think he's pleased I'm marrying Freddie next autumn. But in the meantime ... I am single. And I'm free."

"It's... it's a hard choice," said Eric, his pulse racing.

"So you like them both Eric?"

"Very much."

Sharon then came forward and bent over Eric, cupped his face in her hands, and placed her lips against his. Soon, he felt her tongue caressing and entering his mouth. He gripped her two hands and held them tightly as they rose, their lips still locked. He felt her body thrust against him as her arms went round his shoulders. He slid his hands behind her back and moved them over her spine, caressing it with a firm touch. The two of them lingered, pressing against each other, and then she lifted her head and began to move her lips over his face, kissing him on his eyes and, especially, the scar that now flamed redder than ever on his cheek. Their breathing became heavy, as though they had been running.

Then she gently moved away.

She went to her berth, leaned down to switch off the bright light that illuminated and plainly outlined a full breast as she bent. The cabin was thrown into darkness. She turned on a nightlight above the opposite birth. It cast a gentle glow all around. She opened the sheets on the narrow berth.

Eric stood like a statue.

She slid onto the berth, moved back against the wall and then with painted fingernails patted the sheet.

Need she say more?

Thoughts whirled in Eric's mind. Fond of Sharon? Of course. Desiring her, in fact? Oh yes.

But then, unaccountably, wretchedly, he saw Rene at the railway station where his troop train was leaving for the steamer to Canada, when she had kissed him, oh so chastely, and then stood back to stare into his eyes, as she mouthed the word: Goodbye.

"Last chance," Sharon whispered. She reached out both her arms to him.

* * *

The day following her rejection, Sharon gave Eric only one glance — filled with anger, pointed and sharp as an ice pick.

Hell hath no fury like a woman scorned! Oh yes, how true was that platitude, Eric thought. All night, having been so aroused, he'd tossed and turned in his bunk. How could he ever make it right with her? Why had he been such a damn fool as to turn away, and leave? Of course, he had no answers, which only made it worse. In the short interval before reaching Honolulu, they avoided each other assiduously.

But when they docked, he did come to the rail to watch Sharon step down the gangplank to meet her faithful Freddie, so well dressed, youthful, full of enthusiasm. He wrapped his arms around his bride to be. Eric turned away and hurried back to his cramped stateroom where he lay on his bed and closed his eyes.

The remaining three weeks of the voyage went by without any great excitement. Eric made a point of going ashore in Fiji to poke about the city of Suva, and did the same again when the ship docked at Auckland, New Zealand. But one day blurred into another. Until, finally, the ss *Aorangi*, with a mighty wail from its whistle, pulled in to the docks at Sydney, Australia.

CHAPTER TWELVE

When the RMS *Aorangi* sailed into Sydney Harbour, Eric, on deck, marvelled at the approach spans being constructed for the huge Harbour Bridge. His excitement quickened, and when the ship docked, he was one of the first down the gangplank. He had arrived in Sydney, New South Wales, where Rene lived and worked.

Carrying his bags and trying to calm himself, he got through customs and immigration and made his way with the trickle of passengers towards the gates at one end of the dock. His mind was whirling. This last couple of weeks, he had been pondering his best course of action. He wanted to surprise Rene, but how? And was this all, in the end, just a fruitless pursuit?

He saw a small information office and went in. Being first, right away he asked the lean, whiskery, and somewhat weaselly shipping clerk if he knew the way to the Canadian Legion.

The man frowned and shook his head. "No Canadian legion here. Wrong country."

"Oh I'm sorry, I wasn't thinking." Eric's mind could scarcely calm down. "I meant the club where veterans get together — if you have one?"

"Oh, you must mean the RSL."

Eric frowned. "What's that stand for?"

Grudgingly, it seemed, the man replied, "Returned Sailors and Soldiers Imperial League of Australia."

Eric brightened. "Yes, that would be it. Where is it, do you know?"

"Not the faintest, Mate."

And I heard Aussies were all so nice, thought Eric. But he persevered. "Well, perhaps you know where Macleay Street is?" The address on Rene's letter.

The man gave him a look. "You won't find any RSL in that section."

"Oh? Why ever not?"

The man hesitated, then decided not to reply. Several passengers came in to stand behind Eric, taking an interest in the proceedings. So the man then claimed to know Sydney well. "Macleay? That's the main street in Potts Point. You take the tram to King's Cross, not too far, less than a couple of miles." Giving more directions, he took pains to show off his knowledge. "Started back in the forties by a banker, some fella called Joseph Hyde Potts. Some renovations going on there now, new apartments and such." As Eric turned to go, he added, "You can leave your luggage here behind the counter, but come back before we shut at five. Next please."

Eric set off, mind in a turmoil, alternating between excitement and curiosity. On the boat he had decided that, before trying to meet Rene, he should look for a job. Becoming a surveyor remained at the bottom of his list but, in this great open country, there'd be lots of openings so he was not worried. But what about managing some crew or other, as he'd done in Vancouver? He could always teach, too.

Something else was gnawing at him: he had loved his time at Bishop's and wondered if he should not advance his education, even enrolling in Sydney University, if a job would permit. On the boat he had heard it was a fine institution.

What if Rene were not attached? The likelihood of her being available was too remote even to consider.

But approach her he must. But how exactly? Knock at her door? No, too obvious, and it might confront her in a way that was inadvisable. What about turning up at the school she was establishing? Perhaps pass by there to see what it was like?

But she had mentioned giving talks. That might be best, and even fun — go and hear her talk, learn her theories, absorb all he could, before actually making his presence known. So before catching the tram for Darlinghurst and King's Cross, he bought all three Sydney newspapers, the Sun, the Morning Herald, and the Daily Telegraph. As the streetcar slid forward with a clanging of its bell, he sat on the wooden seat and scanned for signs of Rene or her school. He even checked tiny ads, and then closed the first paper regretfully. Not a thing.

Then half way through the Sun, he saw a notice:

Free lecture demonstrations by Irene Mulvany Gray at David Jones [Department Store] on the art of the dance: Castlereay — Market and Elizabeth streets. Friday, August 27th at 7 PM.

This Friday! In two days! The perfect opportunity.

He got off the tram and walked down Darlinghurst Road until it became Macleay Street. The area charmed him. He could see why the clerk of the shipping company had turned up his nose, for it was certainly Bohemian. A lot of respectable homes had been turned into rooming houses; no shortage of rooms for rent here. Attractive little cafes. Artists' studios, beer taverns, and probably even houses of ill-repute. He kept walking because Number 43 where Rene lived was at the far end, before the road turned slightly left and continued as Wylde Street to the end of Potts Point which jutted into the harbour. As he passed her address, he looked up at the great Victorian house, with its dormer windows and two small balconies. It had clearly been turned into flats: by the door he could pick out a panel with several names. He wondered on which floor she lived. It set his heart aflutter as he hurried on.

Exploring the neighbourhood for the better part of an hour, Eric strode down Victoria Street with its fine terraced houses, then crossed Macleay again towards Elizabeth Bay, checking accommodations until he finally selected one.

The couple who ran it, the Cliffords, were welcoming. "I'm Graeme, spelt G-r-a-e-m-e, and don't you forget it, mate!" mumbled the thick-set and pugnacious gentleman. "And this here is Muriel." Equally heavy set but with a motherly air, she also beamed at Eric: there'd be no nonsense in this rooming house, Eric could see, and he welcomed that. They showed him his room and off he went to collect his luggage and install himself here.

So far so good, thought Eric. In these first few hours, he had taken to this new country and hoped to make a go of it. No turning back now. And he said to himself, if I can find a job, then when Rene rejects me, I shan't be too devastated.

* * *

What an age before Friday evening came! At last Eric found himself heading with others into the great David Jones, Sydney's largest department store, to hear the lecture by Miss Irene Mulvany Gray. He wanted to remain inconspicuous and so sat at the back of the audience — mostly women, unfortunately, so he might stand out. But other men, likely husbands, were scattered about, so Eric scrunched down, hoping she'd not notice. And then, he said to himself, we shall see what we shall see.

The audience of about sixty settled into silence as Harris Johnson, a thin, sharply-dressed executive of the store, stepped forward to introduce Rene. "Miss Mulvany Gray is an authority on the revived Greek dance. She studied at the Ginner-Mawer School of Dance, Drama and Mime in London, and is, by the way, its only graduate here. At present she is busy instructing our public school teachers, as her system is now to be included in our curriculum. Her summer school is flourishing and I'm sure you will all enjoy her talk tonight on the history of dance. And now I present Miss Gray."

In walked Rene. Eric's heart gave a wild leap. Was she beautiful! In person, she was worth any ten visions. She wore a stylish, pale pink and white ensemble, long pleated skirt, and blouse that couldn't hide her ample figure. A light scarf set off her luminescent skin. She looked to Eric more radiant than ever, poised, self-confident and fully prepared.

After thanking everyone for the warm welcome, Rene began her talk. "We all know that dancing is as old as man; it's our natural primitive expression. As an art, it began in Egypt around 4,000 BC, reaching its height two millennia later. Egyptian dance was religious: it reached out to the spirit of the Gods, and the Hebrews, too, used dance as their form of religious worship.

"On it passed to Greece, the great home of dance where it reached its height. You know, in Greece, it was even considered a crime to have a weak and unbeautiful body. Boys started training at seven years and continued to the end of their lives. In Sparta, women did almost the same physical training — except wrestling, of course!" Here Rene paused for chuckles, and went on: "They all believed 'a beautiful soul must be contained in a beautiful body, and a beautiful body must contain a beautiful soul.'"

Those words struck home for Eric — to him, she seemed their

embodiment as she moved across the platform, speaking.

"Then around AD 300..." She gave a dismissive shrug, "we get the Christian Church coming, which stopped dancing — in fact, in 744 AD dancing of any kind was abolished by decree."

Eric noticed that she used no notes. Amazing.

"I apologize if I'm going too quickly through this, but I know we want to get to the present so I'll just mention that in 1000 AD we see the revival of mystery plays in churches, and the beginning of dance in England and France. In 1300 Morris Dancing began – only by men, of course. Strolling players began, going from village to village. As the spirit of Renaissance grew, fashionable people in England sponsored their own companies, and we find magnificent performances around 1400."

Her words washed over him, even unheard, as he watched her crisscross the stage. She seemed too young for her learned discourse — her round face, childlike, defenceless, almost that of a sixteen-year-old, though the sparkling eyes spoke of great experience.

"Then in the early eighteenth century, ballet arrived with a definite plot told through dancing and gesture. And you might not want to know this, but during the Revolutionary Period, public halls were opened in Paris, where – dressed in early Grecian costume — people danced sandalled, bare-armed and bare-breasted."

Laughter greeted this, and as Rene went on quickly, "Of course, that's not what we teach here!" She stepped forward and down some steps to be closer. "Let me explain that the mission of this revival of Greek dance is to induce physical fitness, to encourage a love of the beautiful, and an understanding of the significance of rhythm, regarded by the Greeks as essential qualities of life.

"You see to the Greek, the dance was not a mere pastime; it was intimately connected with his whole life and religion. Through

our revived Greek dance here, using those ideals of beauty, free-
dom, and strength, we seek to be one with the rhythm of the universe."

Eric shook his head. He'd never heard such fine explanations.
More and more, his fellow feeling grew with this talented speaker,
one with such aplomb, such charisma and self-confidence.

When her talk ended, the applause grew. Rene curtsied deeply
and gracefully. Then she gestured to Mr. Johnson, who had introduced her. Eric paled. Had the moment come? Was he about to
meet his Rene face-to-face?

CHAPTER THIRTEEN

Harris Johnson came back to the lectern and announced, "Now we are lucky, because Miss Gray has acceded to my request to answer a few questions."

Thank heaven, a reprieve, Eric breathed. He sat back. The longer she took the better! He truly had stage fright — as well he might after eight long years.

A plump woman got up to pose a question.

Rene came to the lectern to answer, and faced the audiences, whom Eric thought unusually attentive. "Many mothers have remarked that they get quite enough exercise in the house, looking after their children, though today our modern labour-saving devices take away any necessity of physical exertion. Well, you may find yourself sadly overworked, but there are still forms of exercise to help. Co-ordination of mind and movement is all that is required.

"Our secret here is mental and physical relaxation. How few of us today know how to truly relax, either mentally or physically? — A quiet restfulness in mind and body that results in a perfectly poised being." She smiled as the lady sat down. "Anyone else?"

Several hands shot up, which pleased Eric. The moment had been delayed again.

Rene answered the next question, while Eric's mind spun with anxiety. "In Victorian days, deportment was taught, yes, but girls were corsetted and hampered by tradition in clothes and bearing. But the weaker the body is, the more it runs your life. In the haste of modernity, we have lost all rhythm. Look at a street crowd rushing for trains and trams, straining and pushing and fretting. Not hard to realize how far we have departed from real natural movements. We all know that a good walk, a swim, or a game, will brush away the cobwebs, make us forget our depression, our pessimism, our little aches and pains, and so feel beautiful and alive."

Finally, inevitably, Eric heard Harris say, "Time for one last question." He fidgeted while Rene gracefully replied to another question: "Miss Gray, what exactly would you teach us if we came forward to enroll in your new school? The same thing you're putting in the school curriculum?"

"Good question. Each newcomer will be evaluated, of course. You see, Ruby Ginner, the recognized authority on the Revived Greek Dance, has evolved with Irene Mawer a set of exercises based on the old laws of natural movement. The body is trained so that every part is made strong, supple, and rhythmic — no one part more than another, so that your body may become an instrument whereon the mind may play. Music cannot be played upon an instrument that's out of tune."

Now, thought Eric, now she'll stop?

Rene paused, and went on, "A woman is as young as she feels. Why not always be young and beautiful? Let us make our bodies truly expressive of the spirit within and release that spontaneous joy in life — which lends colour to our every thought and magnetizes by its very exuberance everyone we meet."

She curtsied and returned to her corner. But after the applause, several ladies hurried forward to speak to her. Eric couldn't move. This was it. But how should he approach her? Stay back here, or hurry forward with the others clustered about, talking excitedly, asking her questions? Of course not.

But what if she spotted him back here? He hunched over, putting head in hands partially to hide himself as others, chatting, made their way towards the exit. A couple moved past and stopped to touch him on the shoulder. "Feeling all right, mate? Overwhelmed by her talk, I expect," laughed the man.

"A very inspiring talk, it was," said the woman. They could see from the way he looked up, startled, that he was fine.

"Oh yes, very smart, very knowledgeable, no doubt about that!" Eric allowed himself to feel proud of his Rene. His Rene? There you go again, he told himself, as the couple moved on.

He noticed a tall man waiting, smooth attractive face, a dancer's body, standing apart from the few women questioning their speaker. Oh, so that was it! She did have another male friend. His heart sank.

Well, maybe he would come back another day. Not the time to embarrass her in front of that suitor. He got up and started toward the exit; the room had emptied save for the women talking to Rene, a slim young man, and Mr. Johnson who was moving the lectern to one side.

Eric reached the double doors but paused. He saw the young man follow Johnson and join him to chat happily. So not Rene's suitor! Good.

He stood in the doorway, undecided, when Rene caught sight of him.

Even at that distance he could see the blood leave her face. She seemed to waver, and one of the women caught hold of her. He saw her excuse herself from them and, almost as if in a daze, start down the centre aisle towards him, staring all the while. He want-ed to go forward and take her in his arms, but couldn't move.

As if in a dream she drifted forward, lithe, graceful, so beauti-ful. Then she reached him, held out both hands, took his shoul-ders firmly, and looked him full in the face. "I had to touch you. I thought perhaps you were a ghost."

* * *

"We have lots of beer taverns, but I need something stronger!" Rene gave a little laugh as she led the way to a small adjacent café. "I sometimes eat here."

"Something stronger, for sure!" Eric found himself shaking. No shell shock, just strangely intense feelings. After settling them-selves, Rene with her gin and tonic, Eric with a good slug of whis-key, they faced each other across the tiny round table: their hands reached out and held each other.

"When did you get in?"

"The day before yesterday. I came on the *Aorangi*."

"Did you? I've always wanted to travel on that ship. I hear she's marvellous."

"Marvellous indeed." Eric nodded.

They each took another drink and Rene reached into her purse for a pack of cigarettes. She put one in her mouth and Eric lit it for her. "I must stop this. It's not good for my dancing."

She put down the packet and looked hard at Eric. "And so what did you come all this way for, Eric? Have they offered you a good job?"

Eric shook his head, but volunteered no more.

"We're pretty well half way around the world from the Gaspe." She smiled. "I've often thought about that."

Eric lifted his eyes. "Often?"

"Oh yes, dear Eric, often." She nodded, trying to control herself. "So tell me, what did bring you here?"

Eric stared for a moment, and then came out with it. "You."

He paused, then repeated: "I came all this way... just to find you."

The tears welled up in her eyes. Out came a handkerchief from her purse and she touched her cheeks. "I can't believe it," she murmured.

"It was a most impressive talk. I don't think I've learned as much since my years in Philosophy at Bishop's University. You sure know a lot about your subject." He paused. "I'm surprised your man friend didn't come. Perhaps he'd heard it all before?"

"Thank you. But what friend do you mean?"

"Well, you must have someone special?" He had decided to bring it out into the open. No good letting that awful thought drag him down. If she was already attached, he had to know.

Rene reached out and put her hand on his. "Eric, I have made a great many friends here in Sydney. They're such wonderful people, the Australians. We get along wonderfully well." She paused. "But Eric, there is not, and never has been, anyone like you."

They sat, silent, awkward. Then Eric leaned forward. "Rene ..." He paused. "Rene, will you marry me?"

She looked at him again, struck as she had been on the platform. She stared for what seemed an eternity.

Eric looked down at his hands. What would she say?

"Of course, Eric. Of course I will marry you. And the sooner the better."

PART THREE: 1927–1930

CHAPTER FOURTEEN

"**H**is name?"

Rene told him and watched the soft white fingers holding a small black fountain pen trace the letters, Eric Alford, on the form. She heard the next question, "Occupation?"

Rene paused. "Well ..."

Across his desk, the Reverend Clarence Smith looked up and, after a pause, asked gently, "What's his job?"

"He doesn't have one. Yet." Rene saw her Rector's eyebrows rise. "Well, you see, he's just arrived."

"Just?"

"Wednesday or Thursday, I'm not sure. We only met last night."

The Rector leaned back in his heavy leather chair, as well he might. Clarrie, as he was known to his parishioners, was not much older than Rene — far too young, in fact, to have been given the substantial parish of St. John's, Darlington. But then, this clergyman was also substantial: tall, muscular, thin, he had a commanding presence coupled with a warmth that most of his parishioners found exceptional. Rene felt comfortable talking to him.

"I know it sounds dreadful, but it's not what you think."

"Rene, over the months that I've known you, you are definitely not the sort who leaps into things without a good deal of thought." His fingers tapped the arms of his chair. "So perhaps, before we publish the banns of marriage, you ought to tell me a bit more."

Now it was Rene's turn to lean back. The church office was furnished with two bookcases, a small settee, and had the requisite plaques on the wall illuminating Clarence's background. "We met during the war. The Mater felt we should contribute to the war effort, so she told Leo and me take the Daimler into London and join volunteer ladies who drove His Majesty's officers whenever needed. Soon, we were introduced to Colonel John Alford, Eric's much older brother. Later he headed up the Canadian Chaplaincy Corps."

"Aha, so Eric is Canadian?"

Rene nodded. "After Eric arrived in England, we chauffeured him and Father John to lunch, and that's how we met." She smiled. "Just a young farm lad, really, never been anywhere or seen anything. But... there was something about him..." Rene paused, eyes moistening, "the strength of the farm perhaps. You see, his father, and his father before him, they hewed their fields out of real wilderness on the shores of a coast they call the Gaspe. Those trees, Eric told me, sometimes it took all day just to fell one of them and cut it into logs. Two men, of course, doing the sawing. With all sorts of wild animals around. Imagine!" As she went on to amplify Eric's background, Rene felt herself relax. Out the leaded windows could be seen a comfortable spread of lawn and a few trees, although they were in the centre of Sydney.

"And when did you last see him, before he arrived?" Clarence asked.

"Eight years ago."

Clarence frowned in surprise.

"But we wrote.... Though not frequently, in fact." She shook her head, as if just realizing that.

"Now in all those years, have you had other... attachments?"

Rene shook her head. "Clarrie, for me, there has been no one else."

"And Eric? If he is as extraordinary as you seem to think, other young ladies... ?"

Rene moistened her lips. "Odd, but I'm quite sure there's no one else."

"Well," Clarence leaned forward, and picked up the pen again, "that settles it, I suppose." He looked at Rene keenly.

Rene said nothing, thinking hard.

After a good pause, Clarence murmured, "Something you want to tell me, Rene?"

Rene shook her head.

Clarence leaned back again, and folded his hands before him.

"Well, perhaps I should." But she hardly knew how to begin. "I'm not sure, actually, that I haven't been rushed into this." She glanced up to see Clarence barely nod.

"You see, last night, I was so overcome when I saw him — such a shock! Who would ever expect that Eric would come after me like that? I mean, Clarrie, after eight years! He must have something wrong with him to wait eight years, and *then* make that trip all the way from the east coast of Canada, across its Dominion, and then over the Pacific. And I suppose — well, I couldn't sleep all last night, wondering. You see ..." she took a deep breath and stared at her fingernails.

Clarence waited, then murmured, "Go on."

"You see, he has not been entirely well."

"Meaning?"

Rene shrugged, then made herself continue. "He's been beset by that dreadful wartime illness they call shell shock. In fact, he's even been in hospital, I know that because he wrote me from there, just one very short letter. But mostly, he sounds perfectly normal. In his letters, I mean. In fact, I can tell he's led an unexceptional life. He loves gardening, he tells me —" she went on quickly, "but he's very strong, courageous, yes, he's been off in the depths of that untamed wilderness with wild animals, and not a worry. He loves it, in fact. And imagine, he led a Howitzer Brigade through every single one of the horrifying battles those hardy Canadians fought: Ypres, Vimy Ridge, Passchendaele, the Somme... How strong must that make him? It's just that ..."

Clarence nodded. "Many of our brave boys returning home have the same affliction. It occurs so unexpectedly. Ravages anyone it strikes. I do know about it."

"So I'm wondering, should I leap into a marriage where that selfsame, malady... lies lurking?" Then she looked at Clarence, straight in the eyes. "I think that's why I came to see you, Clarrie. I'm... well, I'm having severe doubts."

Clarence nodded to himself, and they both lapsed into silence. Rene looked up, and he met her eyes once again.

"My dear, you mustn't put all this upon me. The decision is yours."

Rene nodded sadly.

Then Clarence went on, as if he realized the weakness of that response. "If you have not been romantically inclined to anyone else for eight years..."

"Oh no."

"... and neither has he, well then... I know you to be a very well grounded person. You've built that school — my wife absolutely adores you, she thinks you're the holy Grail of dancing, she swears by you, and I trust Lyla implicitly. With these qualities, and I'm sure he must have similar ones —"

"Oh yes, he is such a good man. And he has in the past overcome every difficulty. I used to see him after he'd been in that hospital for shell shock cases up in Matlock Bath, and he was fully in balance, yes, he seemed fine. These occurrences, they don't last, they come and go, so briefly, and yet," she paused, "so powerfully. They can be devastating." She nodded to herself. "But then," she went on brightly, "they are over. Quite gone. All is normal again... For long periods."

"Well then, surely together, you and Eric, with God's help, you might as well... get on with it..."

Rene sat up, "Thank you, Clarrie. In fact, now, I don't even know why I spent all night worrying." Relieved, and composed once more, Rene watched a smile grow across her Rector's compassionate features.

* * *

The next day, Rene brought her new fiancé to worship at the eleven o'clock service in St. John's Church with its tall beautiful spire. It served Darlinghurst, Woolloomooloo, Potts Point, and so on. There, the two of them heard the Rector read out:

"I publish the Banns of Marriage between Irene Clarice Mulvany Gray, spinster, of this parish, and Major Eric Alford, retired, of the parish of Shigawake in Canada. If any of you know cause or just impediment why these two persons should not be joined together in Holy Matrimony, ye are to declare it. This is the first time of asking."

It would take two more Sundays for the other Banns, and then, the Saturday afterwards, they had fixed September 18th for their wedding.

After this first service, the couple went to the Rectory for Eric's favourite, the same dinner of fine roast beef, Yorkshire pudding, vegetables and liberal amounts of traditional gravy. Odd, because the Rector was not British, being the first Aussie to lead his prestigious St. John's parish.

"Out of all that big congregation, Rene, why are we being offered such a privilege?" Eric asked on the walk over.

Rene paused before answering. She knew enough to keep her secrets. "I think Clarence has rather taken me under his wing. His wife attends my classes. In fact, we've become good friends."

During the festive meal, having read the Abbott book on St. Paul twice during the voyage, Eric engaged the young Rector, not more than a few years older, in serious discussions. Clarence admitted he had only skimmed the book during his studies at St. John's College in Armidale, a known seat of learning. But Rene could see Clarrie had taken to this companion. With one eye on them, she spent most of the meal talking to Lyla, who wouldn't stop questioning her about dancing.

Afterwards, Eric was delighted to find himself served Spotted Dick, a custard with raisins that he remembered from lunches in London with his brother Jack.

Monday, Rene's usual day off, she had spent putting finishing touches to her apartment, for the special dinner when her future husband would see it for the first time. She had bought another little table, a new throw rug, and had run errands for other neglected oddments. She finished up with groceries and a good bottle of scotch, as well as replenishing her gin.

Eric, on the other hand, had spent his time looking for a job: he wanted to surprise Rene that night. Duly at six he rang the bell and down three flights came Rene to let him in. After their first real embrace, a long one capped by a kiss, they climbed to the top of the old converted Georgian mansion, laughing and chatting.

Eric doffed his light coat — even the early spring here in Sydney was warm. Rene ushered him through the living room to a triangular window looking out across Sydney Harbour.

"My! What a wonderful view," Eric breathed.

"We're on the ridge line of Woolloomooloo Hill. That's why I picked it." She showed Eric around, and then in the bedroom watched him take in the heavy brown rafters exposed in the opened peak above the bed. The apartment had all sorts of interesting nooks and crannies. Not used to such architecture, Eric took his time absorbing it all, but it grew on him. With so many flats like square boxes around these days, Rene offered, it took time to find an interesting nesting place. She paused and looked down at Eric as he sat for a moment on the bed.

"So do you think," he said slowly, "that after the wedding, we might stay here?"

Rene watched. "Whatever you think..."

Eric looked around, and nodded. "I couldn't have imagined anything nicer."

He paused, looking up at her.

"Good. Let's pour a drink."

"Thanks." He shook his head and got up. "So, our first problem solved."

Rene gave her fiancé a good shot of whiskey and herself a gin and tonic. She had already prepared dinner and needed only heat a last-minute dish. They sat talking: no shortage of events of the last few months to run over. Her school was doing exceptionally well, with more women applying every day; Rene had even hired an assistant to deal with appointments and classes. "Everyone seems to have money nowadays."

"They sure do in Canada," Eric agreed. "I met a fellow on the train coming across, he told me that even out West, everything's booming. If one were smart enough to get into the market."

"I'm sure the Mater has all that in hand. The family is mainly in property," Rene told him. "She's always acquiring more houses. When the war was starting, in that recession I believe she snapped up a good many."

"I think Old Poppa is doing well on the farm, too, with Earle. Certainly no shortage of food. Tough in the winter though," Eric added.

"So did you send off your telegram to them? I sent Hilda one in New Zealand, and another to the Mater first thing this morning. You found the telegraph office, all right?"

"Right where you said it was." But then Eric changed the subject, which Rene noticed. Had he not sent one? "Do you remember that pleasant fellow you were telling me about, married to one of your students?"

"An older one? Oh yes, my oldest pupil. She does well, considering." Rene looked at him. What was coming?

"Well, I went to see him."

"Whatever for?"

Eric smiled. He seemed pleased with himself. "Well, you said he was the one arranging for your course to be part of the school curriculum here."

Rene nodded. "Yes."

"I saw him about perhaps doing a bit of teaching." Rene looked at him with appreciative eyes. Eric smiled. "I can't spend all my time sightseeing, you know." He grinned again.

"Eric! You did? So what happened?"

"I think I have a job. Mathematics, actually," Eric stated proudly. "Not full time, because I might be doing something else... But he is going to try to arrange it. They really need teachers. The worthwhile young graduates all want to go into business, with

113

this boom going on. So once we're married, we'll both have jobs!"

He was pleased to see that Rene liked his initiative. In fact, he had quite astonished her.

This evening, filled with laughter, joy, gossip and catching up, augured well for the future, they both agreed. After an embrace that foretold of many pleasures to come, they retired to their separate dwellings, hearts inseparable.

* * *

While Rene spent the rest of the week teaching, organizing, getting invitations printed, setting up the wedding reception, Eric soon discovered, close by, Sydney's beautiful and hilly Botanical Gardens. There, he felt the peace that he had known only in his own garden at the Old Homestead. And one of those days, as he sat on a bench looking down toward the docks where the liners from all the world were coming and going, so slowly, like sleek heavy turtles, he was struck by a dreadful and overwhelming thought: had he forgotten that he was a prey to being attacked, at the most unexpected times, by shell shock?

So what? Wasn't he free of it now? Possibly. But could he really, having won her, impose it on his Rene?

It might strike at any time. He was fully aware that the condition was not under his direct control. Had that stay in military hospital vanquished it completely? Or did that malady lie, lurking beneath the surface, waiting to rise up and swallow them both?

He had asked the doctors, "Will this ever happen again?"

They had no answer. "Possibly. We don't have enough experience. Some men stay cured, some men return." That was all they could offer by way of assurance.

So what should he do about this marriage? Could he honestly burden Rene with his affliction? Had he only been thinking, oh so selfishly, of himself and his own wants, his own love? But if he truly loved her, would he foist a "disabled" veteran on her?

Perish the thought! He remembered a comrade in hospital opening his heart one night: "I'm in pretty bad shape. I would give the world to see an old girl friend of mine." Then the soldier went on, with words that pierced Eric here in the Botanical Gardens: "But who would want a young girl to be tied to a broken soldier — not me! I would shoot myself like a dog first. I let her go, and I just pray for her every night."

Eric heaved a sigh as he slowly came to agree. However painful, he must face up to doing the honourable thing, regardless of his own longing.

CHAPTER FIFTEEN

Thursday evening when Eric came for dinner, Rene noticed how changed her fiancé seemed. Withdrawn, deflated, he even gulped down the first whiskey she poured. Something surely wrong?

She turned down the vegetables and refrained from putting on his choice Australian steak. She came to sit beside him, sipping her drink. Her normally talkative companion was shut tight.

She made small talk for a few moments, telling him about her school. "You know, we're doing awfully well. Word is still getting out, I'm happy to say; we're pretty well full, for our size. If we keep growing at this pace, I shall have to get another teacher. Hilda might come and join me..."

Eric said nothing, but was drinking faster than normal. He held up the empty glass and looked at it, as though surprised.

Rene got up, took it to the sideboard, and then turned and came to stand before him. "Eric, I want you to tell me what's wrong?"

He held out his glass.

Rene shook her head. "No, I want you sober. You have to tell me first. I want to know what's happened."

Eric shifted uncomfortably. Clearly, he did want to speak, but something held him back.

"Eric..." She mouthed the word slowly, tenderly, standing, then turned, poured the drink and brought it over.

Eric took a slug, then another one, with her watching, and then burst out, "Rene, we can't go through with this."

The colour drained from her face. She took a chair, pulled it across, and sat. Her hand went to her brow and wiped her hair back. "Why ever not, Eric?"

"Just because ..."

"No, Eric, that won't do. Because? Because of what?" She asked no more.

Eric forced himself to look at her. She was so lovely, but now her face showed an inner anguish. He took a deep breath. "Rene, in my letters, I never really told you what happened."

"What happened? When?"

"Well, before they put me in hospital."

"I knew, I knew something must have driven them to do that." She leaned back. "Tell me about it. I won't mind, I promise. "

Eric hedged. But Rene persisted, and Eric began. He recounted the details of his time marching with the Officers Training Corps, and coming to believe they faced Passchendaele again. He spared no detail. The whiskey had gone down, and now she could see that he wanted her to know it all. After all, how could he break this off without being utterly honest? If he were not going to see her again, she deserved a complete explanation.

After filling her in about that first episode and how he had re-covered at the Old Homestead and thus been able to return to college, he paused.

Rene nodded. "Keep on, Eric. I'm ready."

So then he told her about the second event in the hotel after the rugby season, and Jack coming to find him in bed, in the depths of despair. How they had checked him in at the Military Hospital in Ste. Anne's, and then Eric gave her a truncated version of his stay there.

After he finished, he sat back on the sofa and held out his tumbler once more. More than ever, he wanted to avoid that hospital, and sink himself into the arms of his new, though long- standing, love. The pressure made him begin, just slightly, to shake. Which made him feel worse, of course. And the more he tried to control it, the worse it got. What was he doing to himself? But the right action was the only action.

Rene got up to pour another. "Now, Eric, don't drink this all at once, please. I want you clearheaded. We have to discuss this."

Eric nodded dumbly and waited as she poured his third drink. "I asked them, you see, the doctors, I pleaded, I had to know. Would it occur again?"

"And what did they say?" Rene sat upright, composing herself, listening.

"Rene, they could give me no assurances. They said that some veterans, they spend the rest of their lives happily, more or less able to deal with everything. Other veterans ..." he shrugged. "It comes back."

Rene nodded.

"And so," Eric sighed deeply, shifted awkwardly, "and so... when I was sitting on that park bench — my gosh, Rene, those gardens are so beautiful. Anyway, as I was sitting there, I knew that I should not ever burden you with this awful — and to me frightening — possibility. And that's why ... that's why I've decided we should perhaps... Just not to go through with our marriage."

Rene sat silent and nodded.

Then she leaned forward. "Eric, my darling Eric, we have waited eight long years. I don't know if you've been to a wedding recently, but there's a phrase in it, "for better or for worse ..." I am ready to take that vow, Eric. Very ready. In fact, I welcome it. That's what marriage is, we both know that. Good times and bad. With luck, there will be only good times." She paused. "But the way things go in life, there are also bound to be bad ones, too."

Eric nodded. "That's what I'm afraid of." His shoulders were hunched, tense.

"Don't be. I think, if we do this together, we can overcome anything. Have you met anyone — in fact, I'm sure you haven't — who could handle all this better than me? I've travelled, I've come here on my own, set up a school, and now, I'm ready to be married, to mingle my soul with yours.."

Eric looked up, and met her steady gaze.

She looked right back, square in the eyes.

"Rene, you know something?" He broke into a big grin. "You always surprise me. And I hope you always will. Surprise, that's one of the great things in life, isn't it."

He jumped up, grabbed her by the arms, hauled her off the chair, wrapped himself around her and kissed her as much and as strongly as he could. "My God, Rene, I love you so much." And that love they consummated at last, under the great brown rafters, in a wild burst of joy.

* * *

Eric had taken to walking everywhere and now knew Potts Point and its surroundings top to bottom. So he felt drawn to investigate Sydney University. He wondered if it compared to Bishop's University, or was it more like McGill? So he caught a tram and got off at the campus.

What a surprise! The great main building before him was indeed, as he had heard, one of the country's best examples of

Gothic Revival architecture. From a superb clock tower two wings extended, the right hand one ending in a chapel with sharply peaked roof, a large window flanked by tall statues in attractive niches, and a narrow tower on guard to the right. No college architecture he'd seen in Canada could rival it and he warmed to the idea of furthering his education here. He began to wander the grounds, the Anderson Medical building, and the new Zoology and Physics building.

Then he went into the aged — well, seventy-five-year-old — quadrangle with its tawny stonework, its cloistered walk, and stood drinking in the pale blue of the jacaranda tree, unknown in the Gaspe. His conversation with Clarence at Sunday dinner came drifting back. "You should take a look at our local college, Moore. Lovely place. Great spot to study. I would have loved doing courses there."

"I shall. But isn't it only for students taking up the cloth?"

Clarence had looked at him. "What's so wrong with that, Eric? You seem to me an ideal candidate."

Eric was taken aback. "Well, I admit that my brother, Jack, often told me I should look into it." Clarence knew of this Canon who had run the Canadian Chaplaincy Corps. "And to be honest, I haven't yet decided what I'm going to do." That did sound a bit odd, Eric knew, and added, "With this wonderful new union coming, Clarence, you may be sure, that I'm giving the future serious thought."

And so, without any predispositions, Eric turned toward the red brick buildings of Moore to the south. Entering it, he found the place rather like Bishop's, in fact. Curious, he thought as he sat on a bench watching the students wander by, I do feel comfortable here. I might even enjoy myself. More learning about St. Paul and more of Him who strode the Holy Land, to whom I pray nightly...

A day or two later, Eric was taking his constitutional around the Botanical Gardens. He felt now, with Rene by his side, he could conquer the world. But he wanted to take on something that would be of use, of help to others. Something that also might afford him the peace and quiet he needed after the devastation of his teenage years on the Firing Line. His thoughts drifted towards his Maker. Ask Him, he prompted himself. Usually he found these conversations soothing.

"You know," he began, "with all the excitement crossing Canada and then the Pacific my search, and then — thanks to who else but You — finding Rene free to marry... Well, You have blessed me so far. But I confess, I've given far too little thought about what comes next.

"Now," he continued in this heavenward conversation, "my marriage is in ten days. So I have to get on with deciding... what to do. Help me, please."

As he strode around, studying the different trees and their leaves, many he'd never seen before, passing colourful plots of flowers so different from the Old Homestead, he kept turning these matters over in his mind.

He came upon a path that turned into some undergrowth by a grove of trees. It wound roughly around hillocks, up and down dips, coming to rest at a clearing with its weathered bench and an attractive man-made pool — empty now, for it was still spring. He sat on the bench and leaned back, reaching his arms along the back of the bench.

He sat, staring into the waterless pool.

To a passerby, this young veteran, only thirty but looking older, might have seemed asleep. But he sat upright, almost rigid, eyes straight ahead; one might take him for blind as they focussed on nothing. A disconcerting sight, but fortunately no one passed, for it was mid-morning when wives were busy making meals, and mothers would never push their prams along this twisted pathway.

A couple of clock towers telling the hour of noon seemed to awaken our veteran. He shook his head and looked about him, then glanced at his watch. He gathered himself, and then, knowing absolutely and firmly what he had to do, set off at a brisk pace for his boarding house.

* * *

That night, as soon as Rene let Eric in she knew something was up. They had only really been together for a few dinners; she herself had been so busy, dealing with new pupils, the well-wishing of friends, the notes arriving, the telegrams of congratulations from the Mater and Hilda. But she knew Eric well enough to realize that all was not as it should be.

As they mounted the stairs, Rene chatted gaily, trying hard to keep an eye on Eric without his noticing.

"I've certainly been looking forward to this dinner," Eric told her. "For someone who claims you haven't done much cooking, you sure know how to make food tasty!" They entered the apartment. "And you know, the more I've thought about it, the more I love this attic flat. Absolutely wonderful, big open beams. Our Homestead has an attic, too, but we closed it in with low ceilings. This is so interesting."

"The builders had just finished the conversion when I saw it," Rene told him. But wasn't he a bit too excited? She went over to the sideboard, got out two tumblers and poured them each a drink. "I don't think too many hereabouts like this sort of thing, so I was able to make rather a good financial agreement with the landlord. I'm glad you like it."

She came across and sat beside him. They exchanged a kiss,

and then another, but before it got too heated, Rene drew back and asked, "Well, so what have you been up to?"

Eric tried to control his excitement. "Oh well, I've been walking around, seeing the neighbourhood. I looked at the University, my goodness, so much more magnificent than anything we have in Canada. Closest I've seen is Oxford, which I did visit once."

"I remember you telling me."

"Then, I even went into Moore Theological College. Clarence suggested it. Amazing, really, how it resembles my old college in Lennoxville."

The first thought that entered Rene's mind was: that's where he had those two episodes of shell shock. But she brushed it aside. "And you loved your time at Bishop's, didn't you?" she said, by way of avoiding the thought.

"Oh yes. Yes indeed." Eric paused as though wanting to continue, but said nothing.

They both sipped their drink. Eric got up and went to the window and looked out. "Just a wonderful view. Just wonderful..." He took a slug of his drink.

Rene watched him. He's avoiding something, she told herself. But she decided to wait.

Eric roamed around the room, his movements erratic. As though he couldn't settle.

Rene watched him but still said nothing. Better, she thought, let this situation, whatever it might be, evolve. She prayed it was not another of those — "We can't go through with the marriage." She had dealt with the last one pretty well, but wasn't looking forward to many more.

Eric seemed to notice his own restlessness, and came to sit beside her again. But he kept wanting to get up, she thought, his hands twitching. He asked for another drink.

Rene got up, went to the sideboard and then, impulsively,

turned to him. "Eric. Eric dear, tell me."

Eric gave her a deep, serious look. Then he shook his head and turned away.

Rene brought him his drink, and sat beside him again. Then she touched him, put her hand on his, and then brought his fingers to her mouth and kissed them. "Eric. I'm to be your wife. We had better start right away not avoiding things. We had better start right now bringing things out."

Eric looked at her. Fear in his look! He turned away.

Rene leaned over and kissed his cheek.

That seemed to do it. Eric leaned back, squeezed himself closer to her, shut his eyes, put his head back, and began. "Rene, after Moore College, I went for a walk in the Botanical Gardens. Aren't they wonderful, as you said? Anyway, I found a quiet place and sat on a bench." He leaned forward. "You see, I've been trying to decide... what I'm going to do..." Rene's heart sank.

Eric nodded slowly. "Yes, I've been doing that a lot these last couple of weeks."

Lord, thought Rene, it's coming again. He's going to go back to Canada. He's going to leave just when everything looks so perfect. How should I deal with that? She braced herself.

He went on, relentless now. "And Rene, I don't know if I was asleep or awake. But I sat for a long, long time. You see ... you see, I do ask God for help. I often do that."

"I quite understand," she murmured. Was Eric going to say God told him to leave her? Dirty trick, if He did, she thought. How did one counter God?

"Well," Eric said, "I sat there and thought. I was staring into that pool, I guess. Built of boulders and smooth rocks, placed together, with cement to hold the water." He shifted. "But at the bottom, there must have been broken glass, for when the sun moved in the heavens, its rays started to flash, they struck into the bottom of the pool and reflected, harshly, brilliantly, into my eyes..."

And then, he became almost rigid.

Shell shock, she thought. Oh no! But she kept silent.

"Rene, staring into that light, into the heart of that light, I saw ... well, the pool was filled with water out of sunlight, and the Lotus rose. And... I saw my Lord standing before me. And he... he pointed, right at me! And told me, what I should do. And you know, Rene," Eric began to shake, "you know, Rene, I swear, I saw my brother next to him. They were both looking at me, with a serious look and yet at the same time, kind of comforting."

Although holding himself rigid, he began to shake even more.

Oh heavens, Rene thought: What do I do? How does one handle this? She wished she'd taken some course. Or perhaps gone into the veteran's hospital to ask them. Instinctively, she found herself putting an arm around him. His shaking grew. "And I knew, really, I knew then, what I had to do."

She began to hug him tightly, as much for herself as for him. Yes, I know, she said to herself — to leave me and go back to Canada. And how to object to that? He was not well, she knew it, but she just could not let him go. What would happen then?

He went on, "I knew that I..." Rene let out a silent sigh. For pity's sake, Lord, tell me how I should react, how I can help him? "...That I must..." he went on, rigid but shaking, "I must become a clergyman. Join Holy Orders."

Rene stared. Then she shook her head and let herself break into a lovely smile.

Only now did Eric let himself turn to her. He saw that smile.

What an experience! Rene thought. A vision...

"Yes," Eric went on, "I'm certain of it, Rene, I'm certain that's what they both wanted. I know it. I'm supposed to become a priest."

With unbounded relief, Rene hugged him as tightly as she

could, and his shaking subsided.

He whispered. "Thank you, thank you, Rene. Thank you."

Rene felt his whole frame slump and gradually, she relaxed her hold. What an experience he had been through. Not to be repeated, she was certain.

Eric leaned down, almost into her lap , and turned to look up at her face. "You won't tell anyone about this... pool thing, will you?"

"No, my darling, that's just between us two."

"So really, you wouldn't mind being the wife of the clergyman?"

She paused. Then she blurted out, "I can't think of a better occupation, Eric. Being the wife of the clergyman, and a teacher of the Revived Greek Dance. What in the world could be a better combination?"

So once again, the marriage was on, and on the appointed Saturday in the Church of St. John's, Darlinghurst, the two of them entered into the state of Holy Matrimony, accompanied by the most glorious bell-ringing of the thirteen tubular bells in the enormous landmark spire.

CHAPTER SIXTEEN

With the wedding and reception past, Eric and Rene set their course for a productive time in Australia. Eric soon found himself in the office of Archdeacon David Davies, the Principal of Moore College, with his friend, the Rev. Clarence Lucas. Passing through some rigorous questioning, he was more than pleased to be accepted — in the middle of the scholastic year, which had begun in February — as a theological student.

Rene continued teaching, always with a weather eye out for her new husband. The shadow of the shadow hung over her. But after a time she saw that he was progressing nicely, enjoying his studies, happy at home, and she allowed herself to forget any looming upheaval from his war years.

Two weeks later on November third, the *Tahiti*, sister ship of the *Aorangi*, cut the Sydney ferry *Greycliffe* in two, killing forty passengers. This tragedy caught everyone by surprise, and now Eric spent his free hours ministering to the survivors. He worked tirelessly, Rene saw, which made her particularly proud. "I don't know how you do it, Eric, all that studying and teaching, and then you spend your time off in hospital helping the victims. But don't overdo it."

"Rene," he replied, "I've seen so much worse, remember. It's no burden. I enjoy this ministry."

The summer passed and before she knew it, she found herself in the Moore Chapel to witness Eric being ordained by the Archbishop of Sydney, John Charles Wright, who the very next week appointed him "curate" in their parish. His years at Bishop's counted, of course, but he hadn't yet passed his final Licentiate in Theology. Not being a full priest, Eric did not find his new duties onerous: helping out on Sundays and doing some pastoral work. But Rene was worried that, in addition to his teaching and studying, these might put another undue strain on him.

One night they sat together eating dinner. Rene had taught and danced all day, hurried home, picked up food and then cooked it for them. Eric was watching her anxiously during the meal, and finally she heard him say: "Rene, I don't know if this will make you feel better, but I don't think I've ever in my entire life been so happy." He looked at her seriously, with a slight frown.

"Do I look tired, my darling?"

Eric nodded.

"Well," she went on, "what you said will surely take away any tiredness. I'm so happy, too. And I thought your ordination just wonderful."

But during 1929, storm clouds of another sort began to gather. "I do hope there's not more bad news," Eric called as he went down to bring up the Daily Telegraph for Rene, who was throwing together breakfast. "Those strikes the last while, they seem contagious: more and more unrest everywhere. I much prefer the papers to bring us news of heroic actions, like they did last year when Bert Hinkler flew in solo from London."

"And what about Kingsford Smith last June? Right across the Pacific! Brave man." She smiled. "I love brave men." She actually winked at Eric and quickly went on: "In a Fokker DVII, wasn't it?"

Eric nodded. "He called it the Southern Cross."

"I love stories like that."

Eric threw the paper down on the table. "Look!"

Rene came to sit. "The Australian election?"

"Yes. They voted out that dreadful Stanley Bruce!"

Rene studied the column. "First sitting PM ever to lose his own seat. Well I never! So James Scullin and his Labour Party have gotten in with a huge majority. I wonder if it'll help?"

"Shouldn't think so..." Already Eric was drifting off in his own world of study and papers that he had to write. "Here it is October 13th, and I've got a whole set of exams beginning. It's my last term, you know, Rene, it ends in December, and that's it."

At the end of October, matters came to a head, oddly enough at another Sunday dinner at the rectory. Walking over after the morning service, Eric remarked, "You know, this reminds me that just over two years ago, we first came to dinner here. Amazing how the time flies."

Rene agreed. "Where did it go? Oh, another couple will be joining us: I think you've met them. A pillar of the church, in fact, very wealthy — perhaps their most important donor, so Lyla told me."

"That will be interesting," Eric said absently.

Rene went on, "You know those lunches three times a week at church when we feed the poor ? Well, Lyla told me that more and more have been coming. I think she invited this couple so her husband could ask for a larger contribution."

Eric opened the door to the rectory for Rene. After exchanging greetings, Clarence introduced Eric to Neal Harcourt, a large florid Mancunian with a red face, perspiring and somewhat jumpy.

His wife, Elsie, was correspondingly small, elflike, with perhaps premature grey hair. She looked worried, and her eyes were red as though she'd been weeping.

Roast lamb was being served along with the usual vegetables and a good red wine. "Another sumptuous meal!" exclaimed Rene as they sat down. Always cheerful, Eric noticed, looking on the bright side.

"Lovely wine, Neal. Thank you very much." The Rector complimented his guest. "Can't you get your friend who owns this vineyard to come to church?"

The others grinned. But Neal seemed in another world.

"Now let us all drink," Clarence went on, "to the future of our parish lunches for the poor." He looked at Neal. "A lot more of the destitute coming these days."

Everyone lifted their glass and drank, but Eric saw that Neal nearly choked on his wine.

The others pretended not to notice.

"Even when things around us aren't going as well as they might, Lyla can be counted on to make a lovely meal," Rene exclaimed again.

Neal glanced up briefly and then buried himself in the roast lamb; he certainly enjoyed his food, if nothing else. But the usual jollity of the meal seemed lacking. "Terrible," Neal mumbled, mouth full, "what's been going on."

"Oh yes?" asked Eric. "I'm afraid I've been so involved in exams this last month, I haven't had enough time to read the papers thoroughly."

"And how do you think your studies are going, Eric?" asked Clarence. "From what I hear, you've been enjoying yourself and doing well to boot."

"Eric's loving it," Rene confirmed. "His graduation is next month, well, at the beginning of December. He'll have his Licentiate in Theology as you know, and the week after that they are arranging for his ordination as full priest."

"Bravo, Eric!" commented Lyla. "I just knew when you took up those courses, you'd do well. Welcome into the clergy!"

"Thank you, Lyla," Eric said. "I just did my best." But he steered the conversation back to Neal, who seemed to be sweating more. "So the economic news is not good, Neal?"

Silence descended on the table while Neal finished a mouthful and wiped his heavy lips on the large white napkin. "Bloody awful. Haven't you heard?" He glanced about him and then dived into the roast potatoes again.

"At classes yesterday," Rene said, "it was all the conversation at the break. Apparently, my women students had heard from their husbands there'd been some sort of awful crash." She glanced at Eric. "I mentioned it last night, my dear."

Eric nodded. "I wish I'd paid more attention."

"Awful is putting it mildly," said Neal. "My brother telegrammed from Manhattan — he's been entirely wiped out." He glanced around the table. "When Elsie and me came out here to New South Wales, Edward opted for New York City. My father, Pa, we call him, he had sent us off. He had made a bit of a fortune, you see·— "

"I'll say he did!" laughed Clarence. "If he was able to send one son to New York and the other to Sydney, who I might add has been as generous as anyone alive!"

"We owned a couple of cotton mills in Manchester. Edward, my brother, he took a good part of his inheritance and put it in the market. Made himself so much, these last years, I even sent him everything I had, too." He shook his head sorrowfully and then mopped his brow.

His little wife, Elsie, added, "You see, with all our contacts in the wool trade from Manchester, it seemed foolish not to come here to Australia with all its sheep. Really, it did. We were sure to do well."

"And you have, my dear," Lyla responded soothingly

"I suppose we did, for some years. But now..." She choked slightly.

"What Elsie's trying to tell you is the last couple of years, our staples, wool and wheat, have tumbled. Almost our whole economy, as you know. Banks won't lend to us fellows who work with real things like sheep and acres of wheat — stuffing their greedy cheeks with market paper. Impossible to do business that way. My partners all say the same. No wonder there's more and more strikes, more and more fellows out of work. The whole Australian economy is going down the drain fast — and pulling us with it!"

Eric had been reading about the number of strikes but he hadn't really absorbed their economic realities.

"Has your school been doing all right?" Clarence leaned over to Rene on his right and touched her arm.

"Well, to be perfectly frank, Clarrie, our enrolment has been dropping. Only yesterday two more women said they can't come back after Christmas. Such a shame. They were doing so well, too: standing more erect, moving gracefully; they need what we can give them."

"I dare say a bunch more will be dropping out, too," growled Neal. He turned to the Rector. "And while we're on this dreadful subject, Clarrie, I'm afraid, the way things are, I'm going to have to stop my support of your weekly luncheons for the poor. In fact," he gave a harsh laugh, "Elsie and I will likely be coming for a hand-out ourselves!"

Elsie gave a little yelp and Eric noticed her eyes brimming again. "It's dreadful," she mumbled, "just dreadful. You don't know the half!"

"Black Thursday, Edward called it. He telegrammed me yesterday again to tell us we'd been wiped out, too." He shook his head, and began to tremble a little. "Black Thursday! Yes, so many finished. Including us." He sat back glumly, and then dived hungrily into the last of his tasty lamb and vegetables.

On their way home together, Eric seemed a new man. He was walking upright like a soldier, and Rene could feel him taking charge. "Now my lovely, Rene," he asked, "what's all this about dancers leaving?"

"Well, I didn't want to worry you, Eric dear, but attendance has been dropping."

"And Neal said it will drop even further. Do you think there's any truth in that?"

"I'm afraid so." Rene left the sentence hanging in the air.

"Is there anything you can do?"

Rene shrugged. "What happens in the country, we just cannot control." She went on, "At least you'll have finished your studies. You'll be a proper clergyman."

"Yes," replied Eric. "And priested on the twenty-first. The Solstice," he added. "Curious. The Pagans used to think of this as the time of maximum conflict between the powers of darkness and the powers of light."

"So finally, the end of studying, and college."

"Yes. And the beginning of something else ..." murmured Eric.

They walked on up Darlinghurst which turned into Macleay St. They still had a way to go.

"So," Rene prompted tentatively, "a beginning?"

"Mmm." He paused. "Well, I've been thinking of trying to find some position in the country or up the coast. All the clergy positions here in Sydney seem pretty well filled. I've been making discreet inquiries."

"You mean, go and stay out in the country?"

"Well, I could come back every weekend, my dear. I don't know what else..."

Rene shook her head. "That's hardly the way I want to live."

"Me neither."

"I noticed when you heard of your mother's death last April, although you tried to hide it, you were thinking long and fully about your Old Homestead."

"A shock, of course. Though expected — we knew she'd not go on forever... You were a great comfort, Rene. I didn't really credit you at the time, as I should have."

"That's what a wife is for. As you are a great comfort to me, Eric."

"Anyway, I try to put morbid thoughts aside," Eric said. Then he was silent. "You're right, Rene, it was difficult. I loved her, as you know."

"I do know," Rene said. "I know a lot more than you imagine," Eric nodded.

"So this might mean, perhaps, that it's time for a trip to Canada? I've never been, you know."

"Oh no," Eric replied. "Your school comes first." They walked on.

"No, in my life, Eric, you come first."

"Even before your school?"

Rene nodded, seeing him look at her. "I've always been intrigued by that wilderness, you know. So romantic. So untouched. No one I know in England, or here for that matter, knows anything about the deep woods, those still lakes you wrote to me about, the call of the loons, the caribou..."

Eric frowned, then looked at her and brightened. "I still have a bit of a nest egg, you know."

"Oh, the travel costs would not be important. As I told you when we got married, the Mater did promise us a honeymoon. I recently suggested a trip around the world — and she agreed!"

Eric looked up, startled. "She did?"

"She can be oddly generous at times. I don't know what possessed her. She never increased my allowance when I left. Leo lives in the lap of luxury at home, but for some reason they both think Hilda and I should get by on our own. Which of course, we do."

"A trip around the world," Eric repeated. And then he said, "Might it include a stop in the Holy Land?"

"Indeed it might."

CHAPTER SEVENTEEN

Ten days after the ordination, Eric and Rene watched their liner's slow progress out of Sydney Harbour. At the rail, Eric shielded his eyes as he looked for the last time at their former apartment, the Georgian house atop Woolloomooloo Hill.

He lifted his arm in farewell and turned to Rene. "Wave good-bye." She followed suit. "Sad at leaving?"

She shook her head. "In fact, I'm pleased at last to have time to relax. These last two months since we decided to leave, I've done nothing but make arrangements, see to the continuation of the school, arrange for Hilda to come. Not a second to myself."

"I know, my dearest Joy." Eric had taken to calling her by this nickname.

"And neither have you, Eric. You've been a wonderful, help."

"But what about the school you built and all that?"

"The pupils, yes, I was sad to say good-bye. But a lot were dropping out. Awful to watch everything weaken and die with this coming slump. What does it say in the Bible? *To everything there is a season.* I loved my time here down under, but now," she turned and brightened, "on to something new."

"Well, I enjoyed helping you. And with everything else, you were just super to put on that little reception after I was priested for Canada by the Archbishop."

Rene smiled. "Didn't he enjoy himself! I don't think he's had as much to drink in a long time!"

Eric laughed. But he kept his eyes fixed on Woolloomooloo Hill as, with the ship picking up speed, it receded from their view.

Countries came and went. They stopped in Ceylon for a couple of days: a wonderful time, sightseeing in rickshaws. Rene noticed how the strain of Eric's exams, his Ministry and his teaching of little scallywags, all drained away. He looked and clearly felt like a new man. Ready for anything. And then, they reached his one much-anticipated destination: the Holy Land.

> The American Colony Hotel,
> Jerusalem, Palestine.
> February, 1930.

Dear Hilda,

We have finally arrived in British Mandated Palestine. We landed at Jaffa and got a bus to Jerusalem where we're installed in the American Colony Hotel, with generous spread-out rooms, just up from Damascus Gate. Its lovely buff-coloured stone has rounded arches like an Arab dwelling, around a charming courtyard.

On the whole, the trip has been wonderful. Eric was pleased with the accommodation on board. Unlike his coming to Australia, when he slept in a six-berth interior cabin, we are on the first-class deck with a lovely large window. I have been mixing with the others perhaps more than Eric, who prefers to lie out and read, but of course, he takes his vigorous constitutional during the morning, which I do with him, and also we love playing quoits and shuffleboard.

I'm not sure I should relate this, but I do feel like telling someone. Make sure it goes no further!

Eric threw the entire steamer trunk of my better dresses, my trousseau, and some fine linens, overboard!

Well, I'm sure it was all my fault. At first I was furious, of course. Then I got worried — not the action of a rational man, I thought. But you see, once I'd called it up out of the hold, I had spent the day going over which dress I should wear for the Gala Dance before we arrived in Ceylon. Eric wanted to read, and I kept asking him about different outfits, trying them on, looking at myself in the mirror — things I normally never do. You know me, I usually throw on anything at hand and get going. So the whole atmosphere of First Class had infected me. Those dreadful women spend all their time commenting on what everyone is wearing, so each woman becomes an object of intense scrutiny.

That night when I was asleep, I suppose Eric had decided enough is enough. He wheeled the trunk out of our cabin onto the deck and then, as he told me later, enlisted the help of one of the cabin boys to throw the whole thing overboard. The next morning, after I got up, I realised there was no trunk.

Eric was washing and I asked him, "Did you see where my trunk went?"

He turned, razor in hand, face half-lathered, and replied, "I think David Jones is delighted. It's safe in his locker."

Davey Jones' Locker is what they call the bottom of the ocean.

I'm sure I must have looked in complete astonishment. I was absolutely staggered, my dear Hilda. "But why?" I asked.

Eric simply returned to his shaving, and then said, "Man is hampered by his possessions."

Well, I tell you! That did take me aback. As I mentioned I was furious. But in the ensuing days, I gradually came to realize that he might have been right. I had become too involved in petty details, such ridiculous things as how I looked, which as you know is not my wont. I think Eric preferred the old me. Well, he got it. No more preening in front of mirrors! First-class women or no first class. And after that, you know what? I enjoyed the voyage even more!

You can make of that what you will, dear Hilda.

I'm hoping you enjoy teaching the students and running the school. You're a brick to have come so quickly to take over. I look forward to hearing word, but I fear that I'll have to wait until we reach Canada. We're going to spend almost a month here in the Holy Land, for this has become, for Eric, the raison d'être of our trip. The closer we got, the more excited he became.

There is so much to see! So many things date from very far back, some places, I am told, to the time of Christ Himself. We are going to be walking in His footsteps, Eric says. Might you take a trip here, too? Though I know you're not particularly religious, in that sense of the word. And neither am I. But I look forward to a wonderful time seeing the Holy Land through Eric's eyes. In fact, now that I'm thinking of it, I shall keep a diary. If it's not too personal, I shall send it one day.

Your devoted sister, Rene

Bethany

Today, we walked to Bethany, beyond the Mount of Olives, as our Lord did many times to visit his friends Martha and Mary, and their brother Lazarus. We began at the Catholic church of St. Peters Gallicantu (cock crow) and it was not long before we were taken down into the bowels of the church to see the dungeons, where the guide claimed our Lord had been held that Thursday night while undergoing his trials.

Eric stood stricken, looking into that darkened hole. No doors. Prisoners were lowered — or thrown down — through that. I began to be afraid that perhaps this whole experience would be too much for him; I am always on the lookout. But no, he was just absolutely drained — I believe putting himself back into those awful times before the crucifixion. He stayed that way for a long time, until the guide became bored and tried to hurry us a long. Eric snapped at him, rare for him, and then we went outside and lo! We stood on the very steps, large, grey paving stones, leading down toward the Kidron Valley, on which the actual feet of Our Lord walked that dreadful night.

Eric knelt and kissed one. I was a bit embarrassed, but not he! For the first time in our lives, we were walking where Jesus himself had actually walked, two thousand years ago. Not hard to understand what it meant for Eric.

Down we went and crossed the Kidron Valley, with its Church of the Assumption of Saint Mary, His mother, facing us just across the little bridge. Amazing, this one lane carries so much traffic: Arabs riding on their little donkeys, bicycles, mule carts, an occasional car — chaos!

We walked up the long slanting road that climbs the Mount of

Olives and at the top we stopped and sat in a grove of olive trees, so very old and twisted. Sheep grazed here, attended by a scrawny Arab urchin in a tunic, nothing else, though I found it quite cold. Snow had fallen during the night but had mostly melted, except for up here. It's mid-winter of course; I'd forgotten, having lived below the equator for so long.

From his old haversack, Eric got out our packed lunch, but I warned him, "He'll come after us..."

"Exactly!" Eric called to the boy, who didn't turn. He called louder. Then he got up, went over and tapped the little lad on his shoulder. It came to me, then, that he was deaf and dumb. Eric held out our lunch pack. The boy drew back, afraid. Eric opened it. The lad looked, saw the food, and then snatched it. Now what would we eat? I wondered. I have never in my entire life seen anyone wolf down food as did that little lad.

Eric smiled and came back to sit, contented. Not for a moment did he regret losing his luncheon picnic.

"The actual Garden of Gethsemane is further down, or so they claim," Eric went on, his mind on the footsteps of Our Lord, unaware of how much he himself was walking in them with his actions. "They can't really know, or guess, where exactly they seized Him. But this is as good a place as any to rest and reflect on that event."

As he was sitting, the little lad came up to him and put his hands together and bowed a little ceremonial thanks. Eric nodded, pleased. Then the boy went back to his sheep.

I got out my Baedeker and read while Eric sat thinking. I love that guidebook.

After a time, we got up, walked over the brow of the hill and on down the old Roman road eastwards towards Bethany, a small cluster of mud and cement huts. Heavens, the people are poor here. No wonder children are forever begging after money or sweets. But I shan't write about this here. What I'm hoping is that later in Canada, my diary will remind us more of the wonderful things we've seen, and how Eric is benefiting from this before he gets a parish.

When we came to the little hovel which the guide fatuously claimed was the genuine original house of Martha and Mary, we were both a bit stunned. What a mess this village is! Imagine! Bethany. But more and more I'm realizing that my British background is interfering with what I grasp must be a very different way of life — perhaps not all that dirty either, which Eric maintains in our evening talks. These disreputable Arabs only appear that way through our own failings.

The guide took us down to what he claimed was the tomb of Lazarus.

"Good a place as any to read about that event." Eric took out his ever-present Bible and read how Our Lord brought Mary's brother back from the dead. But hearing it gives one no sense of what it's really like. I find I'm learning that all the time. Amazing the poverty and simplicity of these people and these mud huts where the Lord of all the world stayed to dine.

Eric hoped to press on towards Jericho for the Monastery on the Mount of Temptation, carved right into those steep high cliffs down the old Roman Road. I felt in the mood for a hike myself; it might have relieved what I realized was my sense of responsibility — and even nervousness — about Eric. But the guide told us it would be too far, there and back, for one afternoon, so we left it to another day when we'll hire a car.

The Sea of Galilee

What a packed couple of days! Full of ups and downs. Yesterday, we did hire a car and drove down to the Jordan Valley and later to Jericho. Eric wanted to see the site where St. John did his baptizing, so our Arab driver brought us to a place among the reeds where we got out and walked forward — to stop in dismay. What a shock! That muddy creek before us — surely not the legendary River Jordan? Eric had been thinking of his St. Lawrence River, which even at its most narrow near the city of Montreal, took an engineering feat to throw a bridge across the vast width. "Not even as big as our salmon rivers in Gaspe," he mumbled.

Afterwards, we did get the most magnificent view at a ruined Crusader castle called Belvoir. Belvoir means "beautiful view" and it certainly was that. But as we climbed into the ruins and looked out, we were both again astonished. The view was marvellous — that whole valley held in its lap the Sea of Galilee. But the sea itself! Again, Eric remarked, smaller than the Quebec lakes he knew. Indeed, that did build my excitement at our heading for his Canadian wilderness. But at the moment, it was hard to see how this lake could generate those great storms one reads about in the Bible.

As we drove down towards the lake, we saw a woman with a huge bundle of sticks on her head, and Eric grew excited again and quoted, "I see women as trees, walking" — something like that, from where Jesus healed a blind man. It made sense to him for the first time. He's learning so much.

We got to the shore and stayed at the Galei Kinneret, an excellent hotel by the standards hereabouts. And then this morning, off we went with our hamper of food round the Sea of Galilee. Although we drove slowly, in only half an hour we reached the north end of the 'sea' to the ruins of Capernaum, now controlled by the Franciscans. Wandering around the tumbled down old synagogue where Jesus once taught, Eric told me about His healing the centurion. This village was apparently home to Peter, and also the apostles Andrew, James and John. I had read in Baedeker that close by stood the village of Cana, where Our Lord turned water into wine – his first miracle.

We must drink to that! Eric said, as though it were part of a ritual he had planned. We sat in the sun on upturned Roman pillars while he broke out our bottle. This winter day turned out to be warm and not many visitors because the site was closed to locals, forced to leave their soliciting at the gates. After a couple of glassfuls, I was a bit alarmed to see Eric break out laughing, almost hysterically. I cautioned him against drinking too much in this heat with nothing on his stomach.

"Do you know," he said through his giggles, "Mother wouldn't let a drop of alcohol in the house? Earle had to keep gin under his bed. That 'religious' Women's Christian Temperance Union used to meet just up from our house — all against drink." He broke out laughing again. "Imagine! — Our Lord turns water into wine, and darn good wine it was too, the Bible says, and yet the women get all fussed over a drop of alcohol."

He got up, shook his head, and we wandered back to the car where our guide, having fallen asleep, woke up and drove us back along the shore till we stopped, as Eric had planned, at one of the rolling grassy slopes. Up we walked and sat to picnic overlooking this "Sea of Galilee". Eric got out his Bible and read the Beatitudes, that collection of sayings. He asked me to imagine the hundreds sitting there, youngsters playing, babies nursing, old men and their families sprawled around, even right up to the feet of where He stood. Lots of the very poor, the sick, the maimed, some with evil spirits as they called crazy people. But each one forgetting their sicknesses, the murmur having gone round, "He's coming soon." Eric talked excitedly, almost possessed.

I'm gradually discovering that these intense emotions don't necessarily bring on that dreadful condition caused by Eric's years in horrible battles. I must teach myself to stop worrying. Who could not be affected, as we both are, by walking in His footsteps? Hearing His sounds: donkeys braying, roosters calling in the dawn, porters shouting in Arabic: "Watch ahead" — and smelling His scents, the flowers, mule dung, wet wool of sheep, all as He did — the Man who brought a new teaching of *love one another* into the Jewish tradition of *an eye for an eye and a tooth for a tooth*. Eric helped me see the enormity of what Jesus preached about the meek being blessed. How radical that must have been at that time. Probably still is today.

We have both been discovering that this land where Jesus walked on foot is a lot smaller than either of us ever dreamed. In the afternoon we motored to the foot of the Mount of Transfiguration. Our driver refused to go up, but Eric insisted, flashing a bit of extra money at him. We went up the really bumpy track to the top, but saw nothing much there of significance. We got out to sit peacefully on the ground while Eric told me a bit more of how Our Lord showed Himself in shining white to his followers, and Eric even flipped pages to read me about the Ascension, which he said could have happened here, too. It's rather small for a mountain, more of a hill I thought, but clouds could have enveloped it, so perhaps He did choose to ascend to His Father on this very spot.

I had intended my journal to be written daily. But so much has been happening, I'm afraid I've only managed to do it in pieces. Evenings after dinner, we spend in the lounge around a good fire, Eric waxing again about what we had discovered during the day and what we might discover the next. And, because this is a private journal, I can write that our nights have been thrilling: Eric seems possessed of a spiritual and physical energy in lovemaking that leaves me breathless, night after night.

PART FOUR: 1930

CHAPTER EIGHTEEN

On Thursday early in April, a group of well-dressed figures waited in Windsor Station, Montreal for the train from New York. In clerical garb, Canon John Alford stood beside his taller, heavy-set son, Gerald, now a well-known lawyer. Eric's diminutive sister Jean and her dapper husband Bert had brought their car to collect the arrivals and chauffeur them back to the apartment on Sherbrooke Street. Their talk, muted, anticipatory, awaited the return of the prodigal son and the dancer about whom, so often and so glowingly, Eric had written to his sister, his brother and, as they had heard, his parents at the Old Homestead.

Before long the train with great clouds of steam screeched into this palatial station built by the Canadian Pacific Railroad in downtown Montreal. The New York passengers streamed through the wrought-iron gates and finally when it seemed as though they might not even be on the train, Eric and Rene arrived with a porter pushing his cart with their few bags.

Amid excited greetings, Eric kissed his sister and introduced her to Rene. Then he presented Jean's husband Albert Finnie, cousin Gerald, and his brother Jack.

"Oh, Father John," Rene shook his hand, "how wonderful to see you again after all this time!"

"And I must say, my dear, you look more flourishing than ever!"

"And your son, Gerald, the brilliant lawyer!" They talked among themselves about the train ride, snatches of the boat ride, and then started to move towards the station entrance.

"I'm dying to see your new church, Father John."

"Well, Rene, I was even hoping you and Eric might pop along this afternoon. If you're not too tired, that is. I might have news for Eric."

"We'd love that!" Eric broke in. "We can get installed this morning in Jean's apartment, and then we'll take the tram back along Sherbrooke Street. Easily done." And so it was arranged.

But Jack took Eric aside first, and with a serious look, told him, "Old Poppa passed away, Eric. While you were in the Holy Land. We didn't know how to reach you. I'm sorry to spoil this happy occasion."

Eric was silent, looking at the ground. Then, he sighed. "Jack, we all expected it, didn't we? He was in his nineties." He nodded, then looked up brightly. "I'll keep his soul in my prayers, this month."

They took their leave, Jack looking relieved that this news hadn't shattered their pleasure at being together at last.

They arrived in the Bert's sparkling Ford. Albert was dressed as always impeccably, with his high starched collar and neat tie setting off an immaculate dark suit. Eric had explained to Rene that Bert owned a clothing factory in some old part of the city. Jean, once a nurse, had given up her profession to marry him.

The Finnies' apartment faced a courtyard on the ground floor, making for easy access. Rene entered and was shown around by an excited Jean, so much shorter than her guest. "Are you sure this isn't too much trouble?" Rene asked. "Perhaps we should find an hotel somewhere?"

"Not at all," Jean said. "I haven't seen my brother for ages."

After Eric had retrieved his bags and haversack, Bert lifted out Rene's two light suitcases. "Is this all you brought, Rene?"

She and Eric exchanged a look. "It's all that arrived. Let's just say it's not all I started out with." She laughed, and Eric smiled broadly. But nothing more was said.

* * *

"What a lovely church you have, Father John! It's enormous," Rene exclaimed, standing with the others on the chancel steps of Trinity Memorial Church in Notre Dame de Grâce.

"Glad you like it. We're rather proud of it. Our architects, Ross and Macdonald, also did the Montreal Star offices here in Montreal, the Château Laurier in Ottawa, and Union Station and the Royal York Hotel in Toronto, among other notable buildings." Father John glanced at his brother with repressed excitement. "We hold nine hundred and fifty. On religious holidays, like Christmas and Easter, we're packed, and I'd say three quarters full most Sundays. Wait until I take you downstairs, Rene: our hall has a stage, with lots of room for concerts, and plays..."

Rene brightened and Eric went on, "You know, Jack, before I left for the West, which turned out to be more of an adventure than anyone expected," Eric chuckled, "I came here while you were off at a conference. I actually got into the pulpit and wondered what it must be like to preach to your congregation. Now that I'm priested, one day in the distant future, I hope to have a church a bit like this."

Jack stepped forward. "Eric, that was part of the good news I had for you. I contacted John, the Bishop of Montreal, and he's agreed, if you like, to install you this Saturday as my curate!"

Rene and Eric were both struck with delight. Rene stepped across to hug Father John as tightly as she could and kissed him warmly on both cheeks. "Oh thank you!"

Eric was surprised at how flustered his brother seemed, not knowing what to say next, having been embraced by such a beautiful woman.

Rene stepped back. "You know, Father John, I confess that, although I've mentioned nothing to Eric, I have been a bit bothered about what would happen after we arrived." Eric glanced at her. "Eric, you know, is not afraid of venturing into the unknown. But we British, we like to know where we're going."

Jack grinned, recovering his composure. "We all know, my dear Rene, that Eric faced uncertain futures in the most horrifying of battle conditions, day after day, week after week, even year after year. I think it's safe to say that nothing would daunt him. You have got yourself a fearless husband. I can say that without any hesitation."

"Now it's me who's getting embarrassed, Jack," his brother said. "I've never heard you talk like that."

Amidst good-natured laughter, the three of them walked down the aisle. "I wonder, Eric, if you've being keeping up with what's been happening over in Europe? To our old enemy, Germany?"

Eric shook his head. "No. I'm afraid in Australia the focus was on the unemployment, and what's been happening in that country."

"Same thing here," Jack said. "Since the crash, we haven't paid as much attention as we should to what's been going on. But I have it on pretty good authority that Germany is in utter disarray. You know, the conditions imposed by the Treaty of Versailles after the war have brought unemployment and economic disarray to far greater heights than it even has here."

"The talk in England was that the Allied powers had made rather a mistake, Father John," Rene said. "I don't know what's going to happen as a result." They passed a couple a little older than Eric, holding hands. The man, rather sunken, was twitching; Eric knew his problem at once. Father John waved cheerily, but allowed them their own space.

"The church secretary has been bound and determined to prepare a little spread of what she calls British afternoon tea for the newcomers."

"I can't think of anything better!" Rene smiled.

In Jack's study, Rene admired the pictures on the wall: one of the Last Supper, and another of a church interior. "That looks to me like Westminster Abbey?"

"It is. I preached there during the war, you know. September 9th 1917."

This impressed Rene no end. The comfortable study had a sofa, bookcases down one wall, and a window looking onto a vine-covered, grey stone wall of the church. Jack moved around his large desk to join them.

"It's going to be so convenient," Eric said, "I can just take the tram along from Jean's. Door to door."

Rene began to pour the tea. "No, Eric, we must immediately set about finding our own accommodation. It's kind of Jean and Bert, but we can't impose. I shall start looking tomorrow."

"Whatever you say, my dear." Eric took his proffered cup of tea and reached for a sandwich of thinly sliced cucumber.

"Real British tea-time!" Rene said. "I must thank your secretary."

Jack asked Rene how she felt, leaving behind a thriving dancing school, and Rene and Eric both recounted the failing economic conditions in Australia.

"We're not much better here in Canada, I'm afraid to say," Jack ventured. "Wheat, our blue-chip export, is actually being over-produced around the world, so we haven't even sold our 1928 crop." He sighed. "Factories are still blasting, but no one's buying. They've got huge stockpiles, my friends in Westmount are telling me."

Eric knew that his brother must be close to the seats of power, having raised over $200,000 to build his church only a few years ago.

"Our revenues in Canada," Jack explained to Rene, "come mostly from export: grain, pulp and paper, metals. Our large neighbour to the south buys almost half, so on Black Thursday when their stock prices fell, the system crashed." He shrugged and held out his hands. "We'd been getting a $1.60 a bushel of wheat — but that has dropped with a bang."

"So what is the government doing?" Rene asked.

"Earlier this month," he explained, "our Liberal prime minister, Mackenzie King, in the course of a long speech in the House, took the position that this whole problem was purely local. No need, he claimed, for any funds from Ottawa to help the devastated workers." Eric shook his head in amazement. "Oh yes, unemployment relief not necessary — no evidence of any emergency! Talk of unemployment is no more than a political move by his opposition." Jack was clearly disgusted.

"And the opposition is?" Rene pressed.

"The Conservatives, led by a millionaire, R.B. Bennett."

"So we must hope that they get in?"

"Rene," Jack said looking at Eric, "we of the cloth mustn't take sides. We shall just have to wait and see. But farmers have stopped buying, so our eastern factories are closing and laying off hundreds. Construction has stopped, banks aren't lending — instead, they're calling in their loans."

"So less and less money in circulation?"

Jack nodded. "And fewer and fewer goods being produced as factories shut down. You'll soon see all around us, the rolls of the poor growing longer and longer. We all feel a sense of despair."

Eric and Rene had both felt this, too, leaving Australia. Times would be hard for everyone. How lucky Eric felt to have an important brother who had arranged his new posting.

In spite of Jack's dire news, especially in Quebec, their excitement at being back in Canada was irrepressible; they talked excitedly on the tram going back to Jean's. Jack had advised them to look further west along Sherbrooke Street, beyond the church. Lots of space available in this economic climate, well within the meagre budget of a curate.

"We'll have to put off going to the Gaspe," Eric said. "I know you've been looking forward to that, and so have I. But apparently, I seem to be starting at once."

"I can't wait to learn how to snowshoe," Rene said, "I hope you'll get a good long time off at Christmas."

"I probably shall in January, as not much happens." Eric reached out and took her hand as she sat next to him on the slatted bench. "In the meantime, I shall have my work cut out for me, helping Jack and, as it appears, ministering to the ever-burgeoning poor."

* * *

Here I am on Palm Sunday, thought Eric, just ten days after arriving, behind two dozen beautifully attired choristers in their purple cassocks and sparkling surplices, my brother bringing up the rear, processing down the centre aisle of Trinity Memorial Church. Wonderful!

None of this pomp and circumstance in the one small church near Sydney where Eric served as part-time curate. But at St.

John's, music had been the passion of the Rev. Lucas, so there they'd had a fine choir of forty voices. Here, Eric decided, our choir rivals that one. The small boys, some only eight or nine years old, led the procession, and then more boy sopranos, male altos, tenors and basses, singing lustily their four part hymn: "All glory laud and honour to thee Redeemer King! To whom the lips of children made sweet hosannas sing." The church was, as Jack had predicted, almost full. Such a moving, glorious experience for Eric to be one of the leaders in such a large and worshipful gathering!

The procession parted and the choir edged into their stalls. Eric had been surprised, and then pleased, to hear his brother offer him on this, his first Sunday, the Passion Gospel from Luke. So at the appointed time, Eric got up to the lectern, a beautiful eagle with outspread wings carved in wood which held the large Bible. The Passion Gospel was the longest passage read in the church year. With what Eric had experienced in the Holy Land and this worshipful congregation before him, he became unusually moved. As the crucifixion narrative carried them along, he had to stop to control his emotions. When he got to the thief saying, "Lord, remember me when thou comest into thy kingdom. And Jesus said unto him, Verily I say unto you, today you will be with me in Paradise..." he was overcome.

Then he looked over and saw Rene sitting tense, stiff, in her pew, but she managed to nod warmly. He pulled himself together, and continued.

The rest of the service was so beautiful with the anthem soaring; the recessional hymn with its descant brought tears to his eyes once again. Such a wonderful service. Afterwards when he apologised to Jack for his emotion, his brother shook it off.

"Well done, Eric. Splendid reading. I'm sure it was Rene's coaching. And the emotion — well placed. You know, I've been talking to the head of our Guild, and we want you to give a talk on the Holy Land at the next meeting, if you can prepare yourself in time."

Lots to do, Eric thought. "Oh yes, I shall be kept busy.

Rene also threw herself into the church activities, joining the Altar Guild and making herself useful elsewhere. With a dancing school no longer taking her attention, she soon became an integral member of the parish. She wasted no time in finding them an apartment not many blocks along Sherbrooke Street, in front of a park with a cenotaph at its centre.

Because this flat was empty, she told Eric of her bright idea to sit on the sidewalk outside their large red-brick building with a placard, saying: *Furniture Bought.* As Eric left for his constitutional, he complimented her. "Very enterprising, Rene. Do you think anyone will sell?"

"I can but try. A parishioner gave me the idea on Sunday. These hard times mean so many need cash. But don't hold out any great hopes for it being things of beauty." Amazed by her ingenuity as always, Eric set off at a good pace. They planned to picnic in the park opposite after he came back; this was their pattern for a few days. Soon Rene had their apartment furnished, albeit with a mish-mash of furniture, though she did find a half decent bed. They moved out of Jean Finnie's and installed themselves here.

For their first dinner, Eric had gotten scotch, gin and a bottle of wine, so they could have a celebration drink before sitting at the table that Rene had laid as best she could, with three candles glowing. "A far cry from the Lions in Brentwood, Essex..." Eric said as he ruefully sipped his whiskey.

"The Lions," Rene was quick to reply, "is not filled with the love that permeates our little home here, my dear. And that is what is important, don't you think?"

"I'll drink to that!" Eric raised his glass. And indeed, it seemed nothing would disturb their happiness...

After Eric's pre-picnic walk a few days later, Rene arrived by the cenotaph with her hamper to find her husband, seemingly exhausted, sitting back and staring up at the marble column with its dark relief of ten weary soldiers in tin hats, marching, the last one carrying a wounded comrade. Ahead, an angel gestured with open arms. Eric seemed fixated, hands twitching.

"Eric!" she exclaimed sharply.

Eric sat up, bewildered. "Rene! What's up? Oh, good. You've brought the lunch. What's wrong?"

"I wonder if you should sit staring at that... at those soldiers. I'm wondering if it's good for you."

"Rene, I told you time and again," Eric snapped, "you must stop worrying about me. I'm perfectly all right! I don't like to think you're watching me. You are, you know. I see it. Always nervous. How am I supposed to function when I know you're so concerned? I don't like it."

Rene realized that she had indeed been showing her concern too much. And what, after all, was there to worry about? Well, if she were honest, a great deal — but she quickly put it aside. "I'm sorry, Eric, I'm truly sorry. I'll stop. Together we can surmount anything. I do know," she reached over and put her hand on his, "I do know that you're cured, you're very well; it will never return, this dreadful illness, I know we're both going to be very happy. I'll just have to stop myself. If you catch me doing it again, please tell me."

And so, it was resolved and not mentioned again. For the moment, at least.

CHAPTER NINETEEN

Piles of furniture on the sidewalk awaited removal, Eric noticed. This particular morning, he passed a couple of apartment buildings only half-built and unattended. After a fine walk along open fields towards Loyola College, he turned back and crossed an avenue to where a family was bringing their belongings onto the sidewalk. He stood for a while, unsure of how to begin. "Another moving day?"

The woman glanced at him as she carried a chair down. Her baby lay in a wicker crib at the foot of the outside stairs. "Not moving day. Eviction day." Eric frowned. "My husband couldn't pay the rent. Landlord threw us out."

"But surely," Eric stuttered, "he wouldn't just put you out on the sidewalk?"

"He would, and he has."

What a piece of work! So that's what he'd been passing: evictions!

"Where are you heading now?"

"My brother, he's gone off to Brockville. Walking. Not a cent for a bus. But Uncle Edward's there, he's got a truck. We're hoping he'll be back tomorra' t'pick this up and maybe take us somewhere." Back she went up the outdoor steps for more belongings, her heavy-set husband trotting down with a chair.

"Where will you go?" asked Eric.

The man obviously didn't want questions, but Eric's garb forced him to be polite. "Father, there's lots like us, with nowhere to go. If we kin get ta Brockville, maybe we'll find someplace. Once I get the wife and three kids installed, I'll hop them rails. For the West."

Eric had heard that the West was even harder hit than Montreal, but he said nothing.

A little girl came down the stairs crying. "Daddy, I asked Mummy for an apple and she wouldn't give it me."

The man looked down at her hopelessly. "She wouldn't, Megan, because there are no apples. But we'll get some when we get to Brockville, don't worry." He turned to Eric. "My wife had a job in a garment factory for two dollars a day, and in came another woman agreed to work for one-fifty." He shook his head. "My wife was out."

A young neighbour came across the street to lend a hand. "That's nothing. My mother operated a sewing machine out the east end. She made pants and things. Her salary for five days a week, nine hours a day, was three dollars. She had to walk four miles to work there and back, and that's what kept me and her and my brother."

Eric wondered what he should do. The man then glanced at Eric. "We're not Catholic, but I hear maybe they serve meals in that Church of St. Augustine." Eric knew it, a huge ungainly basilica at the north end of his park. "Every two days, I heard. If we're lucky, today might be the day, so we're going there."

A good few blocks. So the man would have to carry his baby, and perhaps even the little girl, to find something to eat.

Why didn't he serve food for the needy at Trinity? Talk to Rene; they'd done such a good job with lunches in Sydney at St. Johns. She might agree to spearhead this. Also bring it up with his brother, he decided.

That night, as they were having their meal together, Eric heard rain outside and Rene saw him shift uneasily. "It's not likely a thunderstorm," she said quickly, thinking back to his earlier reactions. And then, realizing her mistake, blurted out, "Of course, I love thunderstorms — I know you do too, Eric."

"I wasn't thinking about thunder, I was thinking about all that furniture out on sidewalks. It'll get ruined. What can we do?"

Rene shrugged and shook her head. "I'm afraid we don't have any tarpaulins here, my dear. Do you know if there are any at the church?

"Too late now, I suspect." In the ensuing weeks, Eric saw he would have needed hundreds of tarpaulins. The poverty and evictions were overwhelming.

* * *

Early one June morning after they had gotten up at sunrise, Eric went out for his usual walk. But instead of heading west along Sherbrooke Street, he thought, this time why don't I head south towards the river? He knew the lower level was covered in railroad tracks, but perhaps the trains coming and going might provide some interest. So he turned right on Sherbrooke Street, and after a short walk headed down Girouard, a rarely travelled dirt lane.

The houses thinned out and their field below fanned into an escarpment that dropped down onto the lower level. Up here, the meadow seemed bountiful with orchards, others with cattle, still others with a few sheep. The farmhouses, though substantial, were in varying states of disrepair. Amazing to find all this agri-culture going on so close to the city. Not enough arable land for fully working farms, perhaps, but enough eggs, apples, and some meat to make do.

Eggs. Of course, why not try and buy some? The farm on his left was mainly an orchard, but on the right the second farm-house held in its yard a sizeable chicken coop and even a couple of turkeys. So he crossed by a small right-of-way behind the first house and walked down beside this weathered dwelling with its attractive red Mansard roof. He stopped as he saw on the veran-da a grizzled farmer, perhaps the grandfather, in a rocking chair smoking his pipe with a shotgun across his lap. On the gate as he had entered he'd seen a sign: *Pas de Vagabonds.* Above it, *oeufs à vendre* under which someone had written: Eggs.

Eric paused at the steps, and called out. "Any eggs?"

The old man motioned inside. Eric climbed the veranda steps and knocked. "*Entrez.*" He went in to find a plump Frenchwom-an with grey hair pulled back into a bun who come forward and asked what he wanted.

"*Oeufs?*"

She nodded, crossed to a sideboard and held out six with a questioning gesture. Eric nodded. "*Cinq cennes.*"

Well, thought Eric, five cents, a good price. Then he saw butter in bricks on the sideboard and he motioned to them. She brought over a pound. "*Dix cennes.*"

Eric nodded. "Milk?"

She squinted. "*Du lait? Après.* (Later) *Huit cennes.*"

Eight cents a quart? Good prices, Eric thought. He handed her a dime and a nickel, thanked her, and left.

He continued on down Girouard towards the rail yards. Beyond them lay the Lachine canal, and further on, crossing the broad St. Lawrence, the Victoria Bridge on which his father had worked some seventy-five years before.

He spotted a trail leading into the woods on his right. He took it and wound along through bushes and trees until he came upon a tent. Good heavens, he thought, someone camping out this close to the city? A man emerged with a knapsack and looked up in surprise.

Eric offered a pleasant greeting. From the surroundings, this was not just the usual camp-out; the fellow obviously lived here. Perhaps one of the hobos?

"Top of the morning to ya, Father," the man said. "Nice sunny day for an outing."

"It is indeed. And where are you off to?"

"Well, Father, I'm goin' up there into town to see if I can get me a day's work. Or a handout, anything that will fill my stomach."

He did look hungry, Eric thought, so he reached into his haversack. "Would you like an egg or two?"

"No, thank you Father, save that for some of the fellas further on down. I'm on my way."

"There are more of you?"

"More?" The fellow broke into a harsh chuckle. "Lots and lots. Regular hobo jungle down there." Eric frowned. "You never heard? We ride the rails, we find a safe place, and that's where we stop."

Eric had brought an apple for himself to eat on the walk so he took that out. "Here, perhaps this might help."

The fellow's eyes gleamed. "Oh, thank you, Father!" He bit into it noisily. "First apple for a long time."

"So you're headed off into Westmount?" The wealthy residential area of the city.

"Oh no, that rich lot won't give you a cent. It's the poor, the ones thrown out on the street, they'll share their last bite. That's where I'm going. Straight above here. Well, good-day to you, Father. And thanks for the treat." The man passed Eric, munching his apple.

Eric kept on, wondering, what he would find. After couple of hovels with no sign of life, he came upon a well-made tent. A woman sat in front, trying to cook over a small fire.

Eric wandered over. "Good morning, ma'am. I didn't think there were any women here."

At the sound of their talk, a man emerged. "Morning, Father." He introduced them both.

"A family! Well, since you're cooking, Ma'am," said Eric, "I have something you might enjoy." Out of his haversack came the six eggs.

They both stared in surprise. "Oh, thank you, thank you, Father. We were down to our last penny. That's most generous of you, sir."

She took them, but before doing anything showed them in her large hands to her husband, whose eyes gleamed. "Now we're just going to eat one each this morning, Harry. We'll save two for tomorrow and two for the next day. That will keep us going, if you don't find no work."

While she cooked, Eric sat on a half-broken crate to chat, not of the Gospel, needless to say, but about how they were getting along and what was happening hereabouts.

"You see," Harry began, "we kept this tent from when we used to go camping. I brought the children with me and we'd go off up in the Laurentians. A decent job I had. But all that stopped a while ago. Then we got evicted. So I sent our three children off to their uncle's down in Drummondville.

"We couldn't impose ourselves as well; my brother's not doing much better than us, just holding onto his job by the skin of his teeth. So we took this tent — they made us sell all the rest of our belongings for the rent, they can do that, you know. We had to stand there on the veranda and watch it all go, a dollar for this, two dollars for that ... broke our hearts..." He sighed and his wife, her tears spent, merely readied her frying pan to cook the precious eggs over a small fire. "We thought we'd be safe here in the hobo jungle. The police don't come, as you know,"

"No, I didn't know."

"It's like those red light districts. The police allow them because then they know where to find all the prostitutes. Same thing here. They know where to find hobos. So nobody bothers us. You see?" He pointed down across the tracks to the canal. "Fresh water, all you want, I just have to lug it here in a bucket. And there's freights coming and going. The fellows are moving in, moving out. Regular bus station." He gave a hearty laugh and his wife forced a smile.

Eric stayed talking for a while and then, as they were eating, he moved on down and passed several more dwellings: cardboard, tin, fragments of signs, anything that could be scrounged to keep the wind out and the rain off. He reached the network of tracks where more men sat cooking up a stew for breakfast. Eric didn't know whether to approach or not. They seemed, though hungry, to be enjoying themselves. Around them, he saw a scattering of small encampments, bits of cardboard laid under trees, likely sleeping quarters, and odd shapes of thrown-together dwellings, though mostly those were higher up the hillside.

One fellow detached himself and came over. "Hello Father. Would you like something to eat?"

Eric shook his head and smiled, reminded of the parable about the widow's mite. "I wish I had brought you all food. I was just wandering, walking... " He felt helpless. "I've not been here before."

"Well, make yourself welcome."

"And how come you're here?" Eric asked pleasantly.

The young man paused, looked at him, and saw he was serious. "Well, I was sleeping in a barn, supposed to get a dollar a week from a farmer."

Eric raised his eyebrows. "A dollar a week?"

"Well, all found! Meals and lodging. But listen to this. He made me sleep in the haymow, only gave us pig mash to eat." He nodded. "Mixed with boiling water, and they threw in a bit of molasses. So I had to leave that haymow after dark and go find a garden to steal myself some carrots, radishes, anything that was growing. That farmer who hired me, he made his own bread, but after a week or more, not fit for dogs. Then he gave it us after chores at eight. Yessir, six to eight. Fourteen hours a day."

"And I gather he did so because a hundred other starving men wanted your job?" Eric was getting the picture — not pretty.

"Right, Father. Well, you can imagine, I up and left. Before that, I went all over begging from the Sally Ann or whoever." Eric frowned. "The Salvation Army. See, my poor old father, he couldn't do nothing for us. Not well. Listen to this: he stole bread and two cans of beans for his family. You know what? Provincial prison for three months. Nobody said anything. Well, we saw he had tuberculosis after that, and there was no curing him. So what could we do? The marble orchard for him! Hope he rests in peace. Never got it when he was alive, leastways, not these last few years..."

The man bowed his head, either in prayer or to hold back tears.

Eric stood awkwardly, when he heard one of the more disreputable hobos stand up and call out, "Eric!"

Eric stood as though struck. Who was this? He peered.

The man came hurrying forward. "Eric, Eric, it's me! Don't you recognize me?"

Eric shook his head.

The man was filthy, ragged, bearded, but smiling. "It's Adam, Adam Hadley, don't you remember? We met on the train. It's me."

Eric shook his head. "Well, I never ..."

CHAPTER TWENTY

When Rene heard the key turn in the apartment door, she wiped her hands on her apron and came forward to greet Eric. Today had been clouding over, so they'd decided not to picnic in the park. Rene was making lunch here, in their apartment on Sherbrooke Street.

In walked Eric, but behind him came a most disreputable figure. He looked so mean. And dangerous. She thought of Eric's small salary, which she hadn't yet taken to the bank. It lay exposed in cash on the sideboard. What should she do? She went towards it but realized this might draw the intruder's attention. She stood uncertain.

"Rene, I want you to meet a friend of mine, Adam Hadley. I met him on that train I took to Vancouver. I've brought him home."

Rene relaxed. "Well, Mr. Hadley, you're certainly welcome." The words almost choked in her throat but she pulled herself together.

"What Adam needs is a bath. I'll see if I can find him some clothes and if we have enough, he'll eat lunch with us."

Later when Adam came out from the bedroom, Rene had to suppress giggles. He looked so odd: Eric's trousers were far too short and his sleeves, too. But he looked presentable, clean, hair brushed and washed, shaven, quite a change!

The three of them sat down, and Rene was treated to all Eric had learned that morning, situations she'd hardly dreamed of. Eric recounted his visit to the farm and the eggs. "That's where we can get farm food, Rene, fresh, and cheaper than our little store on the corner."

"Aye," said Adam, "those farms up there on the escarpment, they're a godsend. Always something to be stolen: chicken, even a lamb, a small porker, the fellas get pretty ingenious. They don't visit the same farms, of course. All spread out they are, a ways west. Sometimes a fellow will go a mile just to get chicken. When he comes back, he cooks it up and we all eat that stew."

"If it's stealing," said Eric, "and there's no other way to stay alive, the Good Lord might sanction it."

"And how is it," Rene asked, "that you all gather down there by the railway yards?"

"Thousands of us are riding the rails, ma'am. Thousands. You can't believe the people had their homes taken, farms ruined — I'm from out West, Winnipeg, maybe your husband here told you. You wouldn't believe the crisis there. Big drought this summer. I seen it coming. Nothing for me but to leave.

"When I met Adam, he was investing in all sorts of things."

"Yes, I had lots of money a couple of years ago. But you know how it is, they gobble it up, and then you don't have a thing."

They sat down at the table, and Eric said Grace.

"I hope you like it." Rene had made a salad and laid out cold meat and a loaf of bread on a board. Eric cut a couple of thick slices for Adam. "But it must be hard, riding the rails, as they call it?"

"Ma'am, there's a science to it. You gotta calculate. I've seen too many guys with their bodies cut in two —" Rene reacted. "Oh yes, legs cut off — I seen one leg just last week layin' beside the rails. You just can't hop a freight like that, too much chance for a green-horn to get himself real hurt."

"So how do you do it?" Rene sampled her salad.

"Well, I'm new myself, only been at it four months. No use staying at home, eating the food that your kid brother and sister could. Sure can't get married, either. So, you grab your turkey and say goodbye and then one day, you send a postcard home."

"A turkey?" Eric broke in. "So you can eat?'

"No no, that's your stuff, your turkey. You see, when I hit the road, I took two blankets wrapped around my Bible and what little clothes I had, tied them up with a couple of thongs. When you hop a freight, you gotta put everything in your pockets, and make damn sure to wear your extra clothes so they won't get stole — maybe two shirts, maybe another pair of pants, all on your-self. Sling extra shoes round your neck. When the train goes by, you run like hell and you jump for the ladder and your speed'll help you swing up." Adam was shovelling in the food as if there were no tomorrow, talking with his mouth full. "Usually you try branch lines, those trains aren't going so fast. If you git dropped off at some little town, chances are — not too many drifters there, handouts better. Besides, no railroad cops. Well, it's a young man's business. Not too many old guys."

"And you ride in between the cars?" Rene took a drink of water, thinking she could have used some wine, listening to all this.

"No, no, inside a boxcar is best, but mostly you ride on top. On sunny days," he shrugged, "well, it's kinda fun, watching the country go by, but in the winter, rain and snow, Lord, it's bad."

"I bet it is." Rene shook her head. How some people lived — well, *had* to live in these times.

"On the freights, you get information, pass it back and forth —

where to go, where to stop, stuff like that. I always had my own salt, a big spoon and a knife, everyone has that. " Adam looked down: he'd already finished his plate, far too fast, he realized. "After a while," he continued, "you get the knack. But you're always dirty. Lice, fleas, just dirty. These jungles have rats, too, big as kittens." Eric nodded: he knew about rats, all right. "You always need a shave..."

"Terrible, terrible," Eric murmured.

"You know, up in Winnipeg North, the immigrants had it even worse — some couldn't even talk English. Last hired and first fired." He took another slice of bread, famished. "Poor fellas, a lot o 'em newly arrived, come to the Land of Plenty." Adam snorted.

"If you was a nice young Polack, well, the oil companies, banks, financial institutions, stockbrokers, even storekeepers, though not the Hudson's Bay, they'd never hire you. All o' them solid against anyone not Anglo-Saxon. If you changed your name, learned better English, maybe you could beat it. But a Jew, well, no name change was good enough. Those damn anti-Semitic Winnipegers, no way a Jew could escape from his Judaism."

Rene felt dreadful. What goings-on!

Eric went to the ice box. "Rene, what else can we find for Adam?"

Rene wanted to stand but was rooted to her chair as Adam went on, "You know, Ma'am, if you left home like I did so your family had one less to feed, they called you a criminal. Cops said, Throw that guy out of town, hustle him along. No more soup or bread here, and none tomorrow, so git! How many times have I heard those words? I never stole so much as a dime or anything, but I was treated like an outlaw. In some people's minds, bein' poor makes a fella a felon." Adam sat back and wiped his mouth and shook his head, overcome with emotion.

Rene reached out and touched him.

When she did, she was shocked to see tears appear in his eyes.

"Excuse me Ma'am." He got up and went into the bedroom, stifling sobs as best he could.

"Poor fellow." Eric shook his head. "And I saw a lot worse off down there..."

Rene wondered if she should follow Adam, but thought better of it. Instead they sat silently, thinking about the Depression and what it was doing to perfectly normal people.

* * *

Sometime in late June, Rene and Eric found themselves on a streetcar heading east along Sherbrooke Street and then turning up Claremont Avenue to climb Westmount Mountain.

"You know, Rene, I never liked these expeditions, these pastoral calls on the well-off, I prefer my hobos..."

"But Jack made a point again last week, didn't he." She watched the houses become larger the higher they went. The streetcar turned along Westmount Avenue.

"It's better when you come," Eric said, "though I have no idea why Jack insisted."

"I think, perhaps, my dear," Rene said gently, "he knows I'm not afraid of bringing up money questions."

They passed Roslyn school on the left, which most of their parishioners had attended before going off to private schools like Lower Canada College further to the west in Notre Dame de Grâce and Bishops College School in Lennoxville, where Eric remembered Andrew McNaughton had gone. Andy was now a General and on all sorts of committees in Ottawa. Well, he wished him Godspeed. And he knew that his old General, Arthur Currie, had become Principal and Chancellor of McGill University, right here in Montreal.

They got off at Murray Park, walked up the next avenue, and

turned in at a splendid house on the right-hand side. They climbed its steps and rang the doorbell. A uniformed maid answered and showed them into a well-appointed living room.

They were greeted by a squat woman festooned with gold necklaces and bracelets, anything to enliven what was, to Eric, a somewhat sour face and over-coiffed hair. On the sofa sat a man ravaged by disease — the reason they had come.

They introduced themselves, and Antonia Petworth frowned. "I thought Father John was coming."

Before Eric could reply, Rene knew at a glance why Jack had delegated them to come and stepped in with a sweetly delivered, though spur-of-the-moment, explanation. "He has some business at the Diocesan Headquarters today, but he was bound and determined that you should not miss your pastoral call on the appointed day. I believe he always comes on the twenty-eighth."

"He does." Mrs. Petworth picked up a small bell and rang it furiously. The maid appeared. "Tell Clancy to give you the coffee tray, Elsie."

"And how are we today?" Eric came to sit next to Mr. Petworth, whose grey skin-colour stated the obvious.

"Doing the best I can in the circumstances." Petworth looked as though he had once been well fed, but now his clothes hung loosely on his frail frame.

Before Elsie arrived with the tray, Mrs. Petworth whispered, "You know, it's just wonderful — you can get help for so little these days. Last week my French maid," she dropped her voice, "had the gall to ask for a bit more money. She claimed her father was sick. Well, of course, I got rid of her, and found someone else, French of course, half the price. She'll take training but then, twenty-five cents a day and all found, of course, I feel fortunate."

Petworth looked up. "Antonia's thanking her lucky day she married me!"

His wife saw that this was her prompt, and took it. "Yes, you know, Harley got out a month before the crash. He saw it coming. Wasn't he clever? Put it all in his bank. Now he's beginning to buy up stocks again. Such a clever man. I don't know what I'll do when..." She stopped herself abruptly, having gone too far already.

She looked at her husband fearfully, but Harley seemed not to notice, turning to Eric. "International Nickel — $72.50 before the crash and now it's $9.50. Can you believe it? Winnipeg Electric, listen to this, $109.50 last year when I got out, and now..." He coughed weakly, and went on with a soft voice, "Now around ten. They're all the same."

In came the salver with silver servers: a tall coffee pot with its graceful spout, small milk jug and sugar bowl, and four fine Wedgewood china cups. Mrs. Petworth poured coffee and passed around the Whippets. Rene had priced them in the market the other day because Eric had asked for some, topped with marshmallow and then coated in a hard shell of pure chocolate, introduced only a couple of years ago in Montreal, but beyond any curate's budget.

"Why the hell King decided to call an election, I have no idea," Petworth grumbled weakly. "Worst time to go to the country for him, but he just didn't seem to understand." He turned to Eric. "You know he'll be booted out the end of July."

"So I hear," said Eric. "Now, is there any way we could help you come to perhaps an early service at Trinity?"

"I gave that up a while ago. I would like to," he added quickly, "but every so often, Father John brings me communion."

Antonia handed round the cookies and Whippets. "You know, King is such a fine man. Look what he's done for the country. We can hire anyone we want at almost any price. Last autumn he went to Rome, you know, and visited Mussolini. They got on like a house on fire. What more could you desire in a leader?"

"Radio is being used far too much," grumbled Petworth in a non sequitur. "First time like this in elections. I hear them at it every day."

Rene sipped her coffee. "So," she asked, trying to hide her incredulity, "you find these times beneficial?"

"Listen, my dear," Antonia leaned over to her, first glancing at the archway which led to the rear. "My second maid gets about ten dollars a month. The French laundress, she scrubs and irons by hand, not every day, of course, and you know what she makes? Two dollars a month. I don't have to give her board; she lives at home. But I pay her carfare."

"Antonia is very generous." Petworth grabbed a Whippet.

"And you know," Antonia went on, "the chef, he got distracted last week and burned the roast. Apparently his two brothers had their homes foreclosed. Well, I made good use of that, didn't I, Harley?"

Harley nodded. "Quick on the uptake, my Antonia."

"Oh yes, I cut his salary from fifty dollars a month down to thirty-five and I dared him to leave." She smiled. "Of course he didn't. He needed the money!"

Eric was downing his coffee as fast as he could, wanting to end this encounter and pronounce his blessing.

"Now Mr. Petworth," Rene broke in, "you have been so awfully clever, we're all so proud of you in the congregation, as I'm sure you must know." Eric frowned as he glanced at his wife — had she gone mad? Harley looked up appreciatively, and actually smiled for the first time. "So Father John wondered if there was a way you might be kind enough to pass on to Trinity a taste of those hard-earned gains. You know in these times, the church is finding it difficult to pay even his salary!"

The man frowned. "Good Lord, we can't have that! Antonia, go upstairs and bring down my cheque-book. I'll see to that at once."

"While she's out," Eric said quickly, "let's pray together for your healing, and I'll pronounce a blessing." Standing above the sick man, Eric made the sign of the cross, prayed with Rene, and gave him an extended Benediction, which continued as Antonia returned, waiting in the archway until he had finished. Then she came, handed the cheque-book to her husband who promptly wrote a cheque for five hundred dollars. He tore it off and handed it to Eric."That should keep them quiet at the church," he barked, then coughed and shook his head weakly.

After thanking him profusely, Rene seized her chance. "I think, perhaps, Eric dear, we should be going."

Later as they walked on up the street, Rene knew that Eric would start venting his anger and thought she had better bring up more cheerful news. "Did you see in the paper this morning that Kingsford Smith flew the Atlantic? Landed in New York yesterday, it said. Remember he came over the Pacific while we were in Australia?"

Eric nodded, his head still churning with annoyance at the previous meeting. "Yes, in the Southern Cross again. Courageous pilot. Adventurous spirits seem everywhere these days."

"Remember how happy we were when Amy Johnson, the young British girl from Hull, flew solo to Australia last month? She touched down in Darwin on the anniversary of my graduation from the Ginner-Mawer school, May 24th, that's how I remember."

Pleased to have diverted the conversation, though momentarily saddened by the loss of her dancing, Rene chatted about the various flights, helping them hike effortlessly up to Westmount Boulevard, just below the summit. On the first crescent winding upwards, they turned in at a palatial grey stone building. Its many terraced steps led up through attractive rock gardens, along a cement path, up more stairs, and Eric rang the bell. A uniformed maid answered and ushered them in.

In the hallway, they were greeted by Freda Winser, tall and white-haired, wearing a smart red suit with a minimum of jewellery. "My brother is waiting for you, Father. Could you go straight in and see him? I think he needs to speak to you alone. Meanwhile, Mrs. Alford might sit with me in the living room. When you return, perhaps you'll join us for a sherry?"

"Oh yes, thank you." Eric went down the hall into a sick room Freda must have converted from her dining room.

Rene preceded Freda into their living room. Above the fireplace, a wonderful oil painting of a young artillery man hung above various military portraits which perched upon the mantelpiece. Freda, seeing Rene studying them, explained: "My sons. Two killed at the front. That centrepiece, Edward, he was in the Artillery."

"Was he? Eric was in the Artillery, too."

"Really? I'm sure your husband would love this then. Edward was in the Firing Line for a long time before... before he died. A Howitzer battery. Tenth Brigade. And that's his older brother, an officer, also lost." She shook her head sadly.

Rene was stricken. Eric's Brigade. Suppose he knew Edward? What if they had even been in the same Battery? She remembered the rugby party in Sherbrooke and how the appearance of Ralph Rideout's brother had shocked her husband. Suppose he recognized this Edward? She brushed aside the thought — Winser was no name Eric ever mentioned. But she needed that glass of sherry to steady her nerves. If only... if only, she prayed, Eric doesn't know him.

The cut glass decanter and crystal glasses had been laid out on a silver tray. Freda poured one for her guest. "I was married to a wonderful man, Norbert Whitehead —" Rene sat up as though struck — Whitehead! She knew that name... "...but now," Freda went on, "I've reverted to my maiden name, Winser, like my brother's, better for the tradespeople."

Rene took rather an unladylike slug of her sherry. She dreaded Eric's return.

CHAPTER TWENTY-ONE

Freda and Rene ended up chatting like old friends. Freda seemed to like the fact that Rene was British and they could reminisce about the Old Country, where Freda had gone soon after the death of her sons, to see if she could help with any form of burial, donate money for cemeteries, and such. Her husband had died shortly after in a motor car accident, she explained to Rene. All she had now was the memory of these sons, and one relative, her brother in the next room, apparently hard on the trail to the Hereafter.

They both rose as Eric walked in, looking down, shaking his head. Clearly, it had been a difficult pastoral visit. He smiled and thanked Freda as she handed him a sherry. He walked towards the fireplace but then stopped. He looked at the portrait. He didn't move.

The young Edward Whitehead stared back at him.

Eric's hand began shaking and the sherry glass fell. His whole body shook. "Oh dear, I'm dreadfully sorry, please excuse me." He rushed out.

"The washroom is on the left," Freda called after him. Then she turned to look at Rene, now most disconcerted. It had happened again!

Rene wanted to rush out, but restrained herself, and tried to divert attention from Eric by bringing up a coming event, the talk of Montreal. "Have you heard that the new R100 is supposed to cross the Atlantic soon?"

"Oh yes, that new dirigible." Freda rang the little crystal bell for the maid to clean the rug, but kept glancing at the archway through which Eric had disappeared. "I believe at the end of next month it leaves Carrington. It's supposed to be flying in with a load of passengers right over the Atlantic to our St. Hubert airport, just over the river."

"I find that so exciting." But Rene knew this conversation could not last. She soon excused herself and went around to the bathroom door, which was shut tight. She knocked on it. "Eric, it's me. Rene."

Hearing nothing she knocked again and heard a lock push back. She paused, squared her shoulders, took a deep breath, and walked in.

Eric was sitting, fluttering, yes, his body fluttering, on the closed toilet seat, wiping his hands on his hair over and over again. "I can't stop it, Rene. I can't. I don't know what's happening. That was Edward. Yes, Edward, he died in my arms. His guts all out. He'd been at the latrine. Imagine! He had... he had that stuff all over him. Rene, he asked me to shoot him. I couldn't. He begged and begged. In my arms, Rene. In my arms. So... I pulled out my revolver." Rene gasped and leaned against the door frame. "I couldn't see him die in such pain so slowly. But Rene, then... he gave up the ghost. Just like that! Just in time. It's all through me, Rene, I can't get rid of it. I see the whole thing right now."

Rene stood. Then she reached out, turned on a tap, filled a

glass of water, and passed it to him. What a fatuous gesture, she thought. And then it occurred to her: "Eric," she said, "Eric listen. Think of this as living water. Baptismal water — from our Lord. Drink. It will help calm you."

Shaking, Eric looked up at her as a child at his mother. He drank the whole glass. And then sat up. The trembling lessened.

"I think we can leave, Eric. You have done your ministry after all, and we can walk all the way home. And we'll talk. You can tell me all about it. And I'm sure, my dearest, I'm sure as I stand here, that by the time we get home, this frightful incident will have passed and you'll be all right again. It wasn't your fault; there was nothing you could do about it." He nodded slowly. "Now, try standing up."

Eric did so. He squared his shoulders.

"Right, let's go. I'll make our excuses. And we'll walk home."

* * *

A month later at the beginning of August, Rene and Eric were having breakfast together. As Rene had foretold, Eric had recovered from the shock of seeing that portrait of his best friend in the Howitzer Battery. He had duly reported the incident, perhaps downplaying it, to his brother, Jack, and then got on with his duties as if nothing had happened.

"You seem excited, Rene." Eric tapped the top of his boiled egg and then stripped off the piping hot, cracked shell. He proceeded to cut his toast into fingers for dipping into the yolk.

"Well, it happened rather suddenly. Hazel called me and wants to us to lunch at the Ritz with Martha Allan."

Hazel and her husband, an immaculate, handsome member of the famous Molson family, were churchgoers, albeit sporadic ones because they went on weekends to their skiing cottage at

Piedmont in the Laurentians. John had been one of the substantial donors to the church's construction.

"That would be just dandy!" Eric dug into his egg. "I've heard that lunch there is quite the thing these days." The Ritz was a new classic hotel, built only twenty years previously, on Sherbrooke Street just by the campus of McGill University. When the Canon and John Molson went to lunch, as they did every few months, that was where John took him.

"You've heard of the Trinity Players?" Rene went on, and Eric shook his head. "Right after they finished building this church, a group here did perform plays, once at the Victoria Hall and three years ago in our auditorium, but since then, nothing has been happening. Last November Martha founded the MRT." Eric looked up. "The Montreal Repertory Theatre, well, it used to be called the Montreal Theatre Guild. She probably supports it with her money, too. She directed their first production last April, A.A. Milne's *The Perfect Alibi*."

"You've been busy!"

Rene smiled. "Well, you know me and theatre. And Hazel, I think, has also been bitten by the theatre bug."

"Well, she's certainly pretty enough," Eric agreed. "I bet she'd make a terrific actress."

"Remember when Father John got us all together with Hazel and John? You saw Hazel and me having a great old time talking about the theatre. She found out from Father John that I had danced in London and taught in Australia, so she's roping me in. We're going to see if we can do something to get the Trinity Players started again. And of course, Martha is *the* theatre here..."

Eric was delighted at this turn of events. Rene might flourish even more with the stage as a possibility.

"And today you're doing early communion?" she asked absently.

Eric shook his head. "That's Wednesdays , remember?"

"Oh yes of course. This is the morning for your hobos, before working at church. Oh by the way, are you preaching this Sunday at Evensong? I enjoy those sermons so much."

Eric shook his head. "Jack will. He asked me to do his turn at the hospitals, and visit other parishioners sick at home — though I drew the line at those Westmount mansions!"

Rene chuckled. "When I told that dreadful man how much we all admired him, I saw you shudder. I hope the Good Lord forgives such a dreadful fib."

Eric turned to her with glowing eyes. "I don't think any other person alive could have wangled five hundred dollars out of that tightwad. Anyway, after my hobos, I have some administration to do in the church. I'll see you back here in the afternoon, hopefully early, to hear all about your lunch."

* * *

During the meal at the Ritz, a mass exodus from the dining room left it deserted. Word had gone round that the R100 was passing overhead. The huge dirigible had arrived at St. Hubert airport a few days earlier and now was off on a one-day tour of Eastern Canada. Everyone wanted to see it. So Rene, Hazel and Martha went out with the others and craned their necks to watch. My! Didn't it seem huge, drifting across the sky, so slowly, giving Montrealers a chance to take it all in. Traffic came to a halt; drivers got out of their cars with everyone watching.

They went back in, talking excitedly. Rene fortunately had kept a couple of her better dresses safe in the locker of their stateroom on the ship. So at least she had something to wear on such an occasion. All the rest of her outfits were, of course, at the bottom of the ocean. But she didn't mind. The simpler she dressed the better, and more becoming a poor curate's wife. It was certainly a new persona for her.

Striking rather than pretty, Martha Allan wore a stylish black hat with a large decoration sprouting wildly above; she had black hair and a definite air of authority, as well she might — being the granddaughter of Sir Hugh Allan, one of the wealthiest men in the world when he died. Martha's father, Montague, another Bishop's College School "old boy", had helped her found the MRT. She lived above McGill on Mount Royal in the imposing *Ravenscrag,* and the dazzling Hazel Molson lived in an attractive mansion atop Clarke Avenue.

Mid-afternoon, Rene turned the key in the lock and entered the apartment bursting with delight, wanting to tell her husband all about it. But no Eric. Still at church, she surmised. She changed into her old clothes — must use this brimming energy! Clean the apartment, give a good scrub to the kitchen floor; she even took the dishes out and cleaned the cupboards, untouched since they'd leased the apartment five months ago. She had bought an old carpet sweeper in an eviction sale and now ran it up and down their two used carpets. Would she and Eric ever afford the kind of furnishings she preferred? Well, Rene told herself, this is a phase; enjoy it while you can. For she was confident that matters would change for the better and, somehow, all would be well.

When suppertime came and still no Eric, worry took over. Finally, she decided to telephone the church. The office was shut: no answer. Well, she thought, he'll be along soon. She set about preparing a small meal for them both. But still no Eric. Then it struck her — that R100 going overhead! Back came all those stories about German Zeppelins in the Great War. Didn't they drop bombs? Eric would have seen it overhead, certainly. So had shell shock struck again? Oh Lord, what should she do?

Calm yourself, just calm down, she told herself, that probably wouldn't bring on any symptoms. But she knew in her heart of hearts it might have. Should she go and tell Father John? No, perhaps try and find Eric first.

Off she went to the church, under a ten-minute walk, and climbed its central steps. The squat grey building was always unlocked, the communion silver kept safe in the Rector's office. She checked the nave and then walked down the long aisle, turning left into the Lady Chapel. There he was, praying!

She went forward. No, wrong. A stranger, praying, and another on the left. Two kneeling separately, silently, veterans she was sure, but not Eric. She walked back to the entry and down into the large auditorium where one day she hoped to stage plays under the banner of the Trinity Players. Up the steps beside the stage she went, into the large side room for meetings, then checked the dressing rooms, passed behind the stage and stepped down into the kitchen where lunches were prepared nowadays. No sign.

Home she came, desperate, mind spinning: what should she do next? Back in the apartment, all sorts of images arose. Had he run off somewhere? Was he hiding in the bushes? Perhaps he'd run across the railway tracks and jumped into the canal for safety? They used to do that to escape mustard gas, she had heard, though erroneously — gas collected on pools. What on earth had happened? Finally, she could stand it no more, put on her jacket and walked firmly along Sherbrooke Street and up Marlowe Avenue to Father John's modest house. She rang the bell.

The Canon opened the door. "Come in, come in, Rene." He quickly saw her state and ushered her into the living room. "Had anything to eat? We've done our supper but Stella can make you a snack in the kitchen. She's there now, washing up."

"No, Father John, I couldn't possibly eat. You see, I think something might have happened to Eric."

Jack went to the sideboard and poured her a slug of gin with tonic. "Here, my dear, this will calm you down. Now sit, and tell me all about it."

She did. She poured out her worries. She even gave Jack a fuller account of his last bout with that dreadful disease.

"Well, I don't think it's a matter for the police yet," Father John said, which pleased Rene. "Let's just you and I make our way down to the hobo jungle. I've been there a couple of times myself with Eric. Mind you, I'm only too happy," he chuckled, "to leave those unfortunates to his ministrations, poor fellows. But I know where it is."

They got into Jack's car, motored along Sherbrooke and down Girouard's gravelled lane. Jack pulled up beside the woods and preceded Rene down an uneven, twisted trail. Dusk was beginning to obscure the way. They passed several empty tents, then cut down towards the tracks.

Jack stopped, put his hand out to caution Rene, who came to stand beside him. They saw before them a small bonfire circled by a listening group. "Let's go ask."

They made their way further, hidden in the woods in case of danger. When none appeared, Jack motioned, and they moved closer. No one paid them any attention, so they advanced within listening distance.

Around a small fire, the men were sitting, standing, or lounging, engrossed in a speaker who sat on a barrel, his back to the two of them. There by the firelight in the growing dusk, Rene peered at hobos, scruffy, ragged — the phrase "the halt, the maimed and the blind" came into her mind. The firelit tableau reminded her of biblical illustrations, too: a lit figure surrounded by listeners in the dusk. She heard snatches of the talk.

Tales of the Holy Land! So it was Eric.

His parables told of a Hobo, like them, who had roamed the uneven hills and deserts in sandals, mixing with those who were as disadvantaged as they. Eric spoke of how He travelled: on foot, sleeping wherever He could, talking to the poor, the unwanted, and the sick. What pictures Eric painted of the peasants he and Rene had seen together, those people who so resembled the crowds in the days of Our Lord. Eric even got in, without being preachy, how He had declared: "Blessed are the poor in spirit, for they shall see God."

At last, after they had listened a good while in astonishment, Jack turned to her. "You're a lucky woman, my dear."

Yes, she thought as tears came into her eyes — in spite of all those tribulations he puts upon me, yes, I'm a very lucky woman.

CHAPTER TWENTY-TWO

A few days later on Wednesday, August 13th, Jack came to collect them at their apartment. Rene led the way downstairs and they got into his motor car. "An exciting occasion, Father John!"

"I thought you'd enjoy our Mayor's reception. Apparently, the R100 doesn't take off till around ten, but we don't have to stay that long."

"You know," Rene said, "at the Ritz the other day when I was having lunch with Hazel, it passed overhead. We all rushed out to see it. Traffic stopped — quite exciting."

"Yes," Eric said, "thank you, Jack. I can't wait to see it up close."

"We both wanted to go and watch it arrive, but the crowds were impossible. They say a hundred thousand people flowed over the Harbour Bridge and down to St. Hubert airport every day since it arrived."

They drove along, chatting pleasantly. Rene had no fears of the dirigible disturbing Eric's tranquillity. That one day he'd been absent, Eric had sent a hobo friend to tell her he'd been inveigled to stay with them. Apparently, the fellow had arrived at their apartment and found it empty.

As they drove along Dorchester Blvd, Jack pointed to the construction of the Sun Life building. "Going to be the tallest office building in the British Empire when it's finished next year," Jack remarked. "And a bit further on, I'll take you through Place d'Armes so you can see the new Aldred building going up. That might even match it."

"Amazing all this construction with times so hard."

"The government must be trying to keep people working."

"Bennett sure got swept in last week!" Eric commented. "Surprised Mackenzie King, I bet! Large majority: one hundred and thirty-seven seats to the Liberals ninety-one."

Jack navigated down towards Place d'Armes. "The new Prime Minister claimed he'd do something about that Smoot Hawley Act. Amazing how those Americans dared erect such high tariffs to shut out most of our exports. But I doubt Bennett can have much effect." They duly passed the Aldred building in progress and then headed east onto the great spans of the just completed Harbour Bridge crossing the St. Lawrence, Montreal being an island.

"Remember Jack, our father is said to have worked on the Victoria Bridge? I don't know how true that is. Longest bridge in the world when it opened in 1860."

"I believe he did, poor old fellow. As a teenager in the eighteen fifties. Snowshoed all the way to Montreal, did you know that Rene? Over six hundred miles."

"On snowshoes?" Rene was suitably impressed. "All the way?"

"Yes. I heard him talking to Old Momma when I was little. He allowed as how he might have drowned right under this bridge on a sleigh. The other one went through the ice with a dozen aboard — of course, no one should have tried so late in spring. But Poppa didn't want to wait weeks to come home and cross the river on a ferry. Times were hard then."

They drove on, high over the houses below them and then on across the river. "I don't know how they ever built this," Rene remarked.

"About time they had a bridge here," Jack said. "Traffic on the Victoria was getting pretty bad."

The road was choked with pedestrians and motor cars, so many heading for the small airfield. At last, they saw the great silvered airship tethered a hundred feet above ground at a slim, seemingly fragile, mast. Rene leaned across to look out the window. Its ribs, clearly delineated, stretched from nose to tail. "Amazing they made it across the Atlantic so easily."

"I expect the crew will be there and we'll hear about it."

After making their way through the crowds on the field, they reached the small airport building where the Mayor's reception was being held. The bigwigs all looked prosperous, with members of the City Council awkward in dress clothes worn especially for the occasion.

Rene was taken aback when approached by a short, heavy dignitary with an enormous nose, dressed in striped trousers, a pale grey waistcoat, Ascot tie and a black coat. Exuberance blossomed from his squat frame. Mayor Camelien Houde greeted Father John, but all the time his small, foxy eyes fastened on Rene. He took her hand, bowed gracefully over it, then kissed the fingers with a loud smack. "You are welcome, Madame, to this humble celebration. It is no surprise the R100 choose our great city for the first visit." Given to hyperboles, Rene had heard.

Mayor Houde hardly looked at Eric when Jack introduced his curate. Jack went on, "You know, Eric, our Mayor is doing some very fine things for the unemployed poor in Montreal." Houde stood listening, his froglike smile stretched across his vast jaw, eyes glued on Rene as the most attractive woman in the room. "He's putting people to work by building new parks, tunnels under the roads —"

"So the lovers, they have place for make love, Madame!" He beamed at Rene and winked.

"And not only tunnels, but he's installing new equipment all over. I don't know how many men he's actually putting to work, but a good many."

"Oh yes oh yes oh yes," the mayor said. "But you have not told this lovely lady about my Vespasiennes..."

Rene looked up. "What are they?"

"Madame, they are where our citizens make pee-pee."

"And Your Honour," Jack quipped, "I've also heard them called Camiliennes..."

They all joined the Mayor in his laughter, and then off he went to greet more visitors.

"Quite a character," Father John told them. "I've been to his office a couple of times. He has a brass spittoon in it."

"Has he?" frowned Eric.

"Oh yes, and a silver shovel for sod turning, and three telephones. You know, he gets up early, works hard, never takes a drink. The French just love him. He's the leader of the provincial Conservative party, too."

Jack went to find a member of the crew, leaving Rene and Eric to sip their champagne and look out at the falling dusk. Then Rene noticed a couple of men and a tall woman looking in their direction. She had become accustomed to men singling her out, so was taken aback when a woman came over and addressed herself to Eric. "Are you Lieut. Alford? I'm Katie Dickson."

Eric nodded. "How you do?"

"I heard from Mrs. Whitehead you visited her last week. We thought we might find you here with your distinguished brother, the Canon." She paused. "I believe you knew Edward Whitehead."

Oh heavens! thought, Rene. Here it comes again. In this crowded room, too. What on earth should I do now?

Eric stared at the young woman — certainly striking, with dark curly hair, flashing eyes, and stunning features. "Bombardier Whitehead? He was my best friend on my gun. We were all so fond of him. But what did you say your name was?"

"Katie Dickson."

"Katie? You mean, Edward's Katie?"

Rene held her breath.

Katie nodded. "He was my fiancé, Father."

Eric was silent for the longest time, staring at her.

Katie went on seriously. "It took me such a long time to get over... But now," she held out her arm and waved over her tall, distinguished companion, "this is my husband, Wallingford." They greeted each other. "We have a lovely family, two girls and a boy. He knows all about Edward. He helped me get over it."

"I often wanted to write, Katie, to tell you what a brave man Edward was. When you said that you were his forever, he told everyone." His voice broke slightly. "He would have been so pleased to know how you have gotten on with your life.

"And his end was sudden?"

"Very sudden," Eric lied. "He died in my arms. Quickly. Painlessly."

Katie nodded to herself and then, perhaps to hide her tears, turned away with her husband to rejoin their group.

Rene looked at Eric anxiously. But it seemed that the pain of that experience had so fully been borne so often before, that now, he was free enough to stare after Edward's love, seeming almost happy at having met her and knowing she was herself at peace. "I can see why Edward was in love with her. An exceptional woman."

"Now, Eric! You're married to me, remember!" She joked, re-lieved.

Just then Jack brought over a slightly taller man with bushy black hair and a prominent nose. "May I present Mr. Nevil Nor-way? Deputy chief engineer of the R100. As you may also know, something of a writer — under the *nom de plume* Nevil Shute. He's been telling me about the trip across."

After the introductions, Nevil went on, "I was saying to the Can-on here, it took us only seventy-eight hours — following the great circle route, about 3,300 miles. Average speed forty-two miles an hour."

"And how high were you flying?" asked Eric.

"Normally fifteen hundred to two thousand feet."

"And not one problem?"

"Oh well, yes, we had leaks in a couple of the gas bags. So up we went to 3,000 feet to let one of the crew mend them. And then, some tears in the fins. I had to go out into the backbone and pull loose the beating fabric to stop the spread till the riggers came. We also had a pretty bad storm between Quebec and Montreal. But that's it."

"I'd like to know how big it really is," continued Eric. "Where do the crew and passengers stay? Inside somehow? Are there bed-rooms?'"

"Oh yes, substantial quarters, about a third of the way back from the bow. Lots of window space to look down on the terrain below, and comfortable beds. The whole envelope is over seven hundred feet long and about a hundred and thirty across."

"And you're leaving with them tonight?"

"Yes, I didn't go when the R100 toured Ottawa, Toronto and Ni-agara Falls," he explained. "I was off at Lake Magog in the East-ern Townships with a friend, instead. But our reception here has been just unbelievable. Functions every day. And you know, when we arrived over Quebec City in the evening, it was still light. They were all massed on the promenades and parks to see us. A tremendous hooting with sirens. Rather exciting, I must confess."

"And I hear your sister ship, the R101, is going to India next," Rene said.

Norway looked worried. "They are supposed to. They've been rushing." He turned to her. "We're in competition, but I don't like what's going on there. They're not taking the care they should. Pushing to get finished." He shook his head again. "Not a good idea. Especially with the novelty of what we're trying to do."

"I do wish them well," said Rene. "I have a mother and sister in England. I can't wait till all this gets to be a normal event, crossing by airship."

"I know, Rene," Eric said, "but it'll probably be far beyond our means. I'm afraid when we go, it may be on a ship."

Soon afterwards, the crew left the reception and climbed the ladder into the dirigible. Rene, worried that the motors overhead might affect her husband, urged him to leave early. But he wanted to wait, as did his brother. So they stayed to see the great ship take off, drinking more champagne and eating assortments from the buffet.

On October 5th, Nevil Norway's worries were realized: on its maiden voyage over France, the R101 crashed, killing 48 people, which effectively ended dirigible transportation.

* * *

The summer passed uneventfully and autumn began with more and more work at the church, as the numbers of the indigent increased daily. Rene was gratified to see Eric in such good spirits. Her vigilance lessened.

Father John was the one to bring up the subject as they were discussing arrangements for the next day's luncheons. "I think perhaps, Rene," he said, "for those Armistice Day ceremonies at the Cenotaph tomorrow, my brother had better not attend."

"Why ever not?" Rene asked. "He's been looking forward to it, you know."

The Canon nodded. "I've even persuaded my old friend Arthur Currie, Eric's commanding officer, to lead the ceremonies. So perhaps I'm being overly cautious," he went on, "but if anything will remind him of the war, surely those disabled veterans, a good number legless in wheelchairs, some without arms, the military band and..." He paused. "The salute being fired..."

Rene thought hard. It had not even crossed her mind. But she knew that Father John respected her, and treated her as his special confidante when it came to matters concerning his brother, so she nodded. "Right-oh, Father, I'll say we need him downstairs to help prepare the special lunch. He's so awfully good at getting people to do things. But I know he'll be disappointed."

Father John seemed relieved. "These last weeks, I've noticed he's becoming a little more agitated. Perhaps I've been giving him too much to do."

The next morning, November 11, 1930, Eric sat down for his modest breakfast having shaved, dressed and said his morning prayers. When Rene brought him his egg, she announced: "I have some rather important news."

"And what is that?" Eric began to tinker with the egg shell.

Rene sat down. "We're going to have a baby."

She thought she saw a look akin to fear cross his face. "Can you be sure?"

"You know the hospital just behind the church down the street?"

"The Queen Elizabeth?"

"I had tests done there; the results came back yesterday. It's true. We are going to have a baby."

"That's ... that's wonderful, dearest, really." Eric came round the breakfast table and hugged Rene tightly.

When he sat down again, Rene was filled with misgivings. For some reason, she felt that he was not as pleased as expected. "Are you not happy, Eric?"

"Of course I am! Why shouldn't I be?"

"I don't know..." She sat down slowly.

"Well, it's confusing. .. You see, I would want the best for the baby. And as a curate ... as a curate, how will I ever provide?"

Rene thought for a moment. "Eric, we've surmounted so much already, you and I. Remember, where there's a will there's a way. We shall certainly be good parents, of that I'm sure. And we shall give our child a lot of love. Let's leave the rest up to the Good Lord Above."

Eric looked at her with genuine admiration. "That is exactly what I might have said myself." He seemed much relieved.

After breakfast, when Eric mentioned the ceremonies, Rene told him what Jack had suggested. Eric looked downcast. "I always mark Armistice Day with the one minute of silence at eleven o'clock. And my prayers. But if my brother asks me to help in the kitchen, of course, I shall. Funny he didn't tell me himself."

Rene made some excuse and went on to say, "We'll have fun, Eric. Not only will we be feeding the hungry, but Father John asked me to make something special for the few officers coming back after the ceremony. They're going to have a drink in his study, and we can join them. Afterwards, they'll come down to eat in the church hall." She smiled. "I think Jack would like to open their eyes to our hungry poor and their families."

Later, after the officers came back to church from the ceremony, Rene left Eric in charge of the kitchen and went upstairs with a tray of *hors d'oeuvres*. Father John introduced her around and brought her to Sir Arthur Currie, superbly decked out in his general's uniform.

Rene could see that he was charmed to meet her and she fell into conversation with him. "I hear one of your professors, Frank Scott, is taking up the cause of our underprivileged citizens. They say he's a real advocate for workers who are being cheated everywhere."

Jack saw that Sir Arthur was taken aback, and so tried to divert the topic. "I told the General here about Eric: how he fought in the Firing Line through every major battle of the Great War. And indeed, how he was an admirer of the General."

Sir Arthur, looking stern, ignored him and turned to Rene. "You mention Frank Scott. You know, as Chancellor, I had to write and ask that he not use our good university's name in his newspaper letters supporting the Communists."

Jack and Rene both looked surprised.

Sir Arthur must have noticed, because he went on lamely, "You see, I did that at the request of our Board of Directors, all industrialists and, of course, wealthy, powerful, men." He shrugged helplessly. "I'm rather at their beck and call. It was, I hope, an innocuous letter."

Again Father John stepped in. "You know, Sir Arthur, I'm a great friend of Frank's father, Fred Scott, one of my finest chaplains in the Great War. We often see each other. In fact, he wrote a poem about the two of us. I'll get it." Jack disappeared into his study, leaving Arthur and Rene together.

"And how is your husband doing, Mrs. Alford?" the General asked. "Fighting through so many battles up in the Firing Line, he bears no scars, I hope? So many of our brave men do, alas."

"He does have bouts of what they call shell shock, General. But he manages to keep them under control. Father John thinks he is doing a great job here at the church. He is a very fine man, my husband."

"I'm sure he is." Sir Arthur turned to see Jack come in with a paper bearing the poem.

"And what is the latest," Jack asked, "from our old enemy, General? I've heard times are really bad."

Currie nodded. "Apparently some demagogue has been rather coming to the fore. Fellow named Hitler. Not sure what he's up to, but they say the results might be rather dangerous. When this blasted Depression caused the U.S. to reduce payments to the Weimar Republic, Germany's struggling new democracy fell apart. Now what did you bring us?"

"Listen to this." Jack read:

Two Archdeacons on the stage,
One shows youth, and one shows age.
One is dark and one is fair,
One is bald and one has hair.

Everyone with eyes can see
Each has got the C.M.G.
Both can duck and both can run,
So they thought the war was fun.

One writes poems, one does not,
One is Alford, one is Scott.
One has eyes of piercing gleam,
One looks always in a dream.
Both wear gaiters now and then
Just to show they're Clergymen.
Woe to Bishops should they dare
To provoke this dauntless pair.

But of this I am most certain:
When they slip behind life's curtain,
They will never, never go
Where they'll have to shovel snow.

The three of them burst out laughing, and then the door opened and Eric came in. At the same time, a loud boom of cannon rattled the windows.

The room fell silent.

"On the mountain," Jack muttered, "always fired on Armistice Day. Twenty-nine-gun salute."

Rene looked anxiously at Eric. He stood as though struck. She could see him staring oddly at the military brass assembled. The cannon sounded again. Eric opened his mouth wide as though he were about to scream. But no sound came out. He turned and rushed out.

Rene glanced at Father John. "I'll be right back."

In the hallway she stood uncertain. Then something told her — the chapel. She hurried down the side aisle and, yes, there was Eric, kneeling at the altar rail of the Lady Chapel, hands clasped, lifted in supplication, his whole body shaking.

She came and knelt beside him.

She put her arm around him and held him as tightly as she could. "Don't worry, Eric, it will pass." As she hugged him, she felt his tension like steel, enwrapping him. "But now," she nodded, "something will have to be done..."

PART FIVE: 1930-33

CHAPTER TWENTY-THREE

Rene lifted the blind. What she saw overwhelmed her.

"Eric. Wake up." She reached across to the seat where Eric was snoozing. She'd pulled down the blind to let him sleep, as she herself had been doing. They had gotten up early in Matapedia to change from the Ocean Limited, the Montreal–Halifax train, to this branch line running on down to Gaspe.

The night before as they pulled out of Montreal, both faces pressed against the window, they had watched the train slide by the many hobos, couples, families, camped, sleeping, and cooking, beside the tracks.

Eric had stared. "So many more than ever before!"

Finally, as the train picked up speed, they both sat back, dazed by the desolation they had seen.

Now, Eric opened his eyes and lifted himself onto one elbow to look out at the bright blue waters speeding by. The autumn trees had lost their leaves, so the view was stunning. "My first look at your beautiful Chaleur Bay," Rene said. "I'm so excited I can hardly stand it."

He shifted over to sit beside her and pulled her close. "So you like it?"

"It's beautiful," Rene breathed, keeping her eyes on the window. Here she was, at last, on the fabled bay, about which she had heard so much.

After watching a long time, she settled back into the corner; Eric moved against her and put his head on her shoulder. As they dozed, she savoured this decision they had made. Father John had been all in favour: yes, Trinity could get along well enough without its curate during these lean winter months; there were plenty of student priests on hand. He would miss his brother and Rene, but clearly, he admitted, it would be best for Eric to have a complete rest at the Old Homestead and to come back in shape for Easter and — he had smiled fulsomely — for the birth of the baby, projected in April.

And what fun she'd had, going with Eric to Eatons to choose her clothes for the Gaspesian winter. Lucky he'd come with her, for Eric picked out — not what she'd have chosen, but surely appropriate, and happily not among the more expensive items: a heavy jacket, boots, sweaters, woolly underwear, exactly what she'd need. Buying the clothes and making arrangements had only increased her excitement.

"You are so clever to get rid of the apartment the way you did, my dear," said Eric. "But aren't you sorry to lose all that furniture that you had collected?"

"Sorry? Eric, I'm pleased it's gone. The man who rented the apartment — it saved him having to do any furnishing. Paid our return train tickets and winter clothing, and even more. You know, I think we got far more than it was worth."

"You made it look so attractive..."

"I may have but it was all junk, Eric, let's be clear about that. I've been thinking I should write the Mater and see if, as our Christmas present and with the baby coming, she might help with furnishing our next apartment."

"You always think of a way," Eric murmured. She felt him relax and drop off to sleep. They were not due at New Carlisle for a good while, where they'd have a meal before continuing on to Port Daniel.

* * *

"Byes me son, what a fine looking woman!" Earle came forward to greet the married couple.

Eric introduced his saucy brother, who grabbed Rene's bags with ease — such a strong man, she thought. Nice broad weather-beaten face, a bit like his brother Jack, not as handsome, but attractive. So what would account for him being still single?

"So you think I 'done good,' Earle?" Eric grinned.

"Fer shore, you done good. Now come, I got Princess waitin' behind."

The red-brown mare stood patiently, hitched in the express wagon — like a buggy, as Rene had seen in pictures, but with the rear extended for luggage. Rene swung up into the seat effortlessly, impressing Earle no end, as Eric clambered in behind. "Giddap, Princess!" Earle slapped the reins and off they went. Lively had passed on, Earle told them.

Rene found herself intrigued by the houses, some whitewashed, others untouched with grey, weathered boards, assortments of barns both small and large, sheds and outhouses, all with tarred rooves and red-ochre trim. The road wound up over Port Daniel mountain and down the other side, a thinner spread of population than any village in her British countryside. Overhead, seagulls were calling and circling and, on the dark bay, a high wind streaked the heavy seas with white caps.

"By Jove, it's freezing!" Rene shivered and her teeth chattered.

"Lord A'mighty, what a fool." Earle turned. "Under the seat, Eric, I put a couple of heavy coats."

The mare slowed to a walk while Eric pulled up the wool jackets and helped Rene into hers, hauling one on himself. "Byes yes, Earle, I should have written to bring these, but we decided to come in a terble hurry."

Rene noticed how easily Eric fell into his homespun manner of talking. She sat again as Earle slapped the reins and Princess trotted off. "And how soon will it snow, do you think?" Rene asked. "I just can't wait to see a blizzard."

"Too soon," Earle answered.

"We need the snow, of course, to protect the roots and crops," Eric said, "but no one likes it when winter descends. Kind of shuts things down."

"Opens 'em up!" Earle contradicted. "We git inta the woods and start cuttin."

"The woods... oh yes. Ow!" She ducked as the mare's hooves shot up a sharp stone; the dashboard only shielded their legs from the clacking of pebbles. "I can't wait to go snowshoeing with Eric. He's promised to take me back into your wilderness."

Earle shook his head in wonder. This was some woman Eric brought, he obviously thought. And Rene herself was pleased that Eric had braved the odd looks of Eaton's salesladies to enter the underwear department and choose her woollen longjohns and bloomers.

They finally passed St. Paul's Church that Eric's father, along with others, had been instrumental in building, and then right away they reached the Brook Hill. How steep! Rene gripped the dash tightly, but Earle reassured her: "Princess, she's has done this hundreds o' times."

Princess held back on the shafts as best she could, but about halfway down the hill, she began to trot more and more furiously and then galloped as they crossed the small wooden bridge over Shigawake brook, and then threw her weight into the traces as she continued trotting up the other side, until forced to a walk. As they crested the hill, Rene got her first look at the Old Homestead. One of the larger houses: a black tarred roof over whitewashed wooden walls and a veranda that wrapped around, with wooden tracery under the eaves.

Princess hauled them up the driveway and Rene saw on her right the great barn with its black tarred roof and wide, white-washed board walls. Ahead of them stood a matching wooden granary.

Lillian must have been waiting because she hurried out the kitchen door, drying her hands on her apron. "Eric, Eric, welcome home." Her brother leapt down and hugged her while Earle got their bags. Rene shook hands with Lillian, plain, shorter than Eric, her dark hair braided and pinned up round on top like a tiara. Lillian stepped back to look at Rene. "Hardly shows. You must be so happy, Eric, becoming a father?"

Eric beamed his response, and in through the back door they went, down the long porch with its indoor pump and water buckets on a shelf, turning right into a small breakfast room with Victorian couch opposite, and a large dining table.

"I've got dinner ready," Lillian said, "I opened a jar of beef I put away this fall, but I 'spect you'll want to see round the house first?"

Eric nodded. "Seems somehow different without Old Momma here. And Old Poppa. You miss them, Lilian?"

She didn't reply, deciding rather to hurry off into the kitchen.

"Where is your son, Lillian?" Rene called after her. "Eric has told me about Henry. He must be sixteen now?"

"Weekdays he boards in New Carlisle. He's at the Academy there. He wants to go to Bishop's, like his uncles."

While Earle left to unhitch Princess, Eric showed Rene through into the next large room, which had been the original main room of the house. A large cooking range heated it; behind, stairs twisted up to his parents' bedroom. But Eric led her diagonally across into what he explained was the 'new wing,' built in the 1880s.

"I guess when they had so many children my parents needed more space." They crossed through that living room into the wide hallway, and Eric opened the closed door facing them to show her the parlour. "For wakes only. Here's where you'll be laid out!" He chuckled at her reaction. "But we also use this for any weddings, oh, and we entertain the vicar here once a month for tea. Lil and everyone are very observant, as you'll see."

Up the stairs they went, Rene thinking it strange to have one whole room saved for such occasions. They reached the upstairs hall with its south-facing window shedding light on a large washbowl, a china jug for hot water, and a white porcelain slop pail hidden by a curtain underneath. "That's where we wash and shave in the morning. Lil brings us up a jug of hot water."

"No running water? I can go down for it. And the bathroom?"

"Chamber pots under the commode — the outhouse is behind the barn."

Rene swallowed. Eric nodded to the room on their left: "Henry's room, so we'll have the one on the right, which has always been mine."

Eric opened that door to let Rene in first. The window faced west. Eric looked out, and gestured. "That's Mae Byers over there. She's an Alford, but her grandmother, my great aunt Maria, married a Byers." Rene was only half-listening; so much to absorb. "After my grandfather cleared the land to build this homestead, right at the beginning of the 1800s, he later stripped off two pieces of land, one for his eldest daughter Maria when she married and the next strip over for his eldest son, John Garrett." Rene was more interested in the large bed, which she sat on: feather-filled mattress, not bad. Amazing he knows and lives with all that lineage, she thought; perhaps one day she'd grasp his antecedents, but not of paramount interest now. In the right-hand corner, she saw covered shelving for clothes; happily, she hadn't brought many.

Eric turned to her. "Well, what do you think?"

"Need you ask?" She spun happily. "Now all I need is to go back into those wild woods, with its bears and wolves, and deer and moose, and foxes and mink and otters —"

"Hold it, hold it!" Eric was delighted at the way his wife couldn't stop talking. "We'll do that soon enough."

* * *

Not long after they arrived, they settled into a routine, which Rene knew would be so good for Eric. Earle and the hired man went out early to do the milking, having had their cup of tea. Lillian got up even earlier to get the fire going from embers left the night before. Then all would assemble for a hearty breakfast sometime around seven. As in the city, the talk often touched on hardships that everyone was facing.

"Ida Young, I went over to give her some eggs, poor old soul, and I seen these here letters on the winda," Earle was saying. "Her daughters have went off south to America. So her letters, she had to wait till she gets ahold of four cents to buy two stamps. Terble job."

"It's hard all around, Earle dear." Lil put down his plate of eggs and bacon. She baked twice a week — the fresh loaf sat next to a jug of molasses. Eric had taken Rene down to Ernie Hayes's store (another relative) a couple of days before, where they'd filled the gallon jug from his puncheon. Rene watched him wind the crank to siphon out the molasses. She wondered at all the items this small store contained: dishes, fence wire, coal oil for lamps, material for clothes, harnesses, groceries in bulk, even caskets!

Back to the stamps: "Doesn't anyone get Relief?" Rene asked. "I thought municipalities were supposed to hand out the government money to their needy."

"Not a lot starving around here. But byes, times is hard. Old Joseph Aubut back on the Second won't cash his relief cheque of three dollars a month because a barl of flour costs five. He's afraid he won't find the other two."

Rene looked shocked. "Could we find two dollars? Eric?"

"No way of us feedin' the entire country," Earle interrupted. "He's not the only one'd like a barrel of flour."

"But no tramps this winter much," Lil remarked.

"Any tramp comes to our door," Earle said, "Old Momma used to give them supper, a good bed, lotsa hot water fer to wash, and send them on their way with a good breakfast. Lil does the same."

"A lot of work, those tramps." Lillian sat to eat her own breakfast. "But the Lord said, the stranger at thy door, it might be Me." Eric smiled: Lil often improvised the Bible.

"So they come mostly in the summer?"

"Land sakes, last summer we had a pile, didn't we, Earle?"

"A lotta tramps, a lotta tramps," breathed Earle. "Lord almighty, yes. Poor fellas too, eh? Not used to work, neither. Seems only the old ones come tramping this way. They have this idea we're gonna feed them."

"And we do," said Lillian. "Poor fellows."

"You do right, Lillian," Eric added. "It's all the Lord's work."

Rene was nonetheless pleased that Eric no longer had the strain of seeing those hobos by the railroad tracks. When he ministered to them, he always came home worried that he hadn't done more.

Just then there was a knock at the door and in came Stan Wellman, short and slight, his stubby beard hiding a cleft palate. He wore a hand-me-down jacket, well patched, and a leather cap with ear-flaps. Behind him came his wife Bess, straight as an arrow, superb posture, Rene noticed, a wad of tobacco wedged in her cheek and fire in her crossed eyes.

"Come in, come in," called Earle. "Come sit fer a bite."

Stan stood uncertainly in the door, and Rene saw Lil give him a push. "Thank you kindly, my dear Mr. Earle," said Bess as they came in. She had the gracious manners of a queen.

Rene and Eric pulled up extra chairs, so the two sat down for a bite. But it wasn't long before Stan brought out a small Redpath sugar bag. "Earle, I wonder if ya got any old chews?"

Rene looked over and discovered small black rolls on the upper window sill. Before he ate, Earle would ball his chewing tobacco and save it.

"I'll take and put in a couple, Stan." Earle went to the window and gave his old chews to Stan.

"Thank you kindly, Mr. Earle," Bess said again as she tucked into her bread and molasses. She held out her teacup for Lillian.

Eric pushed back from the table, having finished. "Well, I'm off to the cabin. See you later, Rene."

Soon after they'd arrived, Eric had set about building a log cabin by the forks of the brook, urged on by some mysterious gene harkening back to that first cabin his grandfather had built. Or perhaps he longed for the woods he'd experienced fishing and trekking over the mountains — his fondest memories.

Their routine became for Rene to walk back to the cabin with a cooked dinner around eleven. But first she stayed to help Lillian with her duties, in spite of protestations. "I don't know how you get through a day," she told Lil. "All those chores: make the beds, empty the slops, bake bread, prepare the meals, heat the water, wash everyone's clothes, clean the house, never-ending!" And in the summer, Lil reminded her, every sunny day she worked in her flower garden, just like Old Momma.

"Enjoy the morning," Rene called as Eric went out into the porch to wrap himself up. It was not yet light but he knew his way in the dark.

"You must have them walls pretty well up?" Earle called. "We drug over good foundation logs last week."

"You did, Earle. Thank you. That Silver, he knows his way in the woods." Once a week, Eric went back where Earle was cutting on his woodlot on the Fourth and returned to the forks with Silver. He'd wrap a chain round the heavier foundation logs and the horse skidded them to the site.

"Byes tomorrow, I'd best be going to see the station-master. I gotta order a bottle from away for that sick cow."

"A bottle of medicine?" asked Rene

Earle put his finger to his lips: sister Lillian was in the kitchen cooking for Stan and Lil. "No, no, a bottle o' whiskey. I gotta get Will Byers fer to come and see to that sick cow. Only way he'll come — a little drink."

Eric, heavily dressed, poked his head in. "We still have to send to Ottawa or Montreal for liquor?"

"Well fer shore."

Usually when Rene arrived at Eric's cabin, they'd eat their lunch and then she'd help with the crosscut saw, slicing through logs for the walls. Now that she was with child, Eric wouldn't let her do any heavy lifting. "But I'm perfectly all right," Rene would say.

"Strong woman," Earle often commented, "strong as an ox, that Rene."

On clear nights, they would frolic and sleep in bedrolls on the flooring of rough boards Joe Hayes had sawn. Nothing Rene loved more than frying trout on Eric's open fire while he recounted tales of the wild woods, of beavers' building dams, of lynx howls — such unearthly yells. "Around here, no loons, only a lynx once in a while, but the most fearsome noise you can ever imagine."

In the clearing around the cabin, you could see straight up into the sky. The stars, so very bright, thrust their darts of light through the inky blackness to pierce your eyeballs, as Eric would say. Rene had never seen anything like it. "Ever since I met you ten years ago, dear Eric, when you would sit in a cozy London pub and tell me about this, I've wanted to come."

"And now, you're here," murmured Eric. "I'm the luckiest man alive."

* * *

Two days before Christmas, Rene put on her snowshoes, hefted up a bunch of shingles with a tump line round her forehead, and picked up the lard pail with their cooked dinner.

Lillian poked her head out the back door. "You'd best stay, Rene. A storm's coming. And leave those shingles! A woman in your condition..." Rene glanced up — the clouds did look a bit heavy, bursting with approaching flurries.

"Oh, I'll make it in under an hour. It should hold off till then." After some six weeks, Rene felt very much a local. She set off up the slanting path behind the house, but when she reached the brow of the hill, the sky did not look promising. She picked up her pace over the flat field and went on round the brow of the Hollow. The first time Eric had taken her, he'd pointed out the shacks on the side hill opposite, and touched on his boyhood romance with a girl from there who had visited him after the war, married and doing well. He pointed out Joe's mill, which made boxes for the Robins codfish company up in Paspebiac.

She was pleased Eric had decided to build this cabin. She just wished he hadn't set himself a deadline of finishing by Christmas Day. Tomorrow was Christmas Eve and all Shigawake went to the service. Before breakfast, she had set out her dress and decided which boots to wear and what jewellery remained after the "accident" with her steamer trunk.

Eric only had the cabin roof to finish, which should be done by the end of the day — the reason she'd insisted on bringing back that last bunch of shingles. A few days ago, they'd fetched boards for the roof on the sleigh, two small window sashes, and a little potbellied stove, but they'd miscalculated the amount of shingles. She knew how much Eric wanted to finish, and it pleased her to do this one last thing to help.

Passing the Mill Road, she paused and put down the shingles. With her dance training she had swung back easily, but even so, hurrying made her short of breath, and the going was harder than she expected. She hoisted the twenty-pound pack onto her back again, but as she set off, the expected blizzard swooped down in force. Much sooner than expected. Too soon, in fact.

CHAPTER TWENTY-FOUR

An almighty gust almost knocked Rene off her snowshoes. She steadied herself and began beating her way up the grade toward the railway crossing. Down came gusting clouds of sharp snowflakes, stinging her face, growing in intensity. With the wind whipping up the loose snow, she could hardly see the way. She turned to the split-rail cedar fence and followed it. This, she told herself, is just a blizzard, the kind one reads about. I'll be able to tell the Mater and Leo, but then again, perhaps not — they'd just think that I'd gone mad. Hilda, that's who she'd write to. And she owed Father John a letter: how well Eric was doing, how the home atmosphere and building his cabin had made him relaxed, happy, and positively charged with energy. Eric was a good letter writer but never prone to commenting on his own health. Father John would be anxious for news, so she made up her mind to write on Boxing Day.

She was getting pretty good on snowshoes but no trail had been beaten alongside the fence where she now tramped, so each snowshoe sank in the accumulated soft snow. Heavy going. But she told herself: keep pressing on! And before long she got to the fence protecting the railway track. In the tearing east wind, she found the gate, slid it open, shut it, then with only a few feet of visibility, did her best to tramp directly across the tracks and reach the opposite gate, more by guess than by God.

Seeing only a few feet ahead, she knew what Eric had meant by a whiteout in some of his letters. She remembered hearing that animals worked more by scent — especially the lynx. She shuddered as she recalled Eric's tale.

Early one morning after Christmas, Earle had gone into the stable with his lantern. Chores began around six, but the sun didn't rise till around eight. He had opened the door and right away sensed something wrong with the cattle. Before he could figure it out, some sinewy creature sped past, a chicken in its mouth. He whirled and jammed the door on its neck. It dropped. He grabbed its hind legs and beat its brains out on the heavy beams.

Rene had timidly brought up the subject on the train coming down. "Eric, are there still lynx around these days?"

"Well," Eric had replied, "you sure hear them sometimes. Awful yowls at night. They did see footprints last winter by the brook."

Rene shivered. "How big are they?"

"Like a small lion. Very shy. But savage, and unbelievably strong. You don't want to meet one — awful hungry in winter."

Rene found her excitement at the wilderness diminish. "Cougars, bears, lynxes —"

"Bears, they always sleep in winter. And no more cougars in the Gaspe."

"But lynxes?"

"Apparently so. I told you about Earle killing one. He was crazy to fight one like that, but little Henry, five at the time, was coming up behind him. The beast could've grabbed the child and taken it off to eat. So Earle had every reason. You get bursts of energy sometimes."

"So how did it get into the closed barn?"

"Likely loose boards in the mow; Earle had meant to fix them..."

Why remember all that now? Being alone like this. And who's to say no lynx was prowling around, waiting for some juicy woman — Stop! she commanded herself, and wrenched the thought from her mind.

Just keep to your left, follow the rail fence — don't try the shorter beaten trail across the open field into that trail in the woods. She snowshoed down to the gully crossed by the Stony Bridge, built by Alford ancestors who cleared their fields of stones. Eric said hayloads rocked precariously, going across.

Hard going through this loose snow. She stopped, panting, and wondered how long blizzards lasted. A few minutes? Fat chance. Keep going, she told herself, and keep going she did. Cross the gully, up the hill towards the head field. Funny what difference a small rise makes. The load of shingles grew heavier, especially as the wood absorbed the moisture. After a few minutes she stopped and tried leaning against the fence. But no such luck: the tapered tails of the Indian snowshoes made it too awkward. Wearily, she forced herself on.

A couple of weeks ago Earle had lent her his old wool trousers. Ladies never wore pants here, but then ladies didn't walk back in the woods with bunches of shingles on their backs either, or with forgotten axes, or warm lunches, or bags of heavy nails. She felt comfortable in them, and warm, too.

By the time she reached the top of the grade, she was exhausted. Now what should she do? Take a little rest? But somewhere, in her dim memory, she heard Eric saying, no one ever stops in a blizzard, you never let up — they'd just find your frozen body in spring. So by sheer force of will, she trudged on step by step, panting and more alarmed. Impossible to see where she was. Finally the fence ended: only trackless woods ahead. Now what?

Put this pack of shingles down, you idiot, she told herself over and over. But she kept imagining the look flooding Eric's face when he saw her arrive carrying it. He wanted so much to finish his cabin by Christmas, and this would make it happen. She'd go to any lengths to help him realize his dream.

But no trail. If only she'd tried their usual path along the floor of the valley? Too late for that. So what now? She wiped her wet sweaty face with a snowy mitten. Good to rest for a moment. But her active imagination threw up visions of succumbing to fatigue and sinking down — Eric finding her huddled body, frozen stiff — if a lynx hadn't gotten to it first.

So on through the woods, go on, try to make for any clearings already logged. But that wind beat at her, the load felt so heavy. Still, she forced herself forward, imagining a fierce cat behind every bushy spruce. Her heart was racing.

The land must dip soon. Go down, find the brook, unless it's too snowed over, and follow that. Yes, so thread through the trees, cross that space already logged — Oh! Trip on a buried stump, pick yourself up, hoist the shingles, slog on. But where was that downward slope? Was she just going in a circle? Don't get yourself frightened, but... well, that lynx WAS seen last fall. Ridiculous to be killed or freeze to death so close to home — and even closer to the cabin. But it had been known to happen; Gaspe was full of such tales.

Do not give up. Pull yourself together. But so tired. Ah! The land is starting to dip. Steeper and steeper. Go down, get to that brook.

Down she headed, panting hard. Difficult to see: only a few feet. But less wind under the trees. Steep — oh my yes, very steep.

Down this hill on snowshoes? But how? Not something Eric had taught her. The load, put it down. But no axe to blaze a tree. So how would they ever come back and find the shingles?

She tripped, fell forward. She and the shingles tumbled over and over down the hill. She struck a tree.

She lay stunned.

Lie still. Check. Your tummy? The baby? Seemed all right. Anything broken? Move your arms and legs. She did so. Dancer's training. She knew how to relax, and fall gracefully. But now, lying here, what a feast for a beast!

She grinned, then panicked — pick yourself up. Find your snowshoes; fortunately they'd come off — saving her from a twisted or broken ankle. She had rolled a good way down. Wait! Was she close to the cabin? Leaning back, she cupped her hands and yelled the Australian, "Cooo-ee!" which was known for its carrying power. "Eric! Eric, help! Cooo-ee!"

She listened for an answering call. None. But a wild animal might have heard. And with no snowshoes, she'd never reach the cabin's safety through this deep snow. Imagining the huge cat bounding toward her, she hurried on hands and knees up the hill, following the marks of her tumble, and found one. Now locate the other. And fast. Again on hands and knees, she headed down, dragging the snowshoe. Awkward, steep. She turned and backed down. Surely any animal would have smelled her by now.

Ah! There, in the branches of a heavy spruce, she saw the other snowshoe and bunch of shingles.

By now, covered in snow, Rene became annoyed — with herself for being so foolish as to bring those shingles back, and with Eric for needing them — she crawled on her hands and knees as fast as she could to the bottom. The flakes fell still thickly but without buffeting winds. She forced herself upright, terror clinging, leaned against a tree, and got her snowshoes on, fingers freezing. Doing up the thongs was agony. Wet, cold, exhausted, and afraid, she thought, what a half-wit I've been!

The snow had not let up, and indeed seemed to be coming down more heavily. She trod quickly, carefully, easier now without the weight, and almost missed the brook, being iced over and covered with snow. She hurried along what she hoped was the course, and then almost before her, log walls! She fumbled at the door latch and stumbled inside. No Eric.

Oh hells bells! Now she did feel sorry for herself and panting hard, almost dissolved in tears, but no — she pulled herself together. The stove was lit, so she stuffed in more wood, and then, brushing the clingy snow off, started to undress.

Later, when Eric returned, covered in snow, and opened the door, he stopped. "Rene! I was up to Vautier's Lake to fish through the ice. Look what I brought! And then I went to find you; I headed down on the woods trail. How did I miss you? I've been so worried."

Rene was sitting naked, clothes hanging by the stove to dry. "Oh, thought I'd just take a stroll down a different path..." They both smiled and fell into each other's arms.

* * *

Later, they sat in front of the fire with fresh-caught trout laid out beside the frying pan ready for cooking. The lard lunch pail had gotten lost in the tumble. Stories told, they both relaxed while Eric fried the trout. What a lovely sizzling sound they made. Insulated by a new blanket of snow, the cabin felt cosy, snug, actually hot.

"Now that's over, I'm pleased I've been through it." She looked out the little side window. Still snowing.

"I could live like this forever," he said simply.

"I'm not sure I could... And anyway, my dearest, we do have a third person joining us in the spring."

"Oh yes, yes. I didn't mean I would. So let's at least enjoy it all now."

"And then in the spring, back to Trinity Memorial."

He nodded. "Yes, back to Trinity."

* * *

The church bell began to toll.

"We're going to be late!" Rene tried to tramp faster on her snowshoes. A light snow had begun again, but she could make out St. Paul's Church beyond, down Kruse's Lane.

"No, we're not. They only start a good bit after the bell."

Eric and Rene had spent the night back at their cabin. Fortunately, Jim, ten, with an older man, had been cutting firewood for his mother, Mae Byers; he'd lost his father early on, and taken on helping with the farm. With his younger brother, Pat they came by the Old Homestead and explained that the couple were spending the night in the woods, so not to worry.

Rene had expected to change for the evening service when the Shigawake ladies put on their finest for this early celebration of the birth of Our Lord. She had laid out her clothes and wanted to wear them. But Eric was so close to realizing his dream of finishing by Christmas Eve that, after they found the bunch of shingles, they had kept on until dusk, which fell early this far north. Then Eric had suggested that, with the darkness they'd better head up the brook to Nelson's bridge and come down Kruse's Lane.

As they approached St. Paul's, they saw a couple of farmers attaching their horses to the fence and throwing blankets over them, the open stable under the church hall being packed. The Minister, Mr. Walters, stood waiting by the church door. The couple arrived, threw off their snowshoes and coats, and hurried in. Only then did Rene realize their situation. She was wearing Earle's old trousers, a borrowed lumberjack coat, and a moth-eaten red wool tuque with its orange tassel that Lillian had found — at least, her head was covered in church.

She and Eric walked down the aisle, drawing astonished stares. Hard to ignore the buzz that rippled through the packed congregation at the sight of their snowy old clothes: Rene in heavy trousers, unheard of in Shigawake. Eric, she saw, was blissfully unaware. He had come to worship his Lord and that's all he thought about: the birth of the baby Jesus.

Mr. Walters led the small choir of plump ladies in procession down the aisle, a few of them casting stern sideways glances at Rene and Eric in the front pew beside Lillian, and her sister Winifred who had come for Christmas from Montreal. Rene could not ignore the shock on Winifred's face at seeing her favourite brother and his wife in their get-ups.

As the service progressed, the snow on their garments melted; Rene noticed pools forming on the pew and the floor beneath. This service would not be forgotten!

And my! What a tongue lashing Winifred gave her young brother outside the church while Earle was getting out the sleigh. "You should be ashamed of yourself, Eric, bringing Rene back there. I saw her beautiful clothes laid out in the bedroom. Why didn't you get back in time? What do you think you're doing, coming to church, the two of you, looking like that!"

Eric actually smiled. "Wyn, do you truly believe Our Lord required his worshippers to be clad in their foolish finery? What did those Bethlehem shepherds wear? You think Mary and Joseph said, Get out, you're not properly dressed?" He shook his head, and threw back his head, and laughed.

Well, that certainly shut his sister up, thought Rene. Bully for you, Eric. But nonetheless, she had felt uncomfortable having caused such an unsightly stir.

And of course, it would be the talk of Shigawake the next week.

CHAPTER TWENTY-FIVE

L ate one Sunday evening at the end of January, the family were gathered around the stove. Eric had been putting finishing touches to his cabin interior, stogging the chinks with moss, making a table and so on. They loved their time back there, cooking and eating crisp trout, reading in the silence of the muffled woods, sprinkling breadcrumbs in front of the door for chickadees. Eric had made a drying rack for their clothes, and their bed more comfortable by fixing springy saplings at each side to bend under the couple's weight.

Here in the Old Homestead, the kettle sang, not boiling, just hissing soothingly above the crackling of the stove. Rene was knitting a tuque; Lillian had taught her almost as soon as she arrived, but what with the chores and working on Eric's cabin she'd not had time to practice. She kept asking Lillian what to do next. Gillis Hayes, their tall lean cousin, had come over with his pretty wife, Jessie; Mae Byers had brought young Pat and Jim around so they could be part of the fun.

The fun, as usual, was storytelling and poetry.

Eric leaned on the table with one arm, smoking thoughtfully; in another rocking chair, Jessie brought out her knitting. Of course, no knitting on Sunday nor playing of cards, no hockey, nothing on the Lord's Day. But Eric assured them that, according to Jewish tradition, though it fell on a Saturday, the Sabbath ended at sundown. So here at the Old Homestead, on Sunday night after the sun went down, you were allowed to knit.

"You mind that rainy spring two year ago?" Earle began.

"Yes, who'll fergit that?" Gillis sipped his tea. Next to him, Lillian rocked by the fire, also knitting.

"Byes, me son, we had terble weather." Earle leaned over to drop a stream of black tobacco juice into his spittoon. "Well, old John Wylie, he was coming up from Chandler and he stopped in at a restaurant for a bite. The waitress brought him his soup and put it down in front of him. 'Looks like rain again,' she sez. Old John looked at his plate. 'Oh no, Ma'am, I see a bit of barley in there.'"

They all burst out laughing. Wonderful, these old stories, Rene thought.

Gillis countered with, "Now you know that Mildred Benwell, terble mean with her food? She had this fellah over for a bite, and she put bread and molasses in front of him, and this here little pat of butter. 'Now Grant,' she sez, 'make a long arm. And don't be afraid of the butter.'

'Thanks, Ma'am, but I seen a bigger piece than that and never got a fright.'

More laughter, after which Jessie prompted, "Now Earle, why don't you do that there Abou ben Adhem."

Earle needed no prodding. Nothing he loved more than reciting poetry.

Abou ben Adhem (may his tribe increase!)
awoke one night from a deep dream of peace,

And saw, within the moonlight of his room,
Making it rich, and like a lily in bloom,
an angel, writing in a book of gold.
Exceeding peace had made Ben Adhem bold,
And to the Presence in the room he said:
"What wrote thou?" The vision raised its head,
And, with a look made of all sweet accord,
Answered, "The names of those who love the Lord."
"And is mine one?" said Abou, "Nay, not so,"
Replied the angel. Abou spoke more low,
But cheerily still, and said, "I pray thee, then,
Write me as one who loves his fellow men."

The angel wrote, and vanished. The next night
It came again, with a great awakening light,
And showed the names whom love of God had blest,
And lo! Ben Adhem's name led all the rest.

Rene, knitting, kept her eyes on Eric. He had lost any lines of worry that used to be on display. Here at the Old Homestead, his broad handsome face was smooth as a baby's. Worry free. This was indeed the life for him.

"Do ya ever hear tell of John James Macpherson and old Mrs. Fitzgerald?"

Gillis nodded, but the others shook their heads. Pat and Jim giggled and bit into their toffee apples, which their cousin Lil had made for them.

Rene had heard from Eric about the great doctor, John James Macpherson, a legend on the Coast, from the Soldiers Memorial Hospital in Campbellton. He would cure people from "down home" when most were too poor to pay. Every weekend, he'd come down to stay at the Macpherson farmhouse, Old Momma's home, in Port Daniel, often stopping for a drink from Earle's bottle of gin hidden under the bed. Old Momma was a Macpherson, so they were all cousins.

"Well, byes," said Earle, "he cut a gall bladder outta Mrs. Fitzgerald. She used to pester him: When kin I get home? So one day, he told her she could leave on the morrow

'Oh Doctor, that's fine news. When will I be able start work?'

'How old are you, Mrs. Fitzgerald?'

'I'm sixty-five, Doctor.'

'No use to start now!"

More laughter.

"You know Will Mackenzie?" Gillis began. "I was a young fella buying fish at the wharf and he come in, soaking wet, boat half-full o' water. My God, out there, he says, she was miserable. Rough, terble rough. I was afeared fer me life. I prayed, Lord Jesus save us. And he did, you know. He used to fish on that there Galilee, so he knowed what it's like."

They all nodded, smiling. "Lovely story," Eric said.

"And now, Earle," Lillian asked, "do 'The Shooting of Dan McGrew' for Rene. I don't think she's heard it yet."

Earle began, his own memory slightly different than the actual poem, but vivid nonetheless.

A bunch of the boys was hoopin' it up
in the Malamute saloon;
The kid that handled the music-box
was hittin' a rag-time tune;
And back of the bar, in a solo game,
sat Dangerous Dan McGrew,
And watching him was his light-o'-love,
the lady that's known as Lou.

As he went on, Rene thought, amazing, the poems Earle knew.

Well, she'd heard that "down home" they all recited poetry. What else was there as entertainment? She loved listening to Robert Service, and resolved to bring one of his books back to London next time she went.

And then a thought formed in her mind. She knew what she must do when they returned to Montreal for Eric to resume his duties. She would speak to Father John, as soon as they got there.

* * *

Three weeks before Easter, which fell this year on April 5th, they sat in facing seats on their way to Matapedia, before transferring to the Ocean Limited for Montreal. Rene checked her husband. Was that familiar frown of worry creeping back? "Are you looking forward to Trinity?"

Eric looked up. "Oh yes, yes. The Lord has called and I must do his bidding."

She nodded to herself. Not a great answer. "We'll be comfortable at Jean's, for a while, don't you think? I'll look for a place after the baby is born. But you never know, they might give you an incumbency somewhere else..."

"And you, Rene, are you all right?" He'd seen her shifting, trying to get comfortable with the baby inside.

"Oh, I'm fine, Eric."

They lapsed into silence again, and watched the blue bay speeding by, slashed by barren trees. Out the other window, weathered farmhouses, some not whitewashed, huddled in the damp retreating snow, few of them as grand as the Old Homestead they had left behind. Eric glanced again at his wife. "So how did you like your first winter in the Gaspe?" He wondered if her mood meant she regretted leaving.

She took a while, staring out the window. "I just cannot fathom why those early explorers ever decided to stay, once they landed on this desolate coast. Why didn't they just go back home to England?"

Eric's eyes widened. "Really?"

"I mean, what a place to live! It may be all right in the summer, but..."

"But," Eric filled in, "you had such dreams for it, the wilderness and all. And now... you've found it wasn't like that?"

She nodded. "I was so looking forward to it." She shook her head, not believing it. Then allowed her eyes to stray to her husband's as if inviting a struggle, and turned back to the view. "I might be overstating it, but..."

"But?"

"How hard a life is that? Look what your sister has to do — every day of her life! Any normal person would have packed it in long ago."

"And done what?"

"I don't know, Lillian told me she used to be a teacher... Anything. But staying as a farm widow..." She shook her head in dismay. "And she's not the only one. Every woman back there..."

Eric sat back and opened a book. "And I thought you were loving it."

Rene shrugged. "Not entirely." She smiled at her understatement. "Not that I didn't love having to put on layers of clothing and heavy boots, trudging out over the snow, just to relieve myself on that freezing two-holer. And then, after sprinkling the lime, coming back to get all undressed again and be faced with helping Lillian make everyone's bed, wash up, empty the slop pails..." She made a face. "I wrecked my knuckles the first time I tried to scrub on those ribbed washboards.... I'd never even made a bed before I got to Australia!"

"The Mater made your bed even when you were old enough to

do it yourself?" Eric sounded incredulous.

"No, of course not. The chambermaid did it. The undercook did the dishes after meals, not me. The washerwoman came in to see to the washing twice a week. The Butler supervised. He answered the door for us and checked the crystal and... I just don't know how Lillian does it, day after day, year after year."

How could Eric answer that? He remained silent. After a time, he saw Rene relax a little, and went on, "You loved those horse races out on the bay — you said so. And I saw you. You were enjoying yourself."

"One race doesn't make a winter."

"It did provide some excitement. Or have you forgotten?"

"Oh no, I could never forget that," Rene admitted, "the jingling and jangling of the harness bells, the sleighs all painted brightly out on that flat bay ice, and Rev. Mr. Walters firing off the starting pistol. But heavens, how cold! Those horses breathing — like little steam engines!" She allowed a smile. "I confess, seeing your breath out in the air like a little cloud, well, it always did impress me." She relaxed slightly. "I don't know how the horses did it on that slippery surface."

"Sharp shod," Eric said. He watched her carefully. Where was all this leading? "And that party at my sister Molly's afterwards?" he prompted. "You seemed to enjoy that."

Joe's house in the Hollow was a convenient stopping place, and the Hayes had thrown open their doors to all comers. Contestants and spectators had trotted up from the Bay on the beaten path by Shigawake brook and crossed the main highway; Route Six had just been completed all the way around the Gaspe Peninsula the year before.

Rene nodded. "Well, the Victrola I liked, I suppose."

"Joe gave it her for Christmas. The only Victrola in Shigawake. My sister was so proud of it!" Eric smiled.

"But with only a few records," Rene said, unable to suppress the mocking tone, "she had to play them over and over." She wondered what had gotten into her. As if to make amends, she went on "Her husband Joe's got quite a mill down there, I did enjoy seeing round that. He's got a good number of men working. Where would Shigawake be without that, I wonder?"

"Oh, I reckon we'd survive," Eric remarked, tartly. He wasn't sure how to handle this new attitude.

They sat in silence for a good while, as the bay sped by. Eric frowned. "Rene, what on earth is wrong?"

Rene shook her head. "I'm sorry. Now that it's over, and I don't have to face... I guess it's all been catching up with me." She pulled herself upright. "Yes, it is all over. At last. We're heading back to civilization —"

"You don't call Shigawake civilized?" Eric snapped.

"Don't you start, Eric. Can't you let me have my little display? I mean, it's not as if I haven't tried. One must let off steam sometimes. You should be more understanding. You should, you know."

Eric sat motionless and then nodded. "Of course, of course. It's just... new to me, dealing with... well, female moods and regrets?"

"Female or not, where I come from they'd have all said I've been crazy. Even Hilda would...."

"Crazy to bring back those shingles when our baby was inside. You could have lost him!"

"How do you know it's a him?"

Eric lapsed into silence. Then he said, "I sure was glad you did, anyhow. I was so happy to see you then. You know, that was one of the best views ever in my life, you there, nothing on, happy and warm, in the very cabin I had built myself. Like Eve. Or maybe, the Virgin Mary, with your tummy out like that." It was as though he'd been speaking to himself. The thoughts overwhelmed him, and he almost radiated a joy.

Rene stared.

Eric went on, "Of course I should be happy when you let off steam, my Joy. Why do I need it always perfect? It never is. But the Lord brought us together. And I'm so lucky to have you. I'm sorry." He shook his head, reached across the space between them, and took her hand. "You've been a real brick, a real companion, my Joy, my love. I'm sorry. Let it all out, it won't bother me any more. You deserve a good grumble! After all you've been through..."

Eric nodded, and they lapsed into silence.

"What did Earle mean by a cowhole?" Rene asked, changing the subject. "I've been meaning to ask you ever since we nearly tipped over on the sleigh? How can a cow make a hole that big in the roadway?"

"No no, it comes from anglicizing the French — *cahot* means a bump or a jolt. Lots of Shigawake words are like that, mangling the French. I told you about *L'Anse au Beau Fils* down the Coast? Lance Abuffy, we call it."

She smiled. Lots of peculiarities to these parts. Peculiarities, and hard work, and a stiffened backbone as a result. Exceptional people in the Gaspe, she decided. "And what about that hockey game? Those lanterns around the rink?"

"Yes, and did you notice what they used for shin pads? Eatons catalogues."

"How enterprising! What was that puck?"

"A horse turd."

"I thought it might be."

"Made their own sticks, too."

As the train sped towards Montreal, their conversation again became full of tales of the winter behind them. Though Rene could not stop wondering what lay ahead.

CHAPTER TWENTY-SIX

Eric felt a jab. He woke sharply. The Hun — coming to attack? Wake up! No, just Rene, nudging him. "I think the baby is on its way, Eric."

The baby! Oh yes, of course. On its way — up we get! Rene kept a small suitcase ready with what she would need in hospital. Several days ago, they had moved from Jean's to Jack's house to be near the Queen Elizabeth Hospital, just below the church. "I'll ring a taxi."

"No, Eric, I feel quite all right. The walk will do me good. It will help the baby along. And we don't want to wake Stella or Jack."

They got up quietly, dressed, and tiptoed downstairs. Eric closed the front door quietly behind and they set off down Marlowe Avenue to Sherbrooke Street, which at one in the morning was deserted. They crossed in front of Trinity Memorial Church and down Northcliffe Avenue, a hundred yards to the hospital.

Rene had done well over the six weeks since they'd arrived. Being tall and strong, she had borne the baby well and in fact had taken part in her usual church work. Eric himself had been extra busy leading up to and during Holy Week, an especial time for any church.

"They may not let you stay." Eric knew that Rene had been in contact with the hospital and her doctor all along.

"Well, I'll stay as long as they let me." In spite of himself, Eric felt anxious. "You all right?"

"As right as rain." But then she stopped and bent over as contractions caught her. In a moment, she straightened and they kept walking.

Checking in and registration were handled gracefully, Eric thought. He accompanied Rene upstairs to the maternity ward on the second floor. After Rene got established, Eric left the room to allow the nurse to check Rene thoroughly, and came back to help as best he could. Finally Rene suggested, "Eric, why not go back to Father John's and get some sleep? We'll need at least one of us in good shape tomorrow." The nurse reassured them that the baby might be born by dawn.

Eric left and went up Northcliffe Avenue and then, instead of going back to bed — he was far too excited — he turned along Sherbrooke to the park opposite their former apartment. His thoughts turned to the future. Clever of Rene not to look for accommodation just yet. After all, they needed to get comfortable with the baby. She should go back to the Gaspe after the baptism: one thing everyone in Shigawake knew was how to look after babies. Soon he might get his own parish and they'd be moving, so no point in renting.

He walked into the park, studying the black shapes of bare branches thrown by the moon on the grass, snow here having disappeared the last while. Peaceful. He sat in front of the Cenotaph and leaned back. How thrilling for them to be producing their own child. A boy or a girl? Either was fine, so long as it was healthy.

All very well for Rene to be confident, or to act as if she were, but how could he stop being consumed with worry? What if something went wrong? What if the baby were born deformed? The doctors had said that all seemed well. But then you never knew, did you? The unexpected could happen. He'd seen that in his years of warfare. Just when you least expected it, when everything seemed jake — bang! The worst happened. He had no confidence in the justice of events. His gaze kept falling on the bronze relief in the centre: a tin hatted platoon marching, the last soldier carrying a wounded comrade. So long ago. But how often had he wrestled with all that, although he never mentioned it. Back in the city now with many duties, especially visiting the poor young men by the train tracks, his hobo jungle had burgeoned with the snow mostly gone. But his memory did often churn up dreadful, disturbing visions from a past left long ago. Not fair! Even now as he sat, that damned maggot crawled out of the nose of the dead German he'd lifted out of the dugout. Sitting here, Eric brushed his face to rub the image away. The bronze relief, maybe that was doing it. So he turned to face the empty park. But oh Lord, look! Down at his feet, Howard's torso from the Firing Line, leaping — hopping awkwardly towards him, bottom half gone, beseeching him with open arms and horribly mangled face — no, get out. Get out! Eric yelled. And fortunately the image did.

He sat up, embarrassed, but nobody had heard. Get up and walk around, he told himself. Exercise. He circled the park, passing that Church of St. Augustine at the north end. Decent lunches for the poor. Good. Well, Catholic, Church of England, what did it matter? Weren't we all servants of Christ, trying to do His will?

Happily, this striding kept those chimeras at bay, but after an hour or more, he began to weaken, feel almost dizzy. The excitement of the baby's imminent arrival was fading. Should he go back to the bench? No. He found a choice piece of dry grass on a knoll and lay down. Before long, he slept.

Later, dreams wrestled him awake once again. He leapt up and looked at his watch. Heavens, what if the baby had come? What if Rene needed him? Was he letting her down? How often would these damnable — dreadful — ghastly — visions step in between them? How long would she put up with his affliction?

To the east, a faint glow. Chilled and stiff, he decided, back to the hospital. Summoning better cheer, he strode across the park and along Sherbrooke Street to Northcliffe and down to the hospital. At the reception desk, he asked after Rene and the night commissionaire, wearing the same veteran pin as his own, welcomed him. Brothers-in-arms. He phoned upstairs and then nodded. Up Eric went, and as he climbed, he could hardly contain his excitement. But anticipation was mixed with trepidation. Would everything be all right?

He came along the corridor and before he went in, a nurse recognized him. "Well, Father, you have a boy."

A boy, Eric thought: Well, well! "Thank you, nurse." He hurried into the room.

His Rene, pale, bathed in sweat, looked exhausted. She opened her lovely eyes and smiled faintly. "Hello, my new Daddy," she breathed.

He came to her bed quickly, bent and kissed her. "Are you all right?" he asked anxiously.

She gave a slight nod. "The baby, Eric, he's perfectly formed, he looks wonderful, they're feeding him already. He's sweet." Her eyes fell shut again. "Go look."

Just then, her nurse came in with the baby. Eric went straight over and stared down into the tiny face. He stood looking for a long time. My son, he thought, my son. He turned. "Rene, I'll just let you sleep."

The nurse nodded. "Yes, let her sleep. She's been through a lot.

Brave woman. I've given her a pill. Come back around noon."

Off went Eric, as excited as any man could be.

When he opened the door to Jack's, he made no attempt to keep quiet. Oh no. Much too excited. He shut it — perhaps too loudly, and went through into the kitchen. His brother Jack was just sitting down to his morning cup of tea. He looked up anxiously, but then smiled as he saw Eric's demeanour .

"It's a boy. I'd like to call him Paul, after the Saint."

Jack nodded. "Good choice. Well, you've been out all night, Eric. You need a good bite to eat."

"I do, I do."

Stella came in wearing a pretty blue dressing gown with pale fur cuffs. Shorter than John, with large blue eyes, she said, "Eric, I'll give you the best breakfast a new father ever had." As Eric sat, she busied herself, full of good cheer.

* * *

Holy, holy, holy, Lord God Almighty.
Early in the morning our song shall rise to thee...

Imagine, Eric thought, singing the processional as lustily as anyone, here I am, a poor curate, walking this Trinity Sunday just ahead of the Lord Bishop of Montreal with mitre and staff, his two clerics in front of him, and my brother Jack. The choir sounded in good voice. And that new organ! What majestic tones! All week, the Casavant people had been here installing it. The Bishop himself was dedicating it to the glory of God. How could Eric not be happier?

As they processed down the aisle, they passed his beautiful Rene, also happily singing. Their son had been baptized that morning in the Lady Chapel by none other than the Bishop himself. Jean and Bert had attended, along with his older sister

Winifred, his nephew Gerald as godparent, and a smattering of friends. Lillian had sent up the family's baptismal garments; little Paul had looked just splendid in the heirloom. He'd behaved beautifully, too, save for the cry of astonishment when that cold water struck him. He and Rene had chuckled, and listened to the Bishop pronounce his christened name: Paul, after the travelling Saint. Perhaps, Eric thought, when he grows up, he'll be a traveller, too.

Eric followed the choristers threading their way into the choir stalls, singing mightily. Was this the apex of his happiness? No, Eric said to himself, it's only going to get better and better. Those wartime flashes would never again disturb his beautiful life, his companionship with Rene, and his new son.

During the sermon, Eric left his seat in the choir stalls to sit in a pew beside Rene, who had left their baby with a volunteer in the church offices. Paul had endured his own christening, so no more church for him today. The words of John Montreal in the Messmer's pulpit with its great carved sounding board came to surround Eric. He revolved in his mind those recent words from Saint Matthew in the Trinity Gospel: *Go ye therefore, and teach all nations, baptizing them in the name of the Father and of the Son and of the Holy Ghost.* Oh yes, the charge to His followers. Just what shall I do now? Eric asked. What about those reassuring words in the King James version that followed: *And, lo, I am with you alway, even unto the end of the world.* Comforting. Eric needed that.

The Anglican Church Woman's Guild had arranged for a fine luncheon as a celebration after the commemoration. But before going into the offices for the reception, Eric strode back up a side aisle into the chancel, still robed, to stand looking down in wonder at the new organ's shiny brass plaque:

To the glory of God and in loving memory of James Alford of

Shigawake, Bonaventure County, Province of Quebec and of Mary Ann MacPherson, his wife, father and mother of Col. the Rev. Canon J.M. Alford, MA DCL CMG CBE *Rector of Trinity Memorial Church, this organ was dedicated Trinity Sunday 1931 by the Right Rev. John Cragg Farthing,* MA DD DCL LLD, *the Lord Bishop of Montreal.*

Whatever would his simple parents in their Old Homestead have thought about this beautiful plaque in Jack's enormous church? He stood a long time, remembering them. But where was the name of the donor, John Molson? He and his wife Hazel, and their three children, Bill, Mary and David had been in the church in the pew behind Rene. What a generous and self-effacing person this John must be.

At the reception as he entered, Eric saw Rene chatting to Hazel, so he went over to speak to her husband. John looked impeccable in his light grey suit, his neat white moustache, small twinkling eyes under a firm forehead, a man of distinction.

"John, if only my parents were alive today... I can't believe how good you are to give this wonderful Casavant organ in their name."

"You know, Eric, we found out that, in this very province, out in Saint Hyacinth —"

Eric grinned, "Yes, which is sort of like Nazareth was to Jerusalem..."

John nodded. "A backyard. Who'd have thought that there, we have perhaps the best organ builder in the entire world! You know," he launched out in what Eric saw was now a pet subject, "that simple blacksmith, Joseph Casavant, decided at twenty-seven to leave his business and go to college!" Eric reacted. "He worked at restoration and, in 1840, he got his first contract for an entirely new organ. When he retired in '66, he'd made seventeen of them."

"I had no idea!"

"His two sons started Casavant Frères in 1879, with workshops in the same place. One of them, over seventy, came this week to oversee the final touches. Wonderful old man."

Eric shook his head. "Amazing!"

"Well, Eric, for that brother of yours, nothing is too good." John smiled. "Hazel and I were determined to get the best. You'll agree, you've never heard a sound like it."

Eric nodded. "Just magnificent tones."

Jack detached himself from a small group around the Bishop and took Eric and Rene to one side. "I have some rather interesting news."

"Yes?" Eric looked up just in time to catch what seemed like a conspiratorial wink between Jack and Rene.

"These last weeks I've been speaking with our Bishop," Jack relayed. "And last Monday, an incumbency opened in the Quebec diocese."

They both looked at Jack with great anticipation.

"Yes, the parish of Iron Hill needs a clergyman. First of September. Our Bishop believes you would be the ideal choice, and he's told Bishop Farthing."

Eric looked surprised, and confused. "Iron Hill? Where on earth is that, Jack?"

"Eastern townships. Not far from Lake Magog, which I'm sure you know. It's a small parish, Eric, but there are one or two other places attached. It's not even on the railway line, I hear. But the church itself, I've seen a picture, it looks charming. The parsonage is a good size — plenty of space for you both to raise children..." He grinned.

Rene stepped over and gave Jack a big hug and a kiss. "Oh, thank you, Father John dear, thank you so much."

"You see, Eric, Rene and I have been discussing this. We both think you'd be much better off in the country."

"Yes, yes, a country parish. Everything I could want."

"So you'll accept?"

"Accept? Indeed, I will!" Eric grinned broadly.

"I shall tell the Bishop at once."

CHAPTER TWENTY-SEVEN

"Whoa, Mack." Selwyn Mason, Eric's new churchwarden, pulled his horse to a halt. Eric jumped out, took Paul's little carrycot and helped Rene step down in front of her new parsonage. Eric's incumbency was due to start on the morrow, Tuesday, Sept 1st, 1931.

"There she is, Holy Trinity Church." Selwyn stood by his horse, looking at the neat white wooden church with its clapboarded sides, and then glanced at Eric. "I hope you like her, Reverend."

"Selwyn, you must call me Eric. Come, Rene, let's look inside."

Rene naturally wanted to check their new home first, but dutifully followed Eric as he strode over to the attractively arched front door flanked by pairs of triple lancet windows, a trio of the same high above, too. Selwyn carried the baby.

Rene watched Eric's excitement as he walked up the steps. All three went in and looked about. What a pretty church, she thought, seven rows of dark wood pews and at the end, three more stained glass lancet windows over the altar.

"Look, Rene, a real pulpit!" Eric couldn't disguise his delight as he came down the aisle. Rene sat down in a back pew with Paul, now asleep. Her husband hopped up the steps into the chancel and turned to read out the scroll running under the roof:

How amiable are thy dwellings, oh Lord of Hosts. My soul hath a desire and longing to enter into the courts of the Lord. Enter into His gates with thanksgiving and into His courts with praise. Be thankful unto him and speak good of his name.

"Painted by one of the daughters of Reverend Fyles, our first clergyman," Selwyn explained. Rene liked this fine farmer who had picked them up from the West Shefford station in an express wagon, just like Earle's. Medium height, with bold features, a tuft of brown hair topping his sunburned face, with good cheekbones and striking blue eyes, their churchwarden would probably be a tower of strength for Eric, Rene decided.

Eric went forward to the altar, moved the candlesticks aside and called out what he saw written on the two white porcelain plaques behind: "My flesh is meat indeed. My blood is drink indeed." He came back to the top step by the lectern similar to the larger wooden eagle gracing Trinity Memorial Church.

"Come see the baptismal font," Selwyn suggested.

Eric came back down the aisle, nodding to himself, clearly delighted with his new posting.

Selwyn bent to read the inscription: *The Rev T.W. Fyles humbly presented this font as a thank offering to Almighty God. Jan 1st, 1865.*

"Just about when the Shigawake church was built, a good long time ago," commented Eric, pleased again.

Rene congratulated herself: so it had really worked out well. On the way from the station, she'd taken in the rolling hills and dales of this part of the Eastern Townships, cattle calmly grazing, flocks of docile sheep, more than on the Coast, maple leaves beginning to don autumnal colours. She knew that here, Eric would enjoy a good long incumbency. Just what she had hoped.

Selwyn rubbed his hands together. "Well, Annie's got a fine dinner waiting for yez, but you'll want to see your home first, I know that." He turned to Rene. "We have a new son too, born in May."

"Oh lovely. They'll grow up together." Rene smiled. Selwyn had also been pleased at Eric's reaction to his new church. They made for the adjacent parsonage, seemingly larger with its parish hall behind, built out over a stable that sheltered horses in wintertime.

Eric looked up at the tree-covered mound behind them. "What's up there?"

"Pine mountain? About an hour's walk to the top. Nice view. Don't know if anyone goes. Might not be much of a trail. I used to hike there Sundays from time to time."

"The young fellows, do they go nowadays?"

Selwyn sighed, shook his head. "They work on the farms all week, but Sundays, apart from church... I don't find there's enough for them to do." He turned to Rene as she entered the parsonage. "Reverend Hatcher left behind some furniture. It might have been here before even he came. But there's lots of room for your own things."

"I'm sure Rene will find just what we need," Eric said.

Rene wasn't so sure; the Mater had written her that times were still hard: the Depression had struck England, too. Rents were not as forthcoming as she'd hoped so she could send the couple nothing; they would have to make do on Eric's clergy stipend. Slightly more than at Trinity Memorial, it was hardly substantial. Rene would have to scrape to make things cheerful.

When Selwyn turned for her opinion, she gave it graciously. "This will be just fine for us, Selwyn. I'm so pleased to have the furniture. I'll supplement it from roadside sales. How are the farmers doing hereabouts?"

"Very hard, Ma'am," said Selwyn, perhaps intimidated by her British accent.

"Oh, do please call me Rene."

"Well, we're all hurting, but we have farms, we got sheep for wool, so we're warmly clad, chickens for eggs, cattle for milk, space for gardens, so we have vegetables. But not a lot of cash to throw around. Hard to keep the tithes going, but we'll do our best." He smiled. Such an infectious grin.

"Probably better than the rest of the country," Eric commented. "I've heard that Germany raised its tariff on wheat to over $1.50 a bushel, and Italy and France raised theirs, too. With them shutting out our Canadian wheat, and our own terrible drought out west, we may be in for long hard times."

Selwyn nodded as they walked back to the express wagon. "There's talk that some o' them stockbrokers finally got stuck in jail."

"Yes," Rene added, "I read that sixteen senior officers from the country's best known brokerage houses have been charged. Unbelievable the graft that goes on. That's why we're so happy to be here in the country."

"Do you think the provincial election last week will help any?" Eric asked.

"We met Houde, you know, Selwyn," Rene said, "at the R100 send-off. His Conservatives lost so badly."

Selwyn knew. "Oh yes, that there Taschereau led them Liberals to seventy-nine seats, and Houde's conservatives only ten."

"Even Houde lost his own seat!" Rene added. "But I find it shocking that women can't vote in Quebec. You know, Selwyn, we were given that right in England three years ago."

"And in Canada, years before that, my dear, in 1919," Eric put in. "Though only in Federal elections. Our beautiful province is just so backward..."

Selwyn helped Rene up onto the wagon. "And now, come have a bite. A real farm dinner."

* * *

Pleased that they'd arrived at the beginning of the week, Eric immediately went on a round of coffee and teas, meeting churchgoers and organizing his three services, two in other churches: St. Augustine's in East Farnham, and St. George's in Adamsville, both about three miles away, half an hour in the buggy. He also wrote a sermon he would deliver at all three.

But most of all, he wanted a staff for his hikes. "In a way," he explained to Rene, "it makes me feel comfortable. A young poplar to dry would be best, but a good bit of straight maple would do. It has to have a cleft for a thumb-hold. Our Lord is often pictured with a staff; Bishops carry them. Good in case you meet some animal that doesn't like you. Though I never have yet."

"But Eric," Rene objected, trying to feed some mashed vegetable into the baby's mouth, "I'm sure there's nothing bigger than a groundhog in these hills."

"Oh yes, there's bears, foxes, bobcats, and cougars, the farmers tell me, even wolves..." He chuckled at the look on Rene's face. "Don't worry, my dear, no danger. Well, off I go. With any luck I'll be back by lunchtime with poles for a staff."

Behind the church, Eric hit on one of the older trails and, zigzagging upward, he could feel himself coming alive. Back in his own environment, his hearing quickened, eyesight grew sharper. In no time he was rewarded by a little pathway running off to the right, made by a rabbit, or perhaps even a fox. Should he follow? Another time. Get to the top first, he told himself, see what else is there. A straight stick for a staff comes first.

He strode down a slight dip and found at the bottom a clear

footprint in the mud. Some large cat. He knelt and studied it. Same size roughly as a cougar's but with smaller palm and toe pads. A bobcat.

Getting interesting, he thought. Not only did he have the parish he wanted, the congregation he had longed for, but right on his doorstep, trails for hiking, woods full of wild creatures. Better and better.

As he climbed further, he kept searching for saplings. A fallen tree blocked the trail. Aha, he thought, I'll just check out those roots. He followed the long trunk and found, under its upturned roots, a burrow. He knelt and inhaled. Fox. Well, that's good. Next trip, he might stop and wait here. Nothing he liked more than watching fox cubs play. Almost as good as having a dog. Poor Marshall Foch. Too bad the old fellow had passed on, albeit peacefully. But Earle had given him a decent burial.

As he neared the summit, the words of Selwyn came back to him: the lads here don't have enough to do. He wondered how many of them were trained in wood-lore. These last few days, he had found out that expeditions so normal in the Gaspe, moose hunting, canoe trips, snowshoeing into the interior, were not a part of daily life here. Lots of forest, yes, but nothing like the miles of uncharted wilderness and caribou plateaus behind Shigawake.

He reached the summit and looked out across at the rolling countryside with its dotting of lakes, fields and woods. A great place for respite, for solitude, for communicating with his God. And then it struck him.

Boy Scouts!

That's what Iron Hill needed: a Scout troop. Yes, he'd start one. Excited by the idea, he gave a last check around, and soon found an ideal stick of maple. He tested it, checked for a notch. Good. Yes sir! Fine place to bring his troop, once formed. The thought excited him more than his forthcoming services. His first sermon he'd already written, and how he looked forward to delivering it. Sure to be a goodly crowd.

And a good crowd there was. All three churches were packed — everyone wanted to see what their new clergyman looked like. Word had gone out from Selwyn that his British wife had been a dancer on the London stage, and many wanted to meet her, too. Rene rose to the occasion, proudly showing off her son to all and sundry. A fine beginning.

CHAPTER TWENTY-EIGHT

Eric had set the date for the first meeting of the Scouts for the last Wednesday of the month. How soon it came! And how gratifying to find the church hall just crowded with rowdy lads, twelve to eighteen, wrestling, shouting, fooling around; they delighted Eric. "Lots of energy to be channelled," he told Rene, who seemed taken aback by his untroubled mien.

"I'll just go over to the house and organize the food. Three parents answered your call to bring sandwiches and soft drinks. We shall have a lovely party at the parsonage when you've finished."

"Thanks. I hope these lads aren't here just for that!"

As Rene left, Eric snapped into his officer's demeanour, calling the meeting to order. No doubting his authority!

Selwyn came forward to introduce their new scoutmaster. "Now boys, we're real lucky. Not only do we have here a veteran of the Great War, but Reverend Alford has been camping and canoeing and exploring all over the back country of Quebec." Eric could see they were looking at him with new eyes. "Now, how many of you ever heard of Vimy Ridge?" Most in the room put up their hands.

"What about Passchendaele?" Again the same response. "The battles around Ypres?" More hands went up. "Well boys, listen to this. Our priest here fought through every one of those battles, commanding a Howitzer group on the Firing Line."

Eric hadn't commanded his gun all through the war, but anything to impress these lads.

"And I don't suppose many here have been off alone with a real Indian guide, and shot your own food and made your own campsites at night. How many fellas faced winter blizzards on snowshoes with only a rifle and pack on your back, and a knife fer to skin the animal when you shot it? Well, that's what this here clergyman's done."

Eric could see all eyes on him; Selwyn's introduction had excited them and his own sermons had whetted his congregation's interests during the month. He had wanted to make sure his parishioners would send their lads. Not enough young fellas in church, but once this Boy Scout troop got going, they'd be there, all right.

So Selwyn handed the meeting over to Eric, and sat down to listen. He seemed as interested as the rest.

Eric took over. "Now boys, you've all heard of Lord Robert Baden Powell?" He looked around the room. Several nodded. "He fought in the Boer war. My brother did too, with that first Canadian force in South Africa for our Queen, who was then -- anyone know?" Several yelled with British accents, "Queen Victoria!"

Eric grinned and nodded. "Good lads. Well, my brother probably met Sir Robert, as he was then. Anyway, that great man started this Scout movement in 1907 and it's spread all over — a million fine scouts, worldwide. So it's high time you fellows around here enjoyed the same manly training: forest lore, and how to serve your country and your fellow man. That's what this movement is all about.

"This is *Scouting for Boys.*" He held the book up. "I'll be getting several copies for you to pass around. You'll read about chivalry, lifesaving, dealing with accidents and your duty as citizens. I want everyone to know trees by their bark and birds by their note, and to climb any tree or crag you come across.

"There's no pleasure that comes near preparing your own meal over wood embers at the end of a long day in the wilderness. And no scent like the smell of that fire. Can you stalk your own stag? Stop a runaway horse? Rescue a drowning person? Close a cut artery? These are some of the skills you're going to learn. He opened his book and read:

"* The tracks of wheels, of men and animals, and how to read them.

* Fire making, and how to find the right tents for camping.

* Sewing with needle and thread — no laughing now! We'll need that, and the use of an axe and how to care for it.

* Map reading — finding your way by landmark, compass, stars, and direction of winds.

* Eyesight — by practice, we're going to strengthen that. Hearing too.

* Your sense of smell — what's down that burrow? A fox? Groundhog?

* Judging distance, and weather— how to read the signs.

"You see, the whole idea of joining the Scouts is to become healthy, happy, and useful citizens. I'll leave you to study the books when they come, but I've printed out the Scout Law." Eric handed it out, and then read:

"A Scouts honour is to be trusted

A Scout is loyal to the King, his officers, and his parents.

A Scout's duty is to be useful and to help others.

A Scout is friend to all and a brother to every other scout.

A Scout is courteous, and a friend to animals.

A Scout obeys orders of his parents, his patrol leader, and his scoutmaster.

A Scout smiles and whistles under all difficulties.

A Scout is thrifty.

And finally, a Scout is clean in thought, word and deed."

"When you've had some training, we'll go on hikes up Pine Mountain and over on Spruce Mountain, and then further into the real wilderness; we'll go in the sun and we'll go in rain. We'll go on snowshoes and in canoes. We'll learn the knots for rope and the tracks of animals. We're going to have the time of our lives. By the time we're finished, you'll all be trained as fine scouts and, when we attend the Scout jamboree next summer, who do you think will be the best troop there?"

The room erupted in cheers: "We will, we will!"

And by the next summer that indeed proved to be true.

* * *

"Have you finished your preparations for the jamboree?" Rene asked. She glanced at her husband, smoking his pipe beside her on the balcony. On this peaceful mid-summer evening in early August, 1932, their little son was playing on the lawn with a toy dump truck.

"Just a few touches tomorrow, but we are as ready now as we'll ever be." He glanced at her. "Did I ever think I'd see the day you sat rocking on a veranda, knitting?" He chuckled. In the distance, a team of horses mowed hay on one of the rolling fields. The year had been good. Eric had all three parishes under control, his Scout troop was the envy of other villages, he'd developed other sports, and intended to set up a soccer team this autumn.

"I've been hearing a bit of that new Canadian radio station," Rene said, casting off stitches, finishing up a wool sweater for little Paul. "This parliament, though they don't seem to be doing much right, did establish the new Canadian Radio Broadcasting Commission in May, funded by the government. I hated having to listen to American stations all the time."

Eric nodded. "Would we ever hear of my brother being made an Archdeacon on an American station?"

"I thought he'd refused that position before."

"He did," Eric replied. "He's done so much administration, he now wants only to minister to a flock. Otherwise he'd have been a bishop long ago."

A load of hay came rattling by on the road. Rene and Eric waved to Walter Mount, from Britain, and his son Stanley lying at the back, waving at his collie dog trotting behind. Not many cars these evenings, just the occasional buggy.

"What about Amelia Earhart's solo flight over the Atlantic?"

"She took off from Newfoundland, didn't she?" asked Eric.

"Yes, in a Lockheed Vega, whatever that is. May 20th, I believe."

"But Amy Johnson did that two years ago. Flew from England to Australia. A lot further in my estimation. And more adventuresome."

"No, Eric, she flew eastward, and in short hops, mostly over land. Never across a great ocean. And look at the dangers she faced. Didn't you read about her weather changing, how her altimeter broke and gasoline was leaking into the cockpit. Her plane even went into a spin but she got out of it. Fifteen hours before she reached the coast of Ireland. May 21st."

"Courageous lady," Eric agreed. "Crossing the Atlantic by plane — seems to be getting easier nowadays." Then he added quickly, "Not to put her down, of course. It was a tremendous achievement. But we're going to see that more and more."

"Talking of achievements..." Rene dropped the knitting in her lap and leaned forward to watch little Paul run off to one side, then soon toddle back. "What do you think of this new CCF formed in Winnipeg? I read in the Family Herald: our first Socialist party! Frank Scott from McGill went out there. And J.S. Woodsworth, he's the head. They do seem to be concerned about our terrible unemployment, the thousands upon thousands riding the rails with no homes and nowhere to go. That awful Bennet, he keeps on saying everything is fine."

"We can but hope." Eric sighed. "I may miss that hobo jungle sometimes, but I do prefer it here. Did you like my sermon the other day about welcoming the stranger at our door as if it were the Lord himself?"

Rene nodded. "Yes, very good. But not a lot of tramps coming by. Two last week."

"Several over in East Farnham." Eric travelled to the other churches on Sundays, and one evening for vestry meetings and such. For his hospital visits, Delmar Hadlock had offered his truck two evenings a week after finishing work. Normally they were much too busy to enjoy gentle evenings like this, when nothing seemed to be happening, and they could bask in a brief communication, soul to soul. Eric took the pipe from his mouth and pointed with the stem. "Our red tailed hawk, I see. Wasn't around the early part of this week."

Rene nodded. Well, she thought, this is a far cry from teaching dancing in Australia. But every day she found something to delight in her little son and to admire in her husband. This country life seemed to be doing them both good. She hoped it would last...

* * *

Eric burst into the house, excited. "We won again, Rene. Last game of the season!" He took off his coat and threw it on the chair. November was cold, bare trees, ground hard. Farmers were battening down their hatches for winter.

"I know, my dear. You must be so excited." Rene was sitting with her son Paul on the floor as he daubed coloured paint onto a large sheet of paper.

"Our team only started this summer and we've ended second in the league. Can you imagine!"

"Your Scout Troop was pretty well best at the jamboree, the soccer team finished strongly. What other worlds will you conquer?"

"And we've been here just over a year."

Rene nodded. "Do you know, I've been thinking about starting a troop of Guides. The girls are getting jealous of your Scouts. Last time I went to Montreal, I bought *The Handbook for Girl Guides* and I've been studying it. I'll start right after Christmas, if that's all right?"

"Wonderful idea." Just then the telephone rang, and Eric sighed. He looked exhausted. He shook his head, rose and went into the dining room to pick it up.

Rene watched him, as he grew serious, then frowned and spoke into mouthpiece of the black upright phone. He came back.

Rene asked, "Who was that?"

"Bishop Farthing."

"Oh?"

"Yes. He wants me to take on West Shefford as well. They don't have enough money for another priest and theirs left last month." Rene shook her head: her husband was taking on far too much.

"It's far too much," echoed Eric, reading her thoughts, and growing agitated. "I can only just handle these three parishes already. You know what a job it's been. And now West Shefford! Right there, that Church of St. John, it's almost a full-time occupation by itself. I can never handle all that."

"Did you tell him?"

"Well, I tried. But he would hear nothing of it. Reports have come back that I'm such a success, he seems to think I can do anything. But he is just asking too much."

Indeed, thought Rene. Her husband did not do well under stress.

Events bore out her misgivings. Two weeks later, after Eric had delivered four church services in one day, he seemed not only worn out, but at the end of his tether. "I can't do it, Rene, I just can't."

"You preached awfully well, Eric." Rene tried calming him. "Your three services in the morning and one in the evening, they worked well."

"But just giving a church service is not enough. What about all the parishioners that need looking after?" He swept his arms wide, clenched his hands into fists. "The sick to be visited? The lonely to be comforted? The rifts and arguments to be healed? The organizations to be managed, churches kept in good repair... It's not just giving a church service!"

Rene said nothing. Not often she had seen him in such a state of agitation. Better keep silent.

"Well, what do you say?" Eric snapped, and looked at her with a frown.

Rene paused. "Would you like me to call the Bishop for you? I'll just tell him it's too much."

"That won't do. That won't do at all. You think Our Lord would have said, no, I can't help? I've been called to do it, and I shall just have to."

"But you won't have to, if I phone —"

"Rene, I want to do everything right."

"You are doing everything right."

"No. The Lord has said, be ye therefore perfect. He never stopped, day or night. I've got to be like Him."

"Eric, you're only human. You're not like Him."

"I've got to try."

Rene could see such arguments were useless. She didn't know where to turn. Even in this quiet parish that had engendered such hope, that ghastly war had once more driven him to despair. "I don't know what I'm going to do." He slammed his palm against the door. "I just don't know, I don't know." He slammed it again and again.

Paul started to cry. Rene picked him up. "Eric dear, do be careful."

"I know, I know." Rene knew that agonising expression. And then he dropped to his knees, lifted his hands in prayer. She almost saw the proverbial drops of blood on his forehead. Well, she thought, we've surmounted everything else, this is just another challenge we must overcome.

CHAPTER TWENTY-NINE

The first Monday of the month, Rene gave a tea for the church guild. She always liked that, a chance to gossip and trade recipes and local news with the ladies. In a sale she had found a British mahogany tea trolley: large wheels behind, small wheels in front and a handle for pulling; on each side leaves lifted for a table. On it she'd laid out her British silver tea service, even the hot water pot with its wick beneath to keep the water on the boil. For this January meeting, the first of 1933, half a dozen women were sitting around the living room and Eric was present. He always opened the guild meetings with a prayer, stayed for a few minutes to chat and be sociable, and then retired upstairs to let Rene get on with the meeting.

Paul was toddling unsteadily about, well-behaved, of course, managing to stagger from one lady to another, who would smile and talk to him. "Eric dear," Rene said, "you keep an eye on Paul. I'll just go out and get the cakes."

She went out to the kitchen to fetch the plate of cucumber sandwiches and cakes that Annie Mason, Selwyn's wife, had baked, because Rene drew the line at baking. She picked up the cakes, and then heard a clatter of tea things falling and the most almighty scream from Paul. She dropped the plates and rushed in.

Eric was standing, frozen, mouth open. Paul lay on the floor, doused in boiling water. After the scream he couldn't catch his breath, seeming to choke. She picked him up quickly.

"He wanted a cookie," Annie said breathlessly as she rushed to the kitchen phone, "but lost his balance. He grabbed the doily and pulled the kittle of bilin' water down — I'll call the doctor." She cranked frantically to ring Central at the Multimode Telephone Company. Others crowded round Rene and then moved back as she tried to walk around, rocking and soothing the stricken child, after getting rid of his wet clothes. They saw he'd been badly scalded all down one side.

Her eyes flicked to Eric, still frozen. From the haunted look on his face, he was devastated. He turned and rushed up the stairs.

Paul caught his breath and let out bloodcurdling yells. Effie Beard huddled with May Mount, discussing what to do with his scalded skin. Annie Mason came back with a horrified look. "Dr. Picardy is not there. He had to go to Sherbrooke. I don't know what to do."

Nellie Hadlock hurried into the kitchen. "I'll call Delmar. He may be home. He has a truck. He'll come. We'll get the baby to the hospital in Sweetsberg."

Rene kept rocking her son, and praying, "Let this not be serious. Let this not be happening." Upstairs, she heard a fist slamming into woodwork again and again. And then it stopped.

Nellie came back. "I got him! He's coming right now. He'll be here soon, less than ten minutes."

Ten minutes, thought Rene. A lifetime. Would Paul still be alive? And what then? The long trip to hospital. But the screams had stopped. The child seemed to have gone into shock. The blood drained from his face. And then he went limp. "Oh heavens!" Rene exclaimed.

"Don't worry, he's passed out." Annie had brought up several children. "It's a protection."

Lenora Hastings stooped to clean the floor and burned her fingers on the steaming water. Nellie came to help. Rene walked back and forth holding her baby, frantic with fear. Slowly, little Paul revived.

"He'll be all right, Rene dear, don't you worry." But the way Effie said it, Rene knew she didn't believe a word. It just made her more distraught.

After what seemed an age, Delmar Hadlock banged on the door. Rene quickly threw on her coat and covered the child, who seemed lifeless, barely stirring. In a coma. She bundled him out into the truck and they rushed off to hospital.

* * *

The next morning, Rene returned without her son. She opened the door and came in. "Eric," she called, "he's going to be fine. He's staying in hospital another two days: they're watching him carefully. But he'll be all right. His side will be scarred, they said, where the worst of the water struck. But he's fine." Having called out, she took off her heavy clothes and then checked the kitchen, only to find her husband not there. Everything had been left exactly as the ladies had cleared it. So where was he? Upstairs she went. Eric's study door was closed. She banged on it.

"Eric. Eric, are you in there?" Oh dear, she thought, he's done something to himself. She knocked again. It was not locked, so she entered. Eric lay on the couch, curled up. She went over and sat. Then she leaned in and hugged him. "Eric, don't worry, he's fine."

"It was all my fault. You said, watch Paul. And he nearly died. I'm no good fer nawthin." He had reverted to Gaspesian.

"Eric dear," she said gently, "you've seen far worse. I know you have. In the war."

"But this was my son, Rene. My only son. I did it to my only son. I did it to us. You and Paul, my whole world — I almost destroyed it."

"I keep telling you, Eric, it wasn't you. It was an accident. Accidents happen. We have to overcome them. They're just there to try us. That's all, my dear. They're just there to test us. And together, we'll meet that test."

He hardly moved.

She straightened. "Now Eric," she said sternly, "this is not the time. Come along. Sit up. Paul is fine." She leaned in and gave him a warm kiss. "I love you, Eric. But now, we must get on. You must sit up. Right now. Come on."

Eric did so. But clearly he had undergone a terrible trauma. Perhaps even worse than their son.

"It's all my fault," he mumbled again. "You told me to watch Paul, and then he nearly died."

"That talk is just ridiculous. You are the most wonderful man in the world. You're a great father. It was an accident. It could have happened to anyone." But she felt as if she were speaking to a piece of granite.

And indeed, as the week progressed with the strain of the extra parish, Eric retreated more and more into himself. With Sunday was coming up, Rene had to do something. She rang the church wardens and told them Eric would not be able to take the services this Sunday: he'd come down with a dreadful flu but she was sure he'd be right as rain after the weekend.

And then on Saturday, she reported to him: "They all want you to take the weekend off, Eric. They know the strain you've been under. In fact they welcome this chance for you to get better. Peter Farrell, that student minister, he's going to help out.

"So we'll go to Brome Lake, to Knowlton. I phoned Robinson's Hotel. It's the oldest in the Eastern townships, and I've heard it's wonderful. No one much is there mid-week; the Christmas rush is over, so I got us a good rate. We're going on holiday, the three of us. Paul will be much better. It was a bad burn, the doctor said, but he's fine now. That's what's important. He's going to be just fine.

"Accidents happen 'in the best of regulated families,' as the Mater used to say. At the lake, you'll get yourself ready for the rest of the month. Won't that be fun?"

And oddly enough, Eric did look better. Did she see his scowl disappear, and even a hint of smile? Funny, she thought, ten minutes ago I would have said he was lost forever.

So Eric, Rene and the baby, holidayed at the best hotel in the Eastern Townships, and Eric slowly revived. Day by day without any responsibility, his bearing became more military, his confidence returned; she could watch him recovering. Paul, too.

Remarkable that fortunes could change so quickly. But happily, their world was getting back together. She congratulated herself on planning this holiday.

When time came to return, the three of them were driven back to the parsonage and Eric wrote his sermon for the next Sunday, and delivered it to all four parishes.

* * *

Toward the end of January, Eric was working with lengths of rope, checking his Scout book and practising the more complicated knots to show his troop the next evening. He heard a car horn outside. "That must be Delmar."

Rene put on her coat with its fur collar, her scarf, and gathered her mittens. Tuesday afternoons, she always went off to buy provisions.

"Not snowing too hard?" asked Eric.

"Delmar said on the phone he wanted to go before the storm got worse. I have a good list; he's such a dear. He only goes to Sweetsberg today. We need things there that Mr. Beard's store doesn't have. I won't be long. And you love these Tuesday afternoons alone with Paul."

"I do. We have fun. He's getting to know his colours. Last week, he learned 'red.'"

She went to give Paul, asleep by the fire, a last check, then bent to kiss Eric, and was off. Eric crossed to the window and watched his wife hurry down to Delmar's waiting truck. The snow was coming down hard and the wind whipping up into a bit of a blizzard. He hoped they'd get back before it got worse.

When Paul woke up, his father gave him milk and biscuits and dressed him. They sat on the floor and Eric interwove his fingers: "Here is the church and here (two forefingers) is the steeple." He turned his hands inside out, and piped, "Open it up, and there's all the people!" He waggled the fingers and Paul chuckled.

With his son, Eric could forget his troubles. All the services, different churches, the meetings and guilds, visiting the sick no matter how cold or blowy, had been overwhelming. Well, of course he'd been agitated. Who wouldn't be? He and Rene would discuss how to handle it after Paul went to sleep at night. The situation could not continue, Rene kept saying. But Eric kept retreating into himself, though he tried not to. No other escape, perhaps. Anyway, nothing he could do about it. Though it certainly disturbed Rene.

"Okay Paul, now we're going to learn some more colours!" He reached for the big picture book he'd got Paul for Christmas, and opened it. But then, he stopped and lifted his head to scent the air. The hairs rose on the back of his neck. What was that smell? He sniffed again. Stood up.

On the stove, some soup spilt from earlier had begun smouldering and one of the round plates had not been put back properly, so smoke was leaking out.

He sniffed again, and frowned. Then it struck him. Every nerve alert, he screamed, "Gas. Gas! Gas attack!"

Not a second to lose. He grabbed the surprised baby in his arms, raced to the door, threw on his coat and charged out.

My God, blowing! Wind fierce, oh yes, driving flakes bit into them both. "Daddy, Daddy," complained Paul.

"Gotta run, me son, gas attack. You never want that in your lungs. Stop ya dead. We gotta get somewhere safe." He plunged down onto the road and set off for the nearest house. "Not far, Paul, not far, don't worry."

The little lad tried to be brave. Eric kept wiping snow from Paul's face and bundle his coat around the two of them but it kept blowing open. The little bare legs were already freezing — he could feel that as he rubbed them, struggling on as fast as he could. "If I had snowshoes, Paul, we'd be there in no time." He just had on light indoor shoes — no time for boots. In a gas attack, every second could save a life. How many soldiers had he seen maimed, coughing blood till they died, or disabled for the rest of their lives. It would have made short work of his baby, that gas, for sure.

"Daddy, cold. Cold, Daddy." Trying hard not to cry.

"Cold, Paullie, yessir, but soon we'll be warm!" Amazing how far that darn house had gotten! On a nice day, only eight minutes' walk. But not a nice day, this. Eric sank in drifts, trying to lift his legs high. Keep thrusting onwards, he encouraged himself. Too bad you can't see further. And too bad no snowshoes.

All at once they fell. Must have stepped off the packed track somehow, lost his footing. Deep in the snowdrift, Paul let out a yell.

"It's all right, Paul, it's all right." Eric struggled to his feet, picked up the child, brushed some snow off his bare face and legs, and hugged him to his chest. He felt Paul freezing, and so was he, and just so tired. The blizzard bit with teeth of glass. He tried to cover Paul's bare head with his coat, but it wasn't working. Would that house never appear?

Not long before Paul was shuddering. Too cold to cry. Hypothermia setting in; Eric knew all about that. "Brave little fellow. We'll be there soon," he kept repeating, lifting his tired legs, forging into the teeth of the gritty wind.

Paul had a cold last week. That's why Rene couldn't come to church. She stayed home with Paul. But what else could he have done? That gas would have finished them both in no time.

A trek from hell. Never been on anything like this. Never had a child with him, of course. Never had gas chasing them in a real blizzard. Been damn cold at the Front, sure. But never like this. Such an everlasting trek.

After more icy minutes, through the snow he could dimly make out a farm house. Yellow walls, on the right by the road. That gave him a burst of energy. He tried to run, nearly tripped again. Watch it!

He reached the door, panting heavily. Banged hard. It came open. Bob Mason, Selwyn's brother, stared. Eric and Paul stumbled in. Belle leapt up from her chair. "Land sakes, Father, what's wrong?" Quickly she took the child, brought him to the stove, began stripping off the wet clothes. "Bob, put in more kindling!"

Eric stood immovable, panting hard. He let his coat drop to the floor, snowy and sopping wet as the snow melted. "Gas attack," he explained. "Huns on their way. Gas first. Always. Then bombardment. Better you get in the cellar!"

"We don't have one. Just the outside root cellar." Belle had hardly listened.

"Bob, take the upstairs window." Eric was barking out commands like an officer. "Where's your rifle?"

Bob, kneeling at the fire, rose and took Eric by the arms. "Father Eric, look. There's no Germans. It's my house. This here's my farm."

"Crazy to have a farm house this close to the Front!" snapped Eric. He ran to the window, peered out. "Don't see them coming yet. Gonna soften us up with shells first."

Belle peered strangely over her shoulder at Eric. With Paul's clothes off, she wrapped him in a blanket and cuddled him to stop his crying. She sat close by the fire and rocked him. "Bob, get that tea from the stove. Pour milk in. Make sure it's just warm. The child needs hot liquid. He's freezing to death."

Paul understood her enough to be thoroughly frightened and began crying loudly.

"Brave soldier!" Eric exclaimed. "Hardly cried all the way here. Now he's safe. Gas will take much longer to enter these locked windows, I can see that. Let him cry all he wants. We've saved our lives." He stared wildly, panting hard.

Bob and Belle traded a look. Clearly, they thought the opposite — that he'd nearly killed his son. And himself.

Bob brought over the hot drink for Paul.

"That's it, you look after him, and I'll take the upstairs window," Eric said. "But where's your rifle? I can break out a pane — anyone comes near, I'll finish them!"

Bob turned with sad eyes. "Father Eric, there's no Germans for thousands of miles. This here is Iron Hill. Never been a German here, never will be. Maybe you had a nightmare. That there war –

what it does to a man, eh Belle? Now come by the stove, Father," he said gently. "I got yez whiskey. I'll pour a drink. You need it."

"I do, I do." Eric stood, staring vacantly, and took in his surroundings. A clean farm kitchen. Yes. True, he was in Iron Hill.

He turned slowly, and walked over to a chair by the stove, shaking his head. Bob handed him a glass of whiskey. He sat by the fire and slipped it slowly.

CHAPTER THIRTY

TWO days later, Rene sat with Father John in his church office. The Archdeacon had never seen her so distraught.

"I wasn't at church, Father John, because Paul had a cold, which made Tuesday's attack... so risky. Anyway, before that, during Eric's sermon — well, Annie phoned first, she's our Warden's wife, but Ida reported the same thing: 'We'll get you now, you sons of bitches!' He was looking out over the congregation, and that's what he said." Rene repeated it. "'...Sons of bitches!' In the pulpit! I heard it from a third parishioner, too: The enemy, the Hun, they're always on his mind.

"His congregation, they just sat quietly, but shocked, oh yes. They knew why, though: I've often heard them say, 'What war does to a man!' They tried to soften the blow for me, saying, not a problem, just the war; he'd been through so much. They thought by telling me, I could do something to help."

"But explain about Tuesday," the Archdeacon prompted.

"Father John, it was the stove, smoking. He thought it was a gas attack. So he ran out with our son, and nothing on! Well, to be fair, in a gas attack, you don't sit around getting dressed, you get out as fast as you can.

"You see, gas it can be such a danger." She looked over at Father John, much wiser and older than she. "But earlier in January, Paul, he got badly scalded – not Eric's fault, of course, but he took it that way. He does mean well. He tries so hard, Father John. He keeps saying, 'I have to be like Christ.' But he isn't like Christ." She was stifling tears; she had to get her full story told.

"When I came back from shopping, he and the baby were gone. I was frantic. Then Belle phoned and told me the whole thing. She and Bob brought them back, and Eric was calmer. I put Paul to bed. But then, Father John," she heaved a sigh, "then, the next day... he realized what he'd done. He went into his room and wouldn't talk to anyone; I couldn't even get him to eat. He lay there like a dead person. I'm no good, he'd say. I'm just not any good. I can't do it... What was he staring at in front of him? Nothing. My own husband. He's such a good man. I love him so much. But I love my baby, too.

"I told him I'd decided that Paul's cold, well, it might be pneumonia, so I was taking him here to Montreal, to Dr. Goldbloom, that's our pediatrician, you know. I think Eric knew that I'd come and talk to you. Apparently Paul will be fine, no after effects, just a bad cold, but that's curable. I left Jean's phone number, and yours, with Selwyn and Annie. He's our warden, you know."

She shook her head. What a struggle not to cry! "I'm torn. I don't know what to do... I just don't know what ... I ... can ... do any more. I've tried, Father John, God knows I've tried so hard. But I just don't know." The tears she had been holding back could be held back no longer.

Father John reached out and touched her. "Quite all right, Rene, quite all right to cry. You've been through so very much." His voice sounded kind and affectionate.

The church secretary heard the crying and came knocking at the door, "Shall I make a nice cup of tea, Father? Might make Mrs. Alford feel better. Would you like that, Rene?"

In a little voice she replied, "Yes, please." And she went on crying, twisting her handkerchief, daubing her eyes, trying to hold back all the anguish building for months, in fact, probably for years.

Just then the phone rang. Jack picked it up, and listened. "I see," he said. "Would you mind telling this to Rene?" He motioned and she took the phone.

"My son Jackson seen him, Mrs. Alford," she heard Emma Hadlock say. "He called me to the window. We all saw it. The Reverend Eric, he was leaving the Parsonage! Had his staff with him, haversack slung over his shoulder. He set off walking in the direction of West Shefford. We reckon he's going to take the train."

"Thank you, thank you, Emma," Rene whispered and put down the phone.

Jack watched her pull herself together. "Father John, he's coming in by train. I must go, I'll have to meet him." She hurriedly put on her coat.

"Rene," the Archdeacon said, "listen. I know why he's coming. Can you guess?"

Rene looked at him and paused, thinking. "To find me?" Then she looked up. "Oh. To go back to hospital?"

The Archdeacon nodded sadly. "We mustn't be downhearted. They may cure him." A forlorn hope, they both knew.

"Rene, when he arrives, even though St. Anne's Military Hospital is close by, he'll still want to go home to Shigawake — to say goodbye. He did that last time. He was adamant. He will insist again. So go with him on the train. Take Paul. He'll only stay a day or two."

* * *

Sunday, February 13, 1933

The sun is blazing off the gleaming iron rails, though the wind is cold. But the icy winter chill is not why the couple are huddled together on a bench outside this Port Daniel station. Even to a casual observer, their pain would be obvious, and so strong that it's almost visible: in the way they hunch over, the way the man clasps the woman's hands; intensity burns from both their features. Though bundled up, the man's lapel can be clearly seen — the veteran's badge: a crown surrounded by the words *For Honourable Service*. Six years ago, he wore that while waiting for another train on this very station. Across the country he went then, to find his love, his Rene. Now, before he leaves, she sits beside him, listening. He is speaking in low tones, but firm and clear.

"You'll wait in Shigawake for Bert and Jean, or perhaps Gerald, to find you a nice apartment, and then you'll both go back." She nods. "This disability..." He pauses. "It... It will get you a bit more of a pension, but it won't be much."

She seems not to care. Her eyes search his features.

"Stay here as long as you can, but then you'll want to get on with life. You might even start a school again. I'll pray for you every day, probably many times a day. You will never be out of my mind." She blinks back tears. "Rene, there's just no other way. I've tried, I've thought, but every option...

"Sometimes I thought I had it beat. College, that first time: I was raring to go." He breathed out a long sigh. "But it came back." He shakes his head. "Put me in hospital for eighteen months. But I beat it. I got out. I went on. I got my degree, I came across this great country, I got to Sydney, and when I saw you — the light broke through, like out of a bank of dark clouds. So I've been happy, oh, I sure have. That first time I saw you up on that stage, giving your dance lecture, and then..." the frown disappears for a few moments, "after we married, those paradises of love... and when we prayed together in those churches round the world, that sun kept breaking through. And all because of you, my Rene, my own Joy. Your presence. So you see," back come the frown and anguish "the worst thing in my whole life ... is leaving you now..."

He lapses into silence, and their hands grip even more tightly. "That's why we came early to the station. I had to explain. I want my son to know, it's not just the big events, no, Rene, all along, it's the every day battle. I had the forces of light on my side. I spent so much time in prayer, or I'd have been lost long ago." Words dredged from his deepest being. "No man knows what I've been through, day after day. I never told you, because I couldn't let you worry."

Rene is about to speak, but he lifts his hand. "No, that wasn't a question. These last months at Iron Hill, I've turned it over and over. When I get real challenges, I love that, I love hard work, I love doing my best, and even more when it gets piled on. But it's just that... it finishes me." He shakes his head. "When I'm most happy, working the hardest, that damn war, it comes back. No man knows..." He breathes hard.

"The war, that did it. I was just like any other young fella — no different. From a farm, and a good life ahead o'me. But then, that howitzer. My friends blown up, torn to pieces, right... beside me. All the time.

"I'm only telling you all this, Rene, to tell my son, to tell anyone, what war done to me so that someone, somewhere, can stop it. Stop any thought of war ever crossing them politicians' minds." He straightens and his jaw tenses. "One thing, promise me, if our son ever gets caught up, like me, by patriotism, stop him. If I'm back home when he gets old enough, I'll explain it myself. But I may... I may not. Last time in hospital: eighteen months. This time, who knows, eighteen more? Or years? We don't know. We're counting on those doctors and nurses to get me cured, once and for all. I need to get out and to do the Lord's work again. I know He wants me to. So the sooner I get there and get back out, the better. It's Valentine's Day tomorrow. Could be our lucky day." He tries to smile.

Tears fall from Rene's eyes.

"I feel as if I've lived a lifetime just in these five years since we met. A lifetime is good enough for any man. How many lifetimes do we need? And with God's help, and the nurses and doctors, I may even start a second lifetime, clear, like any normal man. Wouldn't that be fine?"

Rene nods. She keeps wiping her eyes with a mittened hand.

"Jack'll be meeting me with a car and he'll get me to St. Anne's Military Hospital. He'll keep you posted. Try to write. Don't be downhearted. It will be hard. But harder if I stayed, worrying you every five minutes." Rene shakes her head but he goes on, relentlessly, driven. "No, we were always... waiting for the next explosion. Well, if I can do anything, I can put our minds at rest. By leaving.

"Maybe Hilda can come. It's the worst of times. No man knows how I hate to leave you with this here economic depression. But I've seen how resourceful you are and that's what gives me hope."

He is about to go on, but they both hear, in the distance, a train whistle. He gets up. She does too. Their arms go around each other and they hug in a desperate display of affection.

So perhaps — before we have to watch their unbearable agony as he gets on this one last train — it would be more discreet to leave them now, wrapped in each other's arms.

POST SCRIPTUM

In fact, Eric Alford never did come out of Ste. Anne de Bellevue Military Hospital. His shell shock was apparently interspersed with periods of great clarity when he preached to and comforted inmates at the mediaeval-looking jail of St. Vincent de Paul, or chatted with young MacDonald College students fishing in the dull canal. But often he fell into periods of depression, silences that even caring nurses could not break into. He died in 1953.

ADDENDUM

Excerpts from Lieut Eric Almond's handwritten letters from Ste. Anne's Military Hospital, in the two months before he died, to his wife Rene, and to his son Paul, who was still in England.

From a letter dated June 9, 1953.

For twenty years I have watched and shared in the sufferings of thirteen hundred slowly dying men in this hospital as their priest and their friend.

I have been separated from my work of service in the outside world.

I have been separated from my wife.

I had been separated from my son.

I had been separated from my relatives.

I had been separated from my old gang of friends.

I have been separated from beauty.

I have been separated from humour, etc.

But I may have been placed by Christ in some key position. The chalice I carry in my hands is brim full of suffering.

I have walked through the wards and seen the helpless masses of suffering. Later on I will remember them in intercession. They have won their victory.

It is all placed in God's treasury to be used for sacrificial love, humility and purity on this dying planet.

You will be glad to hear that once again, I have taken up work as an assistant priest. Last Sunday, I assisted in a celebration of the Holy Eucharist in the chapel here. I read the Epistle and served the Holy Bread. Again, I repeated those words which I have said so often before: "Preserve thy body and soul unto everlasting life." I wish you could have been with me. You would have found it strange to see me in clerical collar and robes again.

Well Paul, if you ever get to Florence go to the Pitti Gallery and see Raphael's Madonna — the dead image of your mother.

Now, my lad, Mother and I are with you all the time spiritually, no matter where you go or whatever you do. Carry on. A closed mouth catches no flies.

Keep a stiff upper lip. Get as much fun as you can. Don't worry about your mistakes or failures. That's how you learn.

Well darling ones, I send you all my love. Keep smiling. Sometimes there is a humour and laughter of God.

From a letter two days later dated June 11, 1953

Dear Paul,

This is my last letter to you for some time.

In the third saying from the cross, Jesus made his last will and testament to John, his beloved disciple:

"Woman, behold thy son; son, behold thy mother."
And from that the disciple took her to his own home.
Always take care of Mummy for me.
Dad.

From a letter dated July 23, 1953

I would give the world to see you, so I could jump into you. As I have not seen you for twenty years, you are sort of a fairytale to me. But personalities have a happy faculty of indwelling other personalities so we carry our friends inside of us, but we have to see them and get to know them to do this. We are only one half of ourselves. Our friends are the other half.

The physical does not count an awful lot. It is really only the mental and spiritual that matters. So in a mystic way, I may be in you and we may recognise each other in some other life. (See John 17) Anyhow, our souls, personalities and spiritual bodies may indwell and go into another, as we are all one in the mystical body of Christ.

This planet earth is a training school to prepare us for another life. As we learn service, joy, friendship, love, and humility, we get ready in the beauty of holiness to go into another mansion in the trillions of others in God's universe. The spiritual world is all around.

Here, I send my soul and spiritual body into you at a distance.

I have had four years of war, two years land survey, five years university, two years teaching, four years an active priest, twenty years a sick priest. A pal, friend, companion and sharer of the sufferings of thirteen hundred slowly dying soldier patients.

I have seen much of beauty and friendship in Canada,

USA, Australia, Asia and Europe. I have worshipped in many of the great cathedrals. I have seen much of nature and something of art. I have experienced joy with my pal, partner, playmate, sweetheart, lover, and soulmate.

There has been the humour and laughter of God, at times.

Once in awhile, I saw humility.

There has been an upward look to the stars.

I have drained a chalice of suffering to the bitter dregs. Now, I am tired.

Always take care of Mummy for me. She is my Joy, Angel Saint, and Dove.

Your Dad.

From his last two letters, dated July 28
To Paul Almond, BA Oxon.

Always take care of Mummy for me, this is my last will and testament.

Lieutenant, teacher, priest, Rover Scout, Eric Almond.

To Rene:

This is my second letter to you today. I am so lonesome for you all the time. You know, I love you with my whole heart and soul. The only real joy in this life you have given me.

Please forgive me for all the unhappiness, pain, and sorrow I have caused you. I am full of regret and remorse for that. Again I thank you from the bottom of my heart for all the countless blessings you brought to me in our five years of married life together, physically, mentally, and spiritually.

You brought me joy, beauty, and loving kindness, and

God only knows what you had to put up with all the time. Even building log cabins in the dead of winter.

Now in this last twenty years, we have been completely separated but my love and intercessions have gone out to you constantly, night and day in my sane moments.

I am tremendously proud of your success in your work and in your son Paul.

My life here has been one long hell for twenty years, with sickness night and day of the worst kind, and never a break: no wife, no child, no friends, no beauty, no humour etc. Now I am fifty-eight and tired of the game.

Then there is the thought of the next life. Will we be together then?

Eric Almond, Priest, C. of E.

Ten days later, his life ended.

ACKNOWLEDGEMENTS

First I must acknowledge my mother, whose writings still exist, and my father, Lieut. (later Major) Rev. Eric Almond, on whose story this is based. Such a strange feeling it was, reading his words some ninety years after they were written and forty years after they came into my possession upon the death of my mother, having lain in a safety deposit box, unopened and unread. I have quoted from them with almost no amendments. He wrote himself, "They are rough and ready like the scenes I have depicted for I have made no attempt to polish them." I also opened, twenty five years after her death, the notebooks of my mother, Irene Gray. Every word she spoke that first evening Eric attended her lecture came from these, verbatim — so modern that I should emphasize she wrote them in 1927. Their letters to each other were never kept, so all of them herein were imagined, as were Rene's dairies in the Holy Land.

Some parts of this book come from documents, but still others from oral tradition: such as Rene carrying a bundle of shingles on her back, and the way the couple arrived at church Christmas Eve. The sayings: *A man is hampered by his possessions* and *It's a poor farm that can't afford one gentleman,* were both told by my aunts over and over again. As was the tale of my Uncle Earle, with a boost from his adrenaline, killing the lynx. He went on to become mayor of Shigawake from 1941 to 1945 before his early death in 1953, the same year as his brother, Eric.

I owe much to Douglas Hall, the "antique baker" of Iron Hill, with his prodigious memory and care for the now shuttered Holy Trinity Church, and the genealogy of the village inhabitants. My Iron Hill section is due to his help. He brought me to Stanley Mount, who passed away only a fortnight after my visit, and his wife Ida, who both gave me vivid accounts of their rector. Jackson Hadlock (89 in March 2009) told Douglas about seeing Rev. Eric leaving his parsonage for the last time. Through Doug, this spring I met Wayne Mason, my playmate when we were two. Leslie Ann Ross, Psy.D., an old family friend and senior director of a Child Trauma Centre in Los Angeles, works with combat veterans at the Veteran's Administration there. She gave me a thorough analysis of Post Traumatic Stress Disease, helping me with my father's "shellshock".

I loved James Gray's book on the Great Depression and fashioned my "Adam Hadley" character in the train after him, though not his later manifestation as a hobo. His book *The Winter Years* (1966, Macmillan) is so lively and such a great personal exploration of how the Depression struck Winnipeg, and does far more than my own imagination to illuminate this period. I thank Patricia Fennell, Gray's daughter, for her permission.

Barry Broadfoot's unique collection of quotations *Ten Lost Years*, published by Doubleday Canada, was helpful for the hobo jungle chapters. The real people in his book express themselves wonderfully

Nevil Shute's autobiography "Slide Rule" provided all the details I needed on the R100, and I recommend it.

Laurence Alexander, caretaker of St. John's Church, Darlinghurst in Sydney, found time to help me with that history, between actually pealing the bells for weddings and such.

That wonderful institution, the Canadian Pacific Railroad, is so enlightened as to keep archives, and what is more, to employ a fine archivist in Jo-Anne Colby, who answered every request promptly and kindly. Imagine, finding a Cross-Canada timetable from 1927!

Library and Archives Canada have been keeping all my personal histories, and those of Eric and Rene, thanks to their finest archivist, now retired, Anne Goddard. Sophie Tellier helped us find our way among the classifications on their impossible website, which befuddled even my best researcher.

Jane Nesbitt at the Canadian War Museum, with her staff and wonderful volunteers, have also been very helpful. It's a great place to do research.

Nora Hague at the McCord Museum of Montreal printed valuable pictures from their treasured archive for my reference, and told me about the R100 and other snippets of the day. I was surprised that trans-ocean flights occupied so many newspaper headlines in those years.

Dr. Richard Virr, Curator of Manuscripts, Rare Books and Special Collections at McGill, took valuable time to help (as the volunteer Curator of the Montreal Diocese) with Reverend Eric's various tenures.

I also thank Rachel Lev of the American Colony of Jerusalem Historical Archive for sending me pictures of the American Colony in 1920s. My own time there in 1963 was so special, as it must have been for Rene and Eric thirty years previously.

I must thank the long dead Leigh Hunt (1859) for his poem often heard recited during Shigawake evenings. And of course, Robert Service for his excerpt from *The Shooting of Dan McGrew,* which I myself had memorized. In the same vein, Peter Dale Scott, my good friend for some sixty years, has given the nod to using his grandfather's poem that I found in Archdeacon Almond's papers, and which has never been published in a book.

Out of my admiration for T.S. Eliot I have buried a phrase or two from *Burnt Norton*, the first of his Four Quartets, find it who will. He is the poet who has spoken most powerfully to me over the years.

Leigh Boyle Coffin collected his Uncle Roland's Gaspe diary of fifty-five years into a mimeographed typescript full of his own interpretations. I found this loving volume *Fifty Summers on the Sea,* full of helpful facts about the years 1930 and 1931.

Glenn Bydwell, one of the very few geniuses I know, helped me with the location of railway yards, and the Greek influences of those days. My stepson Chris Elkins also helped with the research.

My loyal readers must be also thanked: Dr. Duncan Steel, the renowned astronomer who lives in Australia, vetted those chapters for me. Oxford friends for over fifty years, John Morrell, a leader in the City of London's financial centre, Peter Duffell, a filmmaker and writer and Diana Colman Webster, a novelist and textbook writer, all came up trumps once again. The Rev. Susan Klein has been an important advisor for all the books that centre on clergymen. Catherine Evans, an English teacher at BCS (who kept winning every prize for her students' literary magazine *Inscape)* brought her brilliant editorial faculties to bear. My good friend Nicholas Etheridge, the retired diplomat, continues to catch anachronisms and other mistakes. Rex King, the only author remaining from our Writers' Group in the nineties, is a faithful reader and a great contributor of felicitous phrasing. Two editors of renown, Clare McKeon (now sadly deceased) and Shannon Wray, both inspired me to add additional scenes. David Stansfield, my new-found writer friend and Cambridge graduate living in Malibu, has been a wonderful support, having gone through it all with a finely honed eye.

My cousin Ted Wright has continued to be a great support and researcher throughout this series. He reads the historic backgrounds and boils them into manageable form for me, and searches endless details on the Internet, at which I still flounder. After early dawns picking raspberries and weeding cabbages, we have creative discussions, after which he goes off to make lobster and crab traps at *La Fine Mouche*. I could never have done this series without him. I also thank my intrepid housekeeper, Francine, who fed me every day and ran the household, leaving me free to write. And the marvellous Joe Dow, who keeps my computer running. I must also thank Red Deer Press publishing the last three books in this series.

And finally, Joan, my wife of well over thirty-five years, who prodded me into doing this series and continues to be my staunch supporter. As with every volume in The Alford Saga, this book is dedicated to her, but she must also be given pride of place in the acknowledgements.